A Baron for Becky

Jude Knight

Cover image: Young Woman in a White Hat, 1780, by Jean-Baptiste Greuze

Dedication

This book is dedicated to my husband, with whom I have learned how hard marriage is, and how rewarding.

Becky is the envy of the courtesans of the demi-monde - the indulged mistress of the wealthy and charismatic Marquis of Aldridge. But she dreams of a normal life; one in which her daughter can have a future that does not depend on beauty, sex, and the whims of a man.

Finding herself with child, she hesitates to tell Aldridge. Will he cast her off, send her away, or keep her and condemn another child to this uncertain shadow world?

The devil-may-care face Hugh shows to the world hides a desperate sorrow; a sorrow he tries to drown with drink and riotous living. His years at war haunt him, but even more, he doesn't want to think about the illness that robbed him of the ability to father a son. When he dies, his barony will die with him. His title will fall into abeyance, and his estate will be scooped up by the Crown.

When Aldridge surprises them both with a daring proposition, they do not expect love to be part of the bargain.

Table of Contents

Prologue

In the nursery, the two little girls waited, sombre in their mourning blacks. Hugh, Baron Overton, had not paused in the hall below. He handed his gloves and his tall hat with its crepe band to the nursemaid, barely caring whether she caught them. He had eyes only for the poor, orphaned mites left in his care.

He knelt, so he didn't loom over them, and they both shrank a little, clinging to one another. Were they frightened of him? He had never hurt them; in the four years he'd been married to their Mama, he'd barely seen them.

He could tell himself he'd been busy putting his unexpected inheritance back on a sound financial footing. And it had worked: those long voyages to secure cotton for the mill in Liverpool, trips to London for buyers, constant scurrying to and from the West Indies and the length and breadth of England.

But the truth was, he'd also been avoiding their Mama. Only after he'd married the widow did she tell him she hated him—only after the birth of her deceased husband's daughter and her own reluctant consent to take him into her bed. Only then did she tell him that she couldn't bear the scars on his face and body; that it made her ill to touch him.

Was it the scars the girls feared? He turned his head a little, so the light fell on the unmarked side of his face. What did one say to little girls of four and seven?

"Are you well, my dears?"

The older one stiffened her thin shoulders and stuck out her chin, all determination. "Papa?" she said. "Have you come to send us to the orfasemery, Papa?'

"I don't plan to send you anywhere, Sophrania," he said, "but I don't understand? What is an orfasemery?"

She frowned with him, and repeated the words, articulating clearly and slowly. "The orfa semery. Where the orfas live. After their Mama dies."

Orphans. He would not have understood, if he'd not been thinking the word himself. Later, he would find out which of the maids had been frightening his daughters with tales of an orphans' seminary. For now...

"You live here, my dears, with me. I am your Papa. This is your home. No one will send you away, I promise. You are not orphans. You have a Papa."

He settled back, so he was sitting on the floor with the wall as a backrest and his legs outstretched. "Come here, Sophrania. Come here, Emmaline."

Cautiously, they approached his welcoming arms, each sitting gingerly upright on a thigh.

He rested a gentle hand on each small back, and—on a sudden inspiration—began telling them stories about his own time in this very nursery with his three cousins. And, moment by moment, they relaxed, until he had a little girl nestled on each shoulder, prompting a surge of tender protectiveness.

He had not been a good Papa, but he was all they had. He would have to do better.

Part One
1807

Chapter One

1807, West Gloucestershire

Aldridge never did find out how he came to be naked, alone, and sleeping in the small summerhouse in the garden of a country cottage. His last memory of the night before had him twenty miles away, and—although not dressed—in a comfortable bed, and in company.

The first time he woke, he had no idea how far he'd come, but the moonlight was bright enough to show him half-trellised window openings, and an archway leading down a short flight of steps into a garden. A house loomed a few hundred feet distant, a dark shape against the star-bright sky. But getting up was too much trouble, particularly with a headache that hung inches above him, threatening to split his head if he moved. The cushioned bench on which he lay invited him to shut his eyes and go back to sleep. Time enough to find out where he was in the morning.

When he woke again, he was facing away from the archway entrance, and someone was behind him. Silence now, but in his memory, the sound of light footsteps shifting the stones on the path outside, followed by twin intakes of breath as the walkers saw him.

One of them spoke; a woman's voice, but low—almost husky. "Sarah, go back to the first rosebush and watch the house."

"Yes, Mama." High and light. A child's voice.

Aldridge waited until he heard the child dance lightly down the steps and away along the path, then shifted his weight slightly letting his body roll over till he was lying on his back.

He waited for the exclamation of shock, but none came. Carefully—he wanted to observe her before he let her know he was awake, and anyway, any sudden movement might start up the hammers above his eye sockets—he cracked open his lids, masking his eyes with his lashes.

He could see more than he expected. The woman was using a shuttered lantern to examine him, starting at his feet. She paused for a long time when she reached his morning salute and it grew even prouder. Then she swept her light up his torso so quickly he barely had time to slam his lids shut before the light reached and lingered over his face.

She was just a vague shadow behind the light. He held himself still while she completed her examination, which she did with a snort of disgust. Not the reaction to which he was accustomed.

"Now what do we do?" she muttered. "Perhaps if Sarah and I...? I will have to cover him. What on earth is he doing here? And like that? Not that it matters. Unless he has something to do with Perry? Or the men he said would come?" Incipient panic showed in the rising pitch and volume, until she rebuked herself. "Stop it." She took a deep breath and let it out slowly. "Stay calm. You must think."

Aldridge risked opening his eyes a mere slit, and was rewarded by a better look at the woman as she paced up and down the summerhouse, in the light of the lantern she'd placed on one of the window ledges.

Spectacular. That was the only appropriate word. Hair that looked black in the poor light, but was probably dark brown, porcelain skin currently flushed with agitation, a heart-shaped face and a perfect cupid's bow of a mouth, the lower lip—which she was currently chewing—larger than the upper.

The redingote she wore fit closely to a shape of amazing promise, obscured, then disclosed, as the shawl over her shoulders swung with her movements. Even more blood surged to his ever-hopeful member. "Down, boy," he told it, silently.

"Mama?" That was the little girl, returning down the path. "Mama, I can hear horses."

The woman froze, every line of her screaming alarm.

Aldridge could hear them too, coming closer through the rustling noises of the night. The quiet clop of walking horses, the riders exchanging a word or two, then nothing. They must have stopped on the other side of the house.

"Sarah." The woman's voice, pitched to carry only as far as her daughter's ears, retreated as she crossed the summerhouse. "Sarah, we must go quickly."

"But, Mama! The escape baskets!" the girl protested.

"I dare not wake the man, my love. He might stop us."

Aldridge responded to the fear in her voice. "I won't stop you. I am not a danger to you." The woman turned to a statue at his voice, her hand on the framework of the arched entrance, as if she would fall without support. He swung himself upright, wincing as the headache closed its vice around his skull. Though he slitted his eyes against the pain, he kept them open just enough.

"Mama?" The girl's fearful voice released the woman from her freeze, and she moved to block the child's sight of him. "Sarah. Watch the house. Do not turn around until I say."

Eyes open, he could confirm his initial assessment as she spun to face him. Spectacular. Then she shone the lantern straight on him, and he flinched from the light. "Not in my eyes, please. I have such a head."

She made that same disgusted sound again, then stripped the shawl from her shoulders and tossed it to him, taking care to stay out of arms' reach.

"Please cover yourself, Sir."

Aldridge stood warily, and made a kilt of the shawl—a long rectangle that wrapped his waist several times and covered him from waist to thigh. "I beg your pardon for my attire, Mrs..." he invited.

But she was ignoring him. While he'd been tucking in the soft wool of the shawl, so it would hold securely, she'd crossed the summerhouse again and lifted the lid of the bench, tipping the cushions onto the floor, pulling various bundles, baskets, and packages from the recess.

"Mama!" The child sounded panicked. "They are in the house."

Aldridge, headache forgotten, moved to a better vantage. Yes. Lights moving through the darkened house. And the men were not bothering to be silent, either, calling to one another as they searched swiftly and methodically: the ground floor, then the next, then the attics.

A rustle and chink came from the other end of the garden, then an eldritch groan that cut through his head like a knife.

"The gate!" The woman's eyes were wide and fearful. Yes, complaining hinges would make that noise, and clearly frightened her more than any unnatural denizen of the night.

"Sarah, come to me."

At the woman's soft command, the child brushed past Aldridge and rushed right into the woman's arms, wrapping herself around her mother's waist. She was a small thing, not quite short enough to fit under the curve of her mother's breasts. The delicate features, a miniature of her mother's, showed fear and a quite adult determination. Aldridge had little experience of children but she was much the size of his cousin's stepdaughter, who was six or seven.

The woman was holding something against the child's temple. In a swift movement, he was almost on her, but he held himself apart, afraid of frightening her into pulling the trigger of the small pistol.

Outside, a rough voice spoke in the kind of argot he'd learned when slumming in St Giles. "Keep by t'prads, I'll see 'tis all bob. I'll crash the culls if uns've banged that Rose." "Wait with the horses," he understood the man to say. "I'll see that all is well at the house. I'll kill the men if they've raped that Rose." Heavy footsteps retreating down the path. If they were quiet, they could talk.

"What the hell are you doing?" he demanded, keeping his voice low enough to carry no further than her ears.

Her whisper was even lower, and he had to strain to hear. "Praying they will pass us by. For the love of all you hold holy, don't give us away!"

"You cannot mean to hurt your child."

"Better death at my hands than what they have planned for her," the woman hissed. Her free hand, the one around the girl's shoulders, returned the frantic hug, patting and soothing even as the other hand held the little pistol firmly in place.

"Better we all live," he retorted. "Who are they?" He needed information. Damn his current state of undress. A fat billfold solved most problems.

"My... Mr Perringworth owes their employer money. He owns... he *used to own* the cottage. He came down this morning, said he had given them the cottage and everything in it, and it wasn't enough. He has fled the country. He said..." She fell silent, her face bleak, but the little girl piped up. "They are very bad men, sir. You should hide until they are gone."

"Why did you not run with this Perry person? Or after he left?" Aldridge was glad he had been woken by the woman rather than the bullies—the heavies of a criminal loan shark, unless he missed his guess.

"He locked us up," the woman said. "We were to be part of the 'everything' he gave this man. It has taken us the whole day to break through the wall into the next room."

Before she had finished, Aldridge was calculating his next move. The pistol was next to useless. Good enough to execute the child, but against at least four men, maybe more?

"I don't suppose you have a sword or another gun in that seat of yours?"

She shook her head.

It would have to be his tongue, then. Well, many a woman had called it his finest weapon.

"Help me drop your bundles out into the garden," he ordered. "I have a plan."

She watched him warily, not moving, as he suited action to words and dropped a covered basket, then a hatbox, then a tied bundle, one from each of the arched sides so they would be hidden in the low shrubbery around the summerhouse.

"Now, let's see how much room there is."

The space inside the bench seat was big enough for a slender woman and a small child. He began clearing out the clutter that accumulates in such places. The woman suddenly seemed to realise what he intended, and bent to whisper in her daughter's ear.

Together, they silently moved around the small room, collecting the bits and pieces he found and dropping them out into the garden.

Aldridge put one of the cushions into the space for their heads, and offered his hand to help the woman in. She ignored it, lifting her skirt with her free hand to show one shapely leg, and then the other, as she climbed inside the space and lay down.

"Here, Sarah," she whispered. "On top of me."

It crossed Aldridge's mind that he would welcome the self-same invitation. Perhaps the woman might be inclined to reward his act of knight errantry in what he had always suspected was the time-honoured manner. "Focus," he told himself.

"Whatever you hear," he told the woman and child, "don't make a sound. Trust me. I'll get you out of this." He closed the seat lid and retrieved the scattered cushions, then opened the woman's lantern to blow out the candle, and lay back down.

Just in time. Multiple boots on the path; voices talking, complaining, or so he understood, that furniture was all well and good, but the real treasure had flown.

He hoped the child couldn't understand what they said. He could, all too well, and the woman—Rose? Was that really her name? It seemed too appropriate to be true. Rose was right to be frightened.

They might get away free and clear, if the thugs believed she was long since gone. One of them suggested the cove had taken the two with him. The cove, this Perringworth, presumably.

But Aldridge's momentary hope was immediately dashed. Another laughed. He and his mate had Perringworth safe and sound, his legs broken so he couldn't run again. And the cull swore he'd left this Rose and her get safely locked up, tied for good measure.

"Swore afore ya bruk 'is munch bones. Won't do no yammerin' now," grumbled one. A broken jaw? Good to know Perringworth couldn't deny whatever lies Aldridge spoke.

The group stopped on the path and argued about what to do next.

The boss was expecting to sell the woman and her child to recover the money he was owed, and more. And breaking

Perringworth an inch at a time might act as a lesson to others, but it wouldn't replace the money.

The London bullies were anxious to get back to the safety of their verminous slums. This wide-open countryside made them nervous. But they were more frightened of their master than the strange environment, and when one of them mentioned a name, Aldridge understood why.

Smite. Whether the single syllable was a given name, a surname, or a nickname that described the terrible power of his fist, nobody knew. But Smite was the uncrowned king of large swaths of the underbelly of London.

And, in some sort, Aldridge's debtor, since the night Aldridge had waded into a fight for the sheer joy of battle, foiling an assassination attempt on Smite by a rival gang. If he could convince these men of his identity, he might pull off the rescue.

But they'd never believe him if they found him hiding. "Shut your noise," he shouted. "I'm trying to sleep in here." Instant silence on the path, then the moonlit entrance was blocked as several large men tried to enter at once.

"Don't shine that lantern in my face," Aldridge ordered, with all the hauteur of his generations of ducal ancestors, and the men—like the curs they were—responded to the voice of command and turned the lantern away. In the returning shadows, six large male shapes loomed over him.

"Who the hell are you, and what are you doing here?" Aldridge demanded. "Do you know where Perry's gone?"

"It be the Merry Marquis," said one of the men, pushing his way through from the back. Now there was a stroke of luck! Smite had sent one of his chief lieutenants. What did they call the man? Tiny. That was it. A typically laconic comment on his enormous size.

"Hello, Tiny," Aldridge said. "You're a step away from your usual haunts."

Big Tiny might be, but he hadn't come unscathed through a life of violence. His nose had been broken several times, was flattened and twisted towards his right cheek, which bore a livid knife scar from the outer edge of the eye to the corner of his thick, misshapen lips. He'd been beaten around the ears, too, many times, leaving them swollen and deformed.

Aldridge knew, though, that the rough appearance hid an incisive mind. Smite looked for intelligence in his lieutenants, and Tiny's presence here, who knew how many days from London, and Smite's control, was evidence of how much Smite trusted him. In this instance, intelligence was all to the good, if Aldridge played his game well.

One of the other men grunted a question. 'Shall I take his head off?' Aldridge translated. Thankfully, Tiny shook his head. "Smite likes 'im." Useful to know, but not something to count on. Rumour had it, Smite's rise to the top had been aided by a childhood friend, killed by his own hand when the friend dared to disagree with him.

The crime lord's lieutenant turned back to Aldridge. "Whacha doin' here, m'lord?" he demanded. "And whassat ya got on?"

Aldridge looked down at his improvised shawl kilt as if he'd never seen it before.

"This? The piece of perfection in the garden was most insistent. Didn't want her daughter seeing my..." he waggled his eyebrows and made a graphic gesture with one hand, prompting a guffaw from the man who wanted to decapitate him.

"A skirt wiv a little un? Where is she?" Tiny wanted to know.

"Gone. She was in a hurry, said she and the little girl had a ship to catch. She couldn't tell me where Perry was, either. Bastard. He'll be sorry when I find him. Drugged me, the lowlife, treacherous cur. Stole my horse and my clothes. Swine. Exquisite female, though. Worth the trip, if she'd have had me. Pity she wouldn't stop to... chat."

Another guffaw from Decapitator, and a pungent comment about a better use for a female than chatting.

"'ow long?" Tiny was not to be distracted.

Enough friendliness. Time to remind them of their place again. He trotted out the ducal manner. Nostrils flared, chin lifted, a glare infused with scorn and disdain.

Tiny flinched, but persisted. "I needs to ask, m'lord; 'ow long since ya seen the skirt? She belongs to Smite. 'Er and the little un."

"Really?" said Aldridge. "Dammit, that's the last straw. I was promised first chance. Perry, damn his cowardly, lying eyes, said he was leaving the country, and she needed a new protector. And all the time... Smite? Really? I say! Do you think he'd consider an offer?"

"We 'ave to find 'er first, m'lord. 'Ow long since ya seen her?"

Aldridge sighed. "Really, I don't know. It was around dusk. How long ago was that? After she left, I... I suppose I passed out again."

Tiny let out a string of profanities, some Aldridge had never heard, and several that sounded painful, if not impossible. "Doxy's got ten hours on us, but we 'ave to search," he told the others, and began organising his men to search the garden, the house, the nearby village of Niddberrow, and the surrounding countryside.

He was near Niddberrow? The last Aldridge remembered, he had been just outside of Bath, half a day's ride away. "If you're off to search the countryside, perhaps one of you would take a message to my cousin in Longford, the Earl of Chirbury at Longford Court."

"No time," Tiny told him.

Aldridge sighed. "So much for Smite's promises," he said. "Ah well. I daresay I can walk to Longford, though it might alarm the local populace. When I get to London, though, I'll be having a little talk with our mutual friend. 'Anything you need, any time,' he said." Aldridge made shooing motions with his hands. "Go on, then. Go, if you're going. I might as well get some more sleep."

Tiny looked a little hunted. He'd witnessed Smite's first meeting with Aldridge. Clearly, Tiny knew no better than Aldridge what the crime lord would expect of him now.

Aldridge let him stew for a minute, then offered him a way out. "I suppose whoever rides over to Longford could just give my note to a villager. That would do."

Tiny agreed, and found a scrap of paper in one pocket and a pencil in the other. Pity. Aldridge had hoped to move the entire meeting up to the house, so Rose and Sarah could release themselves from their prison.

He wrote quickly and handed the message to Tiny, who read it before giving it to the searcher heading for Longford. Would Rede recognise his writing? He had no idea if his cousin had even seen a letter from him. Well, if no carriage came, Aldridge would have to think of something else.

Chapter Two

Trapped in the seat, with Sarah's light weight heavier by the minute, the woman known as the Rose of Frampton listened with growing appreciation as her rescuer played Smite's men like an orchestra. She'd heard of the Merry Marquis—who hadn't? The Marquis of Aldridge: one of the richest men in England, and one of the randiest, too, by all accounts.

Among mistresses and courtesans, his generosity with women of their kind was legendary—and of far more interest to Rose than his rumoured prowess in the act by which she made her living.

Aldridge talked circles around his audience: cajoling, commanding, teasing, amusing, coaxing; by turns haughty, friendly, and bored. Rose understood very little of the London argot, but the tension eased from the air, the men's voices changed as they relaxed their battle-ready awareness and fell under Aldridge's spell.

By the time he sent them off on their wild goose chase around the countryside, Sarah had fallen asleep. Rose hoped they would all leave, but the leader said he would wait here for his followers' reports. Rose felt the bench seat shift slightly as someone sat on it, and she heard Aldridge's voice directly above her, addressing the leader of the heavies.

"You do not have to keep me company, Tiny. I'm happy to go back to sleep until Rede's carriage arrives."

Tiny muttered something, and Aldridge answered as if he could not care a bean. "Search the garden? Why not. Help yourself, old chap." His weight shifted above her, and suddenly his voice was only inches above her head. "I'll just check out the back of my eyelids."

Long moments passed before Tiny grunted, and his boots sounded on their way to the door and down the steps.

Aldridge spoke, his voice a whisper. "Best stay there, ladies. I hope you are not too uncomfortable."

She whispered back. "Sarah is asleep. We can stay as long as we must. Thank you."

"No talking," he warned. She was tempted to tell him he had started it, but she stayed silent.

Sarah slept on as the minutes slowly passed. Rose ignored her increasing discomfort, straining her ears to hear Tiny as he searched the garden, grumbling loudly to himself. He must have a couple of men still here, since she heard him talking to one down by the back gate, and another up near the house. Thank all the powers of Heaven he didn't think to poke in the low shrubbery around the summerhouse, where Aldridge had stowed their bundles.

Several times, he came into the summerhouse to talk. Aldridge asked after the woman they were hunting.

"She, I must suppose," he said, "is this Rose that Perry spoke of so highly. I must say, if she is as good in bed as she is to look at, she's worth every penny Perry wanted for her. If your men find her, I would like to make an offer."

Tiny made an answer, in which 'The Rose of Frampton' was the only familiar phrase, and that only because Rose was accustomed to the label she'd been given, ten years ago, by the abbess who had taken her when her father cast her out.

After the brothel, she had moved from protector to protector. Perry, may he roast in Hell forever, was to have been her last. He'd promised her the cottage, showered her with jewellery, even let her keep Sarah with her. But when he tied her up, he'd told her the cottage was never hers, that the deeds he'd given her were fake. And he'd sorted through her jewels while she sat cuffed to the bed cursing him, leaving the ones he said were paste, and taking the few good pieces.

When she had stashed some clothes and jewellery in the bench seat in case she needed to run, she had laughed at her own fears. Why would she wish to escape from her own house? From her last protector, who was a gambler and a drunkard, but not a violent man? But her escape baskets were a habit established for years, and into the seat they went.

Now her only question was how much of the hidden jewellery was paste? How many of her previous protectors had played her for a fool? Perry, the belly-crawling sack of slime, had given her one piece of good advice: "You should have hired a solicitor, Rose," he told her. "All the smart beauties do. Too late now, though. No lawyers in Smite's world."

If she had to find herself another protector, she'd insist on a written contract, and hire someone to check that he not only seemed wealthy, but actually was. She sighed, taking care to stay silent. She had hoped to leave this life behind her, to give Sarah a fresh start, away from this business. Her hopes were dust now. Even if the rest of her jewellery were real, it wouldn't raise enough for them to survive.

And what were her other choices—assuming she and Sarah got out of this alive? With her past, no one would give her a respectable job, and what marketable skills did she have? It would be the workhouse, where they would separate her from Sarah, or another protector.

Perhaps she should try her luck in London, where rich men were more plentiful, or so she had heard. Perhaps Aldridge would help her. Perhaps...

Her heart, her breathing; everything stopped for a moment while she considered the thought that crept up on her. Perhaps Aldridge meant it when he claimed to be attracted to her, perhaps even when he said he wished to make an offer. Was he in the market for a mistress? And could a provincial whore hope to win his interest?

She was so busy remembering everything she had heard about the Merry Marquis that she almost missed the crunch of footsteps outside.

"Are you 'Tiny'?" Another upper-class voice, consonants so crisp they could cut.

"Rede?" Aldridge said, the boards creaking as he shifted his weight. "Rede, you came yourself?"

The cousin replied, "With a message like that? 'Stuck at Perringworth's cottage just outside Niddberrow. No clothes, no horse, no money. Send closed carriage to the summerhouse, urgently. Your loving cousin, Aldridge.' Fetching kilt, cousin. Pink roses on a green field. Setting a new fashion?"

Aldridge laughed. "I'll bet you a gold guinea, at least a dozen people would imitate me, were I to walk through Hyde Park dressed like this. I did think it rather better than the alternative, especially if I had to walk all the way to the Court."

"I have not been introduced to your friend," the cousin said.

"Ah. A friend of a friend, shall we say. Tiny, *aide-de-camp* to Smite, of Seven Dials in London. He's here on a debt-collecting mission. Our Mr. Perringworth has been a naughty, naughty boy."

"Run orf, 'e as," Tiny said. "An' the skirt too. Smite, 'e's not gonna be 'appy. 'Ad a buyer for the little 'un, 'e did."

"We are talking, I take it, of The Rose of Frampton and her child?" the cousin asked.

"Perringworth left them as payment for his debt, but they seem to have disappeared. I don't suppose I could borrow your jacket, cousin?"

"We can do better, I think." Something was placed on the bench with a thump.

"You've brought clothes? Ah, good chap. I say, Tiny, if you could just wait outside while I change?"

The bully's steps retreated down the stairs, and then up the path towards the house. Suddenly, the seat lid was opened. Rose was dazzled for a moment by the sudden light.

When her eyes cleared, two men were leaning over her. The sun had risen while she was hiding, and was shining directly into the summerhouse, giving both fair heads a halo of gold.

Aldridge was everything she'd heard. If Sarah hadn't been asleep on top of her, she wasn't sure she could have resisted poking his bare chest to see if his muscles were as hard as they looked. Or perhaps just shaping them with her hands... What on earth did Aldridge do for exercise?

She met his amused brown eyes, and he winked as if he knew exactly what she was thinking. She turned her head and met vivid blue, instead. If Aldridge were handsome, then his cousin was beautiful—classic high cheekbones, a firm mouth currently in a stern line, but with a lower lip that suggested a passionate temperament, and golden hair tousled from being trapped under his hat. He could have sat as a model for the archangel Michael. She wouldn't be at all surprised if he slew dragons in his spare time.

"The Rose of Frampton, I presume," he said. The voice was bland, non-committal, not a hint of judgement. Still, she blushed.

"We have no time for introductions," Aldridge said. "My dear, is there another way out of the garden? Tiny has men on the front gate and the back."

"We can get through the hedge," said Sarah with a yawn, as she responded to Rose's hand gently shaking her shoulder.

"Where will that take you?" As he spoke, Aldridge was dressing: stepping into a pair of pantaloons and pulling them up before he unwound the shawl, turning his back to don and tuck in a shirt. "We'll bring the carriage as close as we can to pick you up."

"The lane. It takes a turn past the house and runs beside the hedge for a short way," Rose said. The angel man had helped Sarah from the cavity, and was now holding out a hand for her. Unaccountably shy, Rose held her dress at the knee as she climbed out.

Aldridge was sitting on the floor, pulling on boots. "Over the side with you, and hide. We'll draw Tiny off. Don't run for the hedge until we clear the corner of the house."

"Aldridge," said the angel man, "what am I assisting with here?"

"A rescue, dear cousin. You heard what they said about the child."

The angel man smiled at Sarah with a sweetness Rose did not expect from such a stern man. "A rescue we can manage. Come. Let me lift you over the wall." Sarah went willingly to his arms, and he swung her between the trellises into the garden beyond. Aldridge lifted Rose and did the same, the strength in his arms fulfilling the promise of the muscles now hidden beneath a gentleman's waistcoat and jacket.

"Tiny!" Aldridge's voice moved away from her as he spoke. "Tiny, the Earl of Chirbury and I would like you to take a message for us to Smite."

Aldridge continued talking, and the steps of all three men retreated up the path. Rose waited impatiently until they sounded distant before daring to peek over the bush that was her hiding place. As soon as they disappeared around the corner of the house, she stood cautiously, checking all around her.

No one was in sight.

"Sarah, run for the hedge and hide under it until the carriage comes," she said, before scurrying along the edge of the summerhouse, picking up the bundle, box, and basket.

She checked both ways again before running to join her daughter. Just in time. Tiny rounded the house and started down the path, calling for the man at the back gate.

Moments later, the carriage came slowly up the lane. Aldridge opened the door and leapt down to toss first Sarah, then Rose, then all of their baggage, up into the carriage. He swung in behind them, swiftly shutting the door.

"Stay down," his cousin said to Rose, who was trying to pull herself up from the floor. "We're not out of the woods yet."

Rose sat at the earl's feet, propping herself against the seat, taking Sarah into her arms.

The coachman must have had instructions to spring the horses once all the passengers were aboard, for the coach suddenly lurched forward, and Rose had to brace herself with her feet and one arm.

Aldridge, from the seat opposite his cousin, said, "I expect them to check on us, but they won't follow us to the Court. You'll soon be safe, ladies."

"We have perhaps fifteen minutes until we are on my land," the earl told her, "and then a further ten to the Court." He raised his brows at Aldridge. "Time enough to tell me your story, cousin."

The brief explanation they gave, all they were prepared to say in front of the child, clearly didn't satisfy Rede. But he said nothing, even after they were met at the Court by Rede's countess, the lovely

Anne. But as soon as Aldridge delivered Mrs Rose Darling—a working name if ever he heard one—and Miss Sarah Darling into Lady Chirbury's hands, Aldridge heard the command he'd expected.

"Aldridge, I'll see you in my study."

The courtesan had been subdued in the carriage, but he'd caught a speculative look in her eyes from time to time. Eyes of cornflower blue, in a face that fulfilled the promise he'd glimpsed in the night's shadows. And her body brought his to instant, quivering attention.

He hoped her mind was drifting in the same direction as his. Rede's house had many inviting nooks and crannies to provide cover for a couple in search of privacy.

"Aldridge!" Rede's voice cut through Aldridge's lazy speculation about Mrs Darling's treasures.

Aldridge followed Rede, who went straight to a row of decanters in the spacious study. "Brandy? It's early, but you look like hell, old chap."

"Please."

Now that the crisis was over, Aldridge's headache had returned full force, and he was having trouble focusing his thoughts. Perhaps his lies about being drugged were closer to the truth than he'd thought.

Rede waved him to a chair. "You are planning to offer Mrs Darling *carte blanche*, I assume. Very well. The lady has to make a living. But while she is a guest under my roof, you will not bed her—or tup her anywhere else. Nor will you offend my wife with lewd talk or innuendo. I'll have your promise before you leave this room."

Aldridge didn't have the energy to be offended at Rede's poor opinion of his manners. Besides, he had intended all of those things. Except for lewd talk in front of Rede's countess, obviously.

"I didn't come down to see her," he said. "I didn't even know she existed. How does it happen that you've heard of The Rose of Frampton, and I haven't?"

A two-pronged distraction, and thankfully, Rede picked up one of the lures. "If you didn't come for Mrs Darling, what were you doing in her garden?"

"I have no idea, Rede. Last I remember, I was at a house party just outside of Bath. What's the date?"

"The date?" Rede raised his eyebrows, but answered. "The 17th of October."

"Really? The last day I remember was the 14th. I went to bed on the 14th of October, and woke up in the early morning of the 17th twenty-five miles away and in the garden of a complete stranger."

"Who were you in bed with?" Rede asked dryly.

Aldridge tipped his glass to Rede to acknowledge the point.

A servant arrived in answer to the bell pull. Rede ordered a full breakfast to be brought to the study. "If you've not eaten for two days, you'll be hungry," he observed.

"My stomach thinks my throat's been cut," Aldridge agreed.

He was still thinking about the woman he'd been in bed with, and the others who'd preceded her during the house party.

On the one hand, any husband whose wife warmed the bed of the Marquis of Aldridge had only himself to blame. If they paid more attention to their wives and less to games of chance, drinking, and pursuit of other women at the party, their wives would have no reason to stray.

On the other hand, husbands seldom accepted that point of view. At least six men at the house party would consider themselves entitled to be upset with Aldridge. Make that seven, since one betrothed gentleman also had a neglected lady. Aldridge never made a show of his amorous adventures, but ladies often used an affair with him to punish their spouses, and any of them might have dropped hints designed to do the most damage.

Presumably, the perpetrators did not intend to reward him with the delectable Rose, so what was their purpose in stripping him and leaving him in Perringworth's garden? They couldn't have known, surely, that Smite's boys were on their way?

"Tell me about Perringworth," he said.

Rede steepled his hands and considered for a moment. "He's a younger son. Brother's a baron just south of Bristol. They've had a falling out. Perringworth had a legacy, and he's blown it, by all accounts.

"A loose fish, that's certain. And a big bruiser of a man. Has a reputation as handy with his fists, but lousy with money. Can't resist a game of chance, and always thinks he'll win the next one. Very jealous. Rumour has it, he put the Rose out at Niddberrow to keep her away from competitors. Likely, your friends thought it would be a fine joke for him to find you naked in her garden."

Aldridge nodded. "Not much temptation in Niddberrow, I would think. Not many who would even acknowledge her, I expect."

"Poor girl. It can't have been much of a life for her."

"Better than the one he was selling her into. Her and little Sarah."

Rede swore, low and long, not repeating himself once in a several sentences. Aldridge agreed, but Perringworth had his own problems. He was unlikely to survive the encounter with Smite.

"They're well out of it, and lucky your abductors chose to abandon you in that garden. Do you think they drugged you?"

"Possibly, but perhaps not. I was fairly drunk for most of the party."

"Cousin, I don't believe you've been sober since June—I've never seen you drink so much."

Aldridge shook his head. He'd lost both of his brothers in June. One had fled overseas, and the other had pursued the first. Rede knew that, but didn't need to know that Aldridge blamed himself.

He put the full glass down on the corner of the desk they'd been using as a table.

"No more," he said, decisively. "You're right; it isn't helping. Rede, I'll have to talk to Smite. He has a purchaser set up for the little girl. They'll not be safe unless I can buy him off. Can they stay here till I have it sorted?"

Rede nodded. "If I have your promise not to swive Mrs Darling under my roof," he answered. Aldridge's cousin always had been a tenacious sort.

Chapter Three

Aldridge returned triumphant from his trip to London.

"Smite agreed," he told her, catching her alone in the garden, where two or three late roses clung to the last remnants of their blooms. He sat down beside her on the stone seat, taking up the centre, so she had to lean against the curved arm to keep some distance between them. "You and Sarah are free."

The relief made her breathless. "I had enough?"

She'd given him the jewellery she'd managed to hide in the summerhouse. Paste, most of it, he'd said.

He shrugged, more an action of his head and eyebrows than his shoulders. "It doesn't matter. Here. I used the ones with some value and brought back the rest." The little cloth bag was still full of glittering baubles. He'd used hardly any. How...?

"You paid?" It was barely a question, and he didn't answer, just smiled, rather smugly.

"How can we thank you?" she said. And that wasn't a question either. She knew what he would ask in return. For five days, the Chirburys had treated her like a guest, but her holiday was clearly over.

"I'm sure we can think of something," he replied, crowding her with his strength, but not his weight, his warmth sparking a responding heat. But his complacent assumption, after five days of being treated like a lady, sparked a contrary impulse to deny him, at least for the moment.

She slid sideways off the bench and stood, focusing on smoothing her skirts as she said, "Perhaps you would accept a few pounds a quarter until the debt is repaid?"

"I would accept a kiss on account," he said.

"Certainly," she replied. "Sarah would be delighted to give you a kiss. You are quite her hero."

The moment she spoke, she wanted to take it back. She did not want another protector, but she needed one, and at least servicing this one would not be such a chore.

But no, he was grinning at her, his head cocked to one side and a light in his eyes that said she held his interest. Aha. The man enjoyed the pursuit. Well then, Rose would lead him on a right merry chase.

"If you will excuse me, my lord, I promised to help the countess with her knitting."

She dropped a curtsey and made her escape before he formulated a response. For a few more days, perhaps, Sarah could continue to enjoy life in the upstairs nursery, with the countess's daughter and sister, and Rose could pretend a life further up the ranks of the gentry than she could ever have achieved, even if she hadn't been made a fallen woman before her sixteenth birthday.

Aldridge was waiting for her in the hall outside the countess's sitting room an hour later.

"I had in mind something more personal than soulless pounds," he said, without preamble.

"Perhaps I could bake you a cake," she suggested.

"Certainly, what I have in mind involves tasting," he answered smoothly. "Some sweet, decadent tasting. Licking, undoubtedly. Perhaps a little gentle biting."

Goodness, it was hot for October.

"A single meal, my lord?"

"One... meal... would not be enough, dear Mrs Darling. Do you not agree?"

Sarah. This was not about her pleasure. This was about securing a future for Sarah. If Rose weren't very careful, she would agree to anything he said. "An arrangement, then?"

"An arrangement to please us both." He took her hand as he walked beside her, and placed a single chaste kiss on the tip of her index finger before sucking the whole finger into his mouth in a far-from-chaste gesture.

"Do you garden, my lord?" Her voice was unsteady.

The gambit prompted a quizzical amused quirk of the lips and one eyebrow. "Garden? No, I don't garden."

"I had a garden at Niddberrow. I thought the cottage was mine, you see. Perringworth promised me a house."

"A woman should have her own house," Aldridge agreed. "But a woman like you deserves a town-house in London, rather than a cottage in the country."

She would prefer a cottage in the country, but the Marquis lived mostly in London.

"London is so large, though. If I lived in London, would I not need a carriage?"

"A phaeton, perhaps, that you could drive in Hyde Park during the promenading hour," Aldridge suggested.

"Drive? Myself?" She did her best to sound shocked, not intrigued, but lost her next thought as he whisked her into a curtained alcove and proceeded to kiss her.

She thought she knew kisses. Rough and clumsy connections, rude invasions of her mouth, as the man who had purchased the right, violently mauled her breasts and buttocks. Those weren't kisses.

This; this was a kiss. A firm, but gentle, invitation to a duet, patiently coaxing a response and then turning to a dance, a partnership of giving and taking that spun music through every vein in her body. Rose forgot where she was, almost who she was, as she melted against him, lost in a world of sensation.

Sarah. Campaign plan. She pulled back, and Aldridge let her go.

"Something on account," Aldridge suggested.

"Perhaps." She peeked cautiously around the curtain and then hurried away down the silent hall.

Aldridge next approached her after dinner, sitting on the other side of the love seat she'd deliberately chosen in a shadowed corner of the great parlour, out of the direct view of the earl, who was playing the pianoforte, and the countess, turning the pages of music for him.

"I love that shade of blue on you, Mrs Darling," he said.

She blushed. Her lovers seldom bothered to compliment her, though extravagant, excruciatingly bad, poetry had been written to The Rose of Frampton by those who didn't have her in their keeping.

"It needs something else, though," Aldridge commented. He pulled out a tissue-wrapped package. "Not the diamonds and sapphires I thought of buying, but it is just the colour of your eyes. I had to see it on you."

'This' was a shawl in patterns of blue, so fine it was small enough when rolled to fit into his jacket pocket, but large enough to wrap warmly around her shoulders. She jumped up to examine it in the mirror, and he followed, standing inches away, leaning forward to breathe on her ear as he said, "Exquisite."

She should refuse the gift. Proper ladies did not take gifts from gentlemen. But they both knew she was not a lady, and she was well used to gifts with a price tag attached.

"Something on account?" she asked.

"Not this time. A present, given freely, with no expectation of reward. Because I admire you, lovely Rose."

She had to remind herself of every rumour she had heard about the man. And even then, if she'd not heard him working his charm on Smite's men, she might have unravelled, as he clearly expected. No wonder he had left such a string of broken hearts behind him.

It would be a mistake to give in too easily.

"And in return," she told him, "I freely give you my thanks, my lord."

She was rewarded with a moment's stunned amazement before the amused look reappeared. "Well played, Mrs Darling," he murmured, just before Lady Chirbury called her to the pianoforte.

She had enjoyed music above all things, back when she lived with her father. She'd not had access to a pianoforte for ten years, but when Lady Chirbury found her mooning over the instrument on the first day of her stay, she had insisted Rose start playing again.

With Aldridge watching, she kept to something simple, a country ballad, one of the earliest tunes her mother had taught her. The appreciation brightened in his eyes as she played, and later, when she said goodnight, he whispered, "You are full of surprises, Mrs Darling. The town-house will definitely have a pianoforte."

The following morning, Aldridge caught Rose as she came out of the nursery wing, and led her into a long open gallery with a barrelled ceiling. She stopped just inside the door, staring with her mouth just a little open.

The room ran the length and breadth of the entire east wing, and was easily the size of the countess's private garden. It was a visual cacophony. The panelled walls were painted, and so was the ornate plastered ceiling, features and details picked out in reds and blues and greens and purples and highlighted in gilt. The heavy drapes hanging in the windows along all four sides were embroidered with wonderful beasts and flowers.

Somehow, all the bold, clashing colours worked together to create a thing of beauty.

Aldridge recalled her attention. "I'm pleased by your appreciation, Mrs Darling, truly, though I'd prefer it addressed to myself."

"I've never seen a room like it," she told him. "Whatever is it for? Dancing?"

"Yes, they have dances. And they walk here when the weather is inclement, or play games. It is not used on a fine day like today." He was approaching her with intent, scattering her wits with his masculine aura.

"I enjoy dancing," she said, annoyed when her voice came out in a squeak. In truth, the only dancing she'd done had been at entertainments organised by two of her kinder protectors, and both of them thought 'dancing' simply a euphemism for upright fornication.

"You'd probably enjoy opera, too," he replied. Trying to formulate a reply, she turned and walked the length of the gallery, stopping to exclaim over the views from the windows on the three outer walls.

He prowled after her, content, for the moment, to hold his lusts in check. If he chose to take her here, she doubted she could stop him. Or that she would. This game of tag they were playing was arousing her, too, but she could ignore that. His kindness, though—his willingness to think of ways to please her—those were fast touching the heart she had thought turned to stone a decade ago.

She cast about for something to say. "I am much out of practice on the pianoforte."

"A music master, perhaps? For you and Sarah? It would be a good investment. I appreciate the sound of music in the evening."

For Sarah, too? The thought put a check in her step.

Still, his assumption that she intended to surrender rankled, for all that it was true.

"You assume a great deal, my lord." She didn't have to work at making her voice cold, and a little hurt.

Just then, the door at the far end of the room opened, and the nursery party trooped in: Lady Daisy Redepenning hand-in-hand with Sarah, Lady Meg Haverstock, and a bevy of nursery maids, followed closely by the countess herself. Sarah had quickly become the leader of the three. At seven, she was a year older than Lady Daisy, and Lady Meg—though an adult in years—was younger still in her understanding.

The countess waved her over. "We're going to play Blind Man's Buff, Mrs Darling. Will you join us?"

Rose made her apologies to Aldridge and hurried to the relative safety of a game with children.

Aldridge next saw Mrs Darling when the house gathered for dinner. Her borrowed gown of powder blue intensified the colour of her eyes, echoed in the more vibrant blues of the shawl he'd given her, which she'd draped with studied negligence around her waist and over one shoulder.

Aldridge bowed correctly over Anne's hand, and then that of his lovely quarry. "Ladies, how charming you both look," Rede said, beating Aldridge to the compliment.

At dinner, they did not stand on ceremony, eating in the breakfast parlour around a table that allowed for easy conversation.

"They're sending 2,000 seamen to Denmark to bring back the Danish fleet," Rede told Anne, when she asked if the papers had any news of interest.

Anne frowned. "I cannot like our bombarding a friendly nation."

"War makes for tough choices, Anne," Aldridge said. "The poor Danes were in a dilemma. We were demanding they give up their ships before Napoleon took them, and Napoleon would undoubtedly have punished them had they complied."

"And now they have lost their navy, and Copenhagen lies in ruins," Anne said. "Surely there was another way?"

"Their fate was sealed when Napoleon decided to take their fleet," Aldridge told her.

"Their fate was sealed when they continued to trade with France these last ten years," Mrs Darling corrected. "A neutral nation that trades with both sides? Napoleon's intent, if true, is only an excuse."

"Why do you say 'if true,' Mrs Darling?" Rede asked. "We were acting on information received from merchants and French diplomats."

"What was it Samuel Johnson said?" she retorted. "…'Among the calamities of war may be justly numbered the diminution of the love of truth.'"

Clever, as well as pretty. "Is trade worth going to war?" Aldridge asked, just to see what she would say.

"Trade brings power and money. Are these not the reasons nations take up arms?" she retorted.

Anne disagreed, "The reasons for one nation to attack unprovoked, certainly. But we must defend ourselves from invasion, surely?"

"Certainly, I will fight to protect what is mine," Rede said, "even if that means we must take the battle to the enemy."

Mrs Darling returned them to the point. "Even if it means bombing a neutral nation and taking their entire fleet?"

"A fleet that had been used to supply Napoleon's war effort." Aldridge's voice grew louder at the prospect of a good argument.

But he wasn't to get one. Mrs Darling pulled herself inward, the passion that lit her face smoothing into the calm mask she usually wore. She looked down at her plate, and then up again with a small flash of fire.

"I have never approved of the Fabian strategy," she said, quietly. "It may win wars, but it hurts too many people."

"Steady on, Aldridge," Rede said. "No need to raise your voice. Can I help you to the parsnips, Mrs Darling?"

Apart from murmuring his apologies, Aldridge said little for some time. Mrs Darling was a conundrum. The Fabian strategy? Who had ever heard of a provincial whore who knew about Quintius Fabius Maximus Verrucosus, Roman general, whose war of slow attrition to cut off Hannibal's supply lines had kept the Carthaginian from Rome and spelled his defeat.

He would enjoy matching wits with her. But he would need to be gentle. He had not missed Mrs Darling's flinch. He hoped her previous protectors, starting with the probably-late, unlamented Perringworth, roasted in hell for hurting a defenceless woman.

Mrs Darling, too, remained quiet until near the end of the dinner.

Aldridge was describing a request, received in the mail that morning. One of the ducal estates in Sussex, short of firewood for the new brick kilns they were building, was negotiating to cut a neighbour's woods, but the neighbour wanted a written contract.

"I've never heard the like," Aldridge said. "We're both gentlemen. Is our word not good enough?"

His cousin shrugged. "This is your reward for taking the duchy into trade, Aldridge. We merchants know the value of putting things in writing. With the best will in the world, people can remember different things from the same conversation, and not all gentlemen are as honourable as you and I."

Mrs Darling's murmured comment was clearly not intended for the table at large: "A written contract would be a very good idea," she said to herself.

Mrs Darling and Anne had disappeared up to the nursery immediately after dinner last night, and all day today Aldridge had been unable to snatch more than brief moments with her, though he made full use of every encounter to try to regain the ground he lost the previous evening.

He'd complimented her gown, carried the basket for the flowers she was cutting, suggested several scandalous ways to further enjoy the garden, squeezed her hand, and even managed to divert her into a curtained alcove for another searing kiss that melted her, and had precisely the opposite effect on him. From the sparkle in her eyes and the sway of her hips as she walked off, she appreciated his efforts. But walk off she did.

At first, he had been confident he would win this battle of wills with Mrs Darling. Then his cousin's wife had called him aside and told him she intended to offer Mrs Darling a job in the village. What a waste! Surely, Mrs Darling would prefer to be his mistress rather than a serving woman?

He hoped so. He was so hard he could hammer nails, and his bollocks ached.

By dinner time, he had made progress, if not as much as he'd hoped.

He'd seduced virtuous wives more quickly than this courtesan. He briefly considered accepting the clear invitation one of the maids had been transmitting, but Rede would frown on it, especially since—from the look of her—she was some sort of relative from the wrong side of the blanket. One could never tell when in the stomping ground of the three previous Earls of Chirbury.

In any case, he didn't want another woman. He wanted The Rose of Frampton. He sighed. It had been a long time since he'd required an intimate acquaintance with Mrs Palmer and her five agile daughters.

She was worth waiting for. She was clever; the conversation last night showed that. And there was the music. Clearly, she was both educated and cultured. A fallen daughter of the gentry, undoubtedly. He could certainly do better for her, be better for her, than the provincials who had kept her until now.

So, she wanted a contract, did she? Wise woman. He doubted if the local solicitors had much experience in drafting such things. The current earl was boringly uxorious, and previous earls had been more in favour of *droit de seigneur* than contracts with the *demi-monde*. Still, he'd signed several in the past few years and could, no doubt, draft something that would stand up in court.

Yes. A contract. He'd never offered more than a six-month contract, with mutual right to renew. In bed, he found women largely interchangeable, and outside of bed, he was quickly bored. But Rose, he thought, might amuse him for longer than six months. Perhaps even a year.

That evening, after dinner, Mrs Darling partnered Anne against Aldridge and Rede for cards, and the ladies won. Then Rede and Anne faced him and Mrs Darling, and Mrs Darling led her team to victory again. "What other talents have you, I wonder?" he murmured in her ear in a private moment, while Anne was supervising the tea trolley, and Rede had been called out of the room. She smiled at him, her eyes still full of the triumph of the game, but her gaze faltered when he added, "I look forward to demonstrating my own talents, which are not—I fancy—entirely unheralded."

And he skated one finger in a feather-light touch across her bare arm, from elbow to shoulder.

She had her revenge a few moments later, leaning her breast on his shoulder as she passed him a cup of tea. A small incline of the head, and he would be resting his cheek on that smooth flesh. Rede was watching them, though, so he contented himself with saying, quietly, "A dish very much to my taste, Mrs Darling."

He had to shift though, to ease the strain in his breeches. She cheekily dropped a judicious napkin over his tented fall, and said, her eyes laughing, "In case of spills, my lord."

Witch. She let her thigh brush his as she walked away. He hadn't spilled without intention since he was a boy, and he wasn't about to start now. Mind you, he hadn't been without a woman for more than a week, either, apart from his eighteen-month exile some years back at one of his father's remote properties.

All these fleeting touches, suggestive comments, stolen kisses— he could only hope this seduction was working on her as well as it was working on him.

Mrs Darling and Anne began discussing books. The object of his interest was, it seemed, a member of a circulating library in Bristol, and disliked *The Family Shakespeare*, which Anne had just purchased for the nursery library.

"But surely, Mrs Darling, you cannot object to removing words and expressions that should not be read aloud to gentle ears?" Anne argued.

"I make no complaint about the reader using some discretion, my lady." Mrs Darling said. "But if we can allow such vandalism of our literary treasures, what is next? Shall we let him loose on the Bible? You cannot deny there is much within that is indecorous."

Anne laughed in agreement. "But still, a noble intent, do you not think?"

"I prefer the retellings in *Tales from Shakespeare*, my lady. Mr and Miss Lamb make no attempt to keep to the original words, but just retell the stories. It is very good fare for the schoolroom, I think. Then, when our girls are old enough, let them hear the true poetry in Shakespeare's own words. And all of his own words, for the Bowdler volumes not only cut passages, but whole plays!"

Perhaps a two-year contract? He couldn't imagine being bored with her in less than two years.

Chapter Four

The entire next day, Rede and Anne must have been conspiring to keep them apart. Anne took Mrs Darling to the village in the morning. Since she wasn't about, Aldridge accepted Rede's invitation to go riding after he'd dealt with the day's mail, and regretted it when the two men on horseback passed the carriage returning through the gate.

He and Mrs Darling met over lunch in the company of the Chirburys, and he found her alone four times during the afternoon, only to have Rede, Anne, or both enter before they could exchange more than one or two moves in their game.

Had he ever desired a woman this much? Perhaps it was the chase; mostly, they fell into his bed with little effort. Or they didn't, and he looked elsewhere. And she wanted him, too. She might manufacture the shiver of desire when he breathed on her ear, the way she moulded herself to him when they managed a stolen kiss. But the flush of colour on that perfect skin? That was genuine. And he saw no artifice, no calculation, in the lovely eyes.

When Aldridge joined Rede for a drink after dinner, he asked, "Rede, are you and Anne deliberately trying to stop me from talking to Mrs Darling?"

Rede laughed. "Whatever makes you think that, cousin?"

"Please desist? I promised I wouldn't bed her under your roof, but I am trying to negotiate a contract. And it is damned difficult when I can't even talk to the lady."

"Why not leave it till you get to London?"

"First," Aldridge explained, "Mrs Darling has no place to live in London, nor the money to rent anything, until I have the right to provide for her. Second, I am not letting those wolves in London get a glimpse of her until she is under my protection."

"Anne thinks I should protect her from you. She wants to find her a job here in Longford. Or, at the very least, she wants me to ensure you give the woman a fair contract."

"I don't mind a contract. A contract is a good idea. But a job? A jewel like that? She's a courtesan, Rede. It's not as if I'm seducing a virgin."

Rede grinned and slid the port along the table. "Pour yourself another, Aldridge. Mrs Darling has the right to make her own choices. I've told Anne that Mrs Darling can stay in Longford if that is what the lady wants, but I won't stand in your way, either."

"Then please stop trying to keep us apart."

"Very well, cousin," Rede agreed, and conceded, "I'll take Anne out visiting tomorrow with the girls and leave you with Mrs Darling. Good enough? But I will tell her if she wants advice on the contract, I am happy to be at her service."

Aldridge went to find Mrs Darling, but she had already retired for the night.

Rose bundled Sarah well against the cold, blustery day before sending the girl off to the market in Chipping Niddwick with the earl and his family, hopping up and down and chattering like a starling. When Rose turned back to the house, after waving farewell, Aldridge was waiting.

"Mrs Darling, I've asked the housekeeper to set out tea in the library. Will you join me?"

She brushed against him as she moved through the doorway, which clearly set him off-balance, but she gained no advantage because it affected her as much. They had to end this negotiation soon. It was killing her.

Last night, Lady Chirbury had followed her to her room and offered to help her find 'honest work.' She could be a seamstress or serve in a shop, and Lord Chirbury would lease her and Sarah a cottage at favourable terms. "I would suggest teaching, Mrs Darling, since you are obviously well educated, but if your past were to come out... The Longford villagers are good people, but they can be very hard on those they don't understand."

Rose's sewing was mediocre, and neither occupation would earn her more than a pittance. "Forgive me," she told Anne. "I need to make more than that, if I am to give Sarah a chance at a better life than mine..." She could not meet Lady Chirbury's eyes, fearing the scorn and rejection. But the countess surprised her. "I understand better than you might think, Mrs Darling. Make sure he gives you a favourable contract, then. My husband will read it for you, if you wish."

In the library, several closely-written pages were lying on a table under the window. "You suggested a contract, Mrs Darling," he said. "Here is a start. Everything is negotiable. I want you to be happy." He looked nervous. Did he really think she had a choice?

She took the chair in front of the table and began reading.

Two years? He wanted *two years*? An upfront payment, hers to keep plus an allowance. Was two hundred and fifty guineas a quarter low? But wait; he would pay all her costs: the wages for servants, unlimited accounts at the grocer, the butcher, and the candlemaker, as well as her choice of milliner, *modiste*, bootmaker, and any other makers of clothing and adornments.

Dear Heavens. Her eyes must be out on stalks!

He would pay for, and keep, a carriage and horses for her use, including grooms and stabling. He would pay for a nurse for Sarah, and teachers for Rose in dance and pianoforte.

She read on. She couldn't help the grin, though she managed not to dance in her seat.

Aldridge would purchase and staff a town-house within easy distance of Haverford House. At the end of two years, the house would be hers, free and clear.

Two years. She could do anything for two years.

Surely between the value of the town-house and what she could save, she would be able to start again in the country? Be free? Give Sarah a decent life?

He wanted a key to the house. He wanted her to be available whenever he wished, and travel if he wanted her company. He wanted the right of renewal after two years, should he wish to continue to keep her.

He would expect her to host and accompany him to entertainments and activities. She frowned a little.

He was watching closely. "Something wrong?" he asked.

"Would you... would you expect me to 'entertain' other men?" She hated that. Her third protector had used a night with her to reward his friends or bribe his allies.

"I'm not good at sharing what is mine," Aldridge said. "Mrs Darling, I won't insist on you doing anything that makes you feel diminished. Though I hope you'll try new things, even if they seem a bit odd or uncomfortable at first."

She considered him carefully. Even in Bristol, even in her circles, Aldridge's parties were discussed in scandalised whispers. But rumours were seldom accurate.

His usual twinkle deserted him, and his eyes were level and serious as he said, "Mrs Darling, I ask one thing of my lovers, and I ask it of you. Tell me what pleases you. Tell what does not please you. Never pretend pleasure you do not feel."

"My lord," she protested, "this arrangement is about your pleasure, not mine."

He rejected that with a swift shake of the head. "My pleasure is enhanced by your pleasure. Women know this; that is why they pretend. But I will know if you pretend, Mrs Darling, and that will destroy my pleasure. If you wish to please me in intimate matters, then you must first allow me to please you."

Rose's mouth was hanging open. She closed it, gathering her scattered thoughts.

"I want Sarah to have her own apartments, and not to..." she blushed again, not sure quite how to say she was ashamed to let her daughter to see her being the harlot she was. And afraid those attending Aldridge's entertainments might be a danger to Sarah.

Aldridge nodded. "A town-house with a top floor that has its own entrance."

She studied the papers some more. She was sure she must be missing something. At her age, this might be her last chance. And Sarah was growing older, too, and better able to understand what she observed. Rose had to be careful. "My lord, Lady Chirbury said... I wish to discuss the contract with the earl."

Aldridge nodded again, smiling. "Good idea. He's not a solicitor, but he is a good businessman and has read many hundreds of contracts. Not this sort, precisely, or not that I've heard. But he will give you good advice."

"You have no objection?" The man was a miracle.

No. A miracle would save her without expecting the use of her body as a reward. But he was kind and generous, and that was miracle enough.

"I want you to be happy," Aldridge said again.

To give her hands something to do, besides trembling and shaking pages of parchment, Rose prepared a cup of tea for Aldridge the way he liked it—black and strong with lemon. Then she sliced into the cake.

Aldridge put out a hand to stop her. "That's not what I'm hungry for, Rose." She glanced at his fall. The fashion for tight knit pantaloons left a man with nowhere to hide his lust. Her mouth suddenly dry at the size of what she saw, she met his eyes. For once, he was not smiling.

"I promised Rede I'd not bed you under his roof," he told her. "So perhaps we could think of something quenching to discuss?"

Rose reached out and ran a fingernail along the object of her fascination. "Did he specify bed?" she asked.

Aldridge had to make two attempts to speak, which she counted a success. "Bed or otherwise tup," he told her. "Have you another suggestion?"

Her voice dropped into another register. "I wouldn't encourage you to break your word to your cousin. Nor will I—complete the act with you until I decide whether or not to accept your contract. But can we not find a way to enjoy one another short of...?" She slipped her sleeve down her arm as she spoke, revealing more and more of her breast.

He swallowed again, and croaked, "Several ways. Give me one moment to lock the door."

But before he could, it opened. Rose just had time to pull her dress to decency before an imperious little woman sailed into the room, talking over her shoulder as she entered the room.

"No, indeed, my dear Cole, no need to announce me. I know my own nephew's home. Not that it ever was my sister's, of course, but we often visited. Do you not remember, Aldridge, my dear? Hello, darling, do you not have a kiss for your Mama?"

Her Grace of Haverford, for it must be she, presented one perfumed cheek to her son, then glanced around the room.

Rose attempted to gather up the pages on the table before the duchess saw them.

The duchess frowned, clearly taking in Rose's dishevelled state and perhaps the rampant erection Aldridge was valiantly trying to hide behind an occasional table, too low to do a good job. "Oh, but I have interrupted. Cole tried to tell me... Oh dear. Shall I go out and come in again, my love?"

Aldridge, in a tone equidistant between exasperation, amusement, and despair, said, "No need, Mama. May I beg your permission to present Mrs Rose Darling, a guest of the earl and countess? Mrs Darling, this, as you may have guessed, is Her Grace, the Duchess of Haverford. My mother."

Rose performed her best curtsey, grateful for the training that allowed her to perform the manoeuvre while shrinking inside, and then made her escape while the Marquis was interrogating his mother on her unexpected appearance.

She had no idea how she felt. Elated, undoubtedly. She had never imagined such a contract. Shamed, embarrassed... Aldridge's mother clearly thought... And she was right. And she was a duchess! If she had arrived two minutes later... no, Aldridge was going to lock the door.

Rose giggled nervously at the thought of the Duchess of Haverford knocking on the door, demanding her son's attention while he attempted to put himself back into his pants. Not that the actual scene was much better. A bucket of cold water could have separated them no more quickly.

The duchess's arrival would not change Aldridge's mind, would it?

The entrance hall was full of people—no doubt ducal servants and attendants. Rose took the contract papers up to her guest room and sat studying them until the earl and countess returned and she had to go down to be sociable.

The Duchess of Haverford had been visiting friends in Cirencester and was on her way to call on a goddaughter in Bath. "You will remember Polly, Anne, dear. She married the Viscount Sudding. And she has been delivered of a son, which is such a relief for the family. Three daughters, you know, and the cousin a very odd man. One would not want him to inherit. And she is still young, so there may be more."

The thought clearly reminded her of her own offspring. "Rede, I had such a comfortable coze with Aldridge today." Aldridge was seated on the floor at her feet, and she patted his cheek lovingly. "I had no idea you were here, darling. So pleased. I thought you and your friend, Lord Overton, had gone off to a party somewhere."

"Overton returned home, Mama," Aldridge told her. They had separated in London two months ago, after Overton read Aldridge a lecture on his drinking, refusing to 'follow him to perdition.' Overton headed back north to his estate, his wife, and his stepdaughters, and Aldridge rambled from house party to house party. "His wife is in expectation of a happy event."

"How lovely! Lord Overton was at school with Aldridge, my dears. You remember, Rede. Such a nice boy. Injured in the war, you know, then came home to inherit the barony."

She patted her son's cheek again. "He has settled down nicely since he wed. Aldridge quite misses him, do you not, my love?"

"He is staid and boring."

"And a new baby," the Duchess continued, taking no notice. "How lovely."

Aldridge shifted from under his mother's hand, and got to his feet. "Perhaps Mrs Darling would play for us. Would you be so kind?"

Rose nodded, taking the message from the abrupt change of subject. His Lordship's friend was not a topic to be discussed in front of a mistress, however expensive.

Her Grace watched her son thoughtfully as he arranged music for Rose, then turned pages for her. "You play beautifully, my dear," she said, when Rose returned to her seat.

"Simple things, Your Grace," Rose said. "I fear anything difficult is beyond me."

"You do well, my dear, to know your limits and stay within them," the duchess replied, her grave look giving the words another layer of meaning.

By the time dinner was called, Rose knew where Aldridge came by his conversational dexterity. The duchess swooped, with butterfly ease, from family to family, throughout the *ton*, and up and down society. Her Grace, it seemed, knew everybody in England, was related to half of them, and was godmother to the other half.

The addition of a duchess to the table did not change the informality with which they dined, and the conversation ranged freely around the table. Her Grace had news of Lady Chirbury's sister, Kitty, who had been staying with her in London. "Dear Kitty; she is meant to be refreshing her winter wardrobe, but she and Mia will be spending their pin money on music and books, I dare say." And she had spent half an hour with the nursery party. "Your Sarah is such a pretty child, Mrs Darling. And lovely manners."

After dinner, the ladies withdrew to the great parlour, leaving the two men to the port.

"I am travelling in the morning, so will go up to bed," the duchess announced. "Mrs Darling, perhaps you would give me a few moments of your time?"

"Be nice, aunt," warned Lady Chirbury, making Rose even more nervous. The duchess gave an enigmatic smile and led the way upstairs.

"Leave us, dear," she said to the maid who was standing ready by the bed. "I shall ring when I want you." She took a chair by the fire and waved Rose to the other.

"Do not look so nervous, Mrs Darling. I do not intend to bite you."

Rose blushed scarlet. Aldridge had promised to bite her, and had explained exactly where. No. She must not think of that. She sat, as commanded.

"Mrs Darling, you were raised gentry, were you not?"

Rose nodded, cautiously. Where was the duchess going with this?

"The manners, the speech, the accomplishments—they can all be taught, of course. But one who has learned them from the cradle..." Her Grace waved a hand as if to flick away counterfeits.

"The usual story, I imagine? Seduction or rape? And no father to defend your honour?"

"My father..." Rose swallowed hard to remove the lump that closed her throat at the memories. "My father was a librarian. He took the part of his employer."

"Ah." Her Grace nodded. "And the employer was the cause of your downfall. Or his son, perhaps?"

"His son," Rose confirmed. His sons, in fact, but she would not say that.

"And Sarah was the...?"

"No, Your Grace. Sarah... came later."

"Mr. Darling?"

"There was no Mr. Darling," Rose admitted.

The maid must have added a fresh log to the fire just before they arrived. The top was still uncharred, but flames licked up from the bed of hot embers. A twig that jutted from one side suddenly flared, turned black, and shrivelled. The bottom of the log began to glow red.

The duchess spoke again, startling Rose out of her flame-induced trance.

"What do you want for your daughter, Mrs Darling?"

"A better life," Rose said immediately, suddenly fierce. "A chance to be respectable. A life that does not depend on the whims of a man."

"The first two may be achievable," the duchess said, dryly. "The third is highly unlikely for any woman of any station. You expect my son to help you to these goals, I take it."

Rose was suddenly tired of polite circling. "I was saving so that I could leave this life, start again in another place under another name. But my last protector cheated me and stole from me.

"I do what I must, Your Grace. Should I have killed myself when I was disgraced? I had no skills anyone wanted to buy. I could play the piano, a little; sew, but others were faster and better; paint, but indifferently; parse a Latin sentence, but of what use was that in my circumstances? Should I have starved in the gutter where they threw me?

"Well, I was not given that choice. Those who took me from the gutter knew precisely what I had that others would pay for. As soon as I could, I began selling it for myself, and I. Will. Not. Be. Ashamed."

Her vehemence did not ruffle the duchess's calm. "We all do what we must, my dear. I am not judging you. Men have the power in this world, and women of the gentry are raised to depend on them for our survival. But you must know that Aldridge cannot offer marriage to a woman with your history."

The mere thought startled a laugh out of Rose. Marriage had never crossed Aldridge's mind. Of that she was certain. "His Lordship has offered me a two-year contract as his mistress," she said, "with very favourable terms. If I accept, and if I save carefully, I will never need to take a protector again."

"Two years!" The duchess arched a delicate eyebrow. "Aldridge seldom keeps a mistress beyond six months. He must be utterly besotted."

"He has no thought of marriage," Rose found herself reassuring the duchess. "And neither do I. I like him, but do not love him, and I think only love could make marriage tolerable."

It was only partly true. She could easily fall in love with Aldridge... was, perhaps, beginning to do so already. That way, she knew, led to heartache, for the duchess was right. Aldridge would never offer her marriage, or even permanence.

The duchess nodded, decisively. "You are wise. I think you will be good for him, Mrs Darling—which is a ridiculous name. May I call you 'Rose'?" Her Grace's smile was a wonderful thing, another feature her son had inherited.

"Would you..." Rose had never imagined having such a conversation, but there was something about this woman. Nothing shocked her, and she listened. "Would you call me Becky? It is my real name."

"Becky, then. Becky, as long as you remember that you will never be accepted as a fit mate for the future Duke of Haverford—which is a great shame, for you seem to be a fine young woman, but we must live in the world as it is—you and I shall be friends, and I shall support you and little Sarah to find the new life you seek when Aldridge is finished with you. He needs someone like you. He is not happy, poor boy."

That squashed the nascent hope that the duchess's sponsorship might mean she could avoid accepting Aldridge's protection. Still, it was a good offer. Becky accepted the duchess's outstretched hands. "Thank you, Your Grace. I will do my best to make him happy."

Chapter Five

When Aldridge and Rede returned to the ladies, only Anne was left. Mama had carried Mrs Darling off for a private interview. His alarm propelled him up the stairs to retrieve her, but by the time he reached Mama's room, she was alone.

"I hope you did not frighten Mrs Darling, Mama," he grumbled.

What had Mama said to Mrs Darling? What had Mrs Darling said to Mama?

The duchess just laughed, patted his cheek, and told him he was a naughty boy. "Now off with you, dearest, and let this old woman seek her bed."

Rose must have gone to bed herself, for she was nowhere to be found, and didn't appear again until just before the duchess left in the morning.

Her Grace went down the line, enfolding each of them in a perfumed hug.

"Take care, now, Anne," she said to the countess. "You must eat wisely and exercise a little each day."

"Let me know if you hear from David," she told Rede. "Jonathan always falls on his feet, but I cannot help but be a little anxious."

She hugged Mrs Darling next, and Mrs Darling looked as surprised as Aldridge. "Remember, dear," was all she said, ratcheting Aldridge's alarm up another couple of notches.

Aldridge was last in the line, Her Grace having farewelled the nursery party upstairs.

"Do not look so worried," she told him, patting one cheek while she kissed the other. He wished she would stop treating him as if he were twelve. Though knowing Her Grace, that would be the point.

"Relax, dear," she told him. "The world is not on your shoulders. Have a little fun."

Her Grace might be the only person in the world who thought his life wasn't wholly devoted to fun. Even his father, who had off-loaded almost the entire work of running the ducal estates, continued to insist Aldridge was a useless ne'er-do-well with no occupation beyond enjoying himself.

Mind you, Aldridge was, himself, at pains to project that impression.

How long would Mrs Darling be fooled? Aldridge smiled. Not long, probably.

He waved off his mother's carriage. Right. Time to bring this long negotiation to an end. With luck, they could be on the road tomorrow. His promise to Rede did not extend beyond the boundary of Longford Court.

"Mrs Darling," he murmured, as they went back up the steps to the house, "have you made a decision? Will you accept my contract?"

Rede overheard, and held back, letting Anne go into the house without him. "Mrs Darling has asked me to look over the papers for her, Aldridge. You don't mind, do you?"

He was rational enough to know he should not mind. If he'd met Mrs Darling in London, and she had a bit of Town bronze, he'd be dealing with a solicitor experienced in such matters, and would think nothing of it. However much he would prefer his relatives stay out of his business, Mrs Darling had a right to good advice.

"Of course not," he assured Rede. "I am willing to make changes, of course. But I hope we can settle this today."

Rede looked pointedly at Aldridge's fall and snickered. "This way, Mrs Darling."

Instead of following them into the house, Aldridge crossed the porch to the outside door of the estate office. It opened. Good. On the other side of the room, an interior door let onto the study, and he opened it a crack before Rede showed Mrs Darling to a seat.

"I have had a look through," Rede said, "and it is a fair contract, on the whole. I would like to make a couple of suggestions, however."

"Go on."

"The contract specifies a nurse for Sarah. I suggest changing that to a governess. Anne tells me she is a bright little girl. You have been teaching her yourself, I understand, and I expect you will continue. But your time will be at my cousin's disposal, and a governess will provide structure and continuity."

Aldridge nodded. Perhaps Rede's intervention was a good thing.

"Also," Rede continued, "as she grows older, you will want to hire other teachers for particular skills. I suggest you broaden the bit about teachers for you to include her."

That was fair. Aldridge had no objection to that.

"And I would write in a clause that says you have the hiring and firing of staff. You will know best what you want, particularly for Sarah, and you will be more comfortable if they answer to you.

"The town-house. Make sure you have the right to refuse one that is unsuitable, and for God's sake, reserve full control of its decoration. I have seen Aldridge's bedchamber in the heir's wing at Haverford House." Rede lingered meaningfully on the word 'seen'.

"What is wrong with his bedchamber?" Mrs Darling asked. Aldridge wanted to know, too. He'd spent a lot of thought and effort getting it just the way he wanted it.

"It is clearly designed for one thing, and one thing only," Rede said. "And sleeping is not that thing."

Yes, true. And none the worse for that, Aldridge thought.

"You do not want your daughter to grow up in a fornicatorium," Rede continued, "if you will excuse my blunt language, Mrs Darling."

"Decoration," Mrs Darling said, firmly. "Is there anything else, Lord Chirbury?"

"It is a two-year contract, and if you wish to leave early, you do not keep the house."

"Yes," Mrs Darling acknowledged. "That is fair, is it not?"

"Add a clause to say, if he wishes to dismiss you early, you do keep the house, and also any quarterly payments owed to the end of the term."

Really? Aldridge bristled. Whose cousin did Rede think he was? But on reflection, it was fair enough.

Rede hadn't finished. "He has given himself right of renewal at the end of the two years. Make that 'renewal upon mutual agreement.'"

Aldridge shifted uneasily and caught himself in the movement. Again, a fair clause. And one that would not affect him, besides. He'd never kept a mistress even a year, let alone longer, nor ever given one reason to want to leave him.

"You have written a note about... er... intimate services." For the first time, Rede sounded a little embarrassed.

"Yes. Aldridge said he would not require... that is to say, I would have the right to..."

"Yes, quite," Rede interrupted. "Mrs Darling, such a clause... it would be unenforceable in law, you understand. Property rights are one thing, but the courts would hold that anything Aldridge does to a woman under his protection—mistress, wife, sister, or child— short of causing serious bodily harm, is perfectly acceptable."

At that, Aldridge very nearly opened the door. He would never hurt any woman, let alone one he had in his keeping. The idea! But Rede was still talking.

"But you do need not worry on that account. Aldridge, whatever you might have heard about him, is a good man. I have never known him to break a promise, nor deliberately hurt a woman or child. He is a careless son of a devil, though. Don't give him your heart, Mrs Darling."

"I have no heart left, Lord Chirbury. But thank you."

The two in the study were silent after that exchange. Aldridge didn't want Mrs Darling's heart, or anyone else's. Having his lovers profess such feelings left him embarrassed and slightly guilty, as if he owed them an apology for retaining his own. Certainly, if he were capable of this kind of love (and he rather thought he wasn't), he'd not be offering it to a woman he had purchased. He'd cheerfully share the rest of his anatomy, though. One part, in particular, thought it had waited long enough.

In the next room, Rede said, "One last thing. Your name. The contract should bear your full legal name, though I well understand your wish to bear a working name while you are active in the *demi-*

monde. I think it unlikely in the extreme you will need to sue Aldridge, but if anything happened to him, you might end up fighting his father, and in that, you will need all the advantages you can get."

"Let us pray that never happens," answered Mrs Darling.

Aldridge should have thought of that. He had no intention of breaching the agreement, but Rede was right again. Life was a chancy thing, and His Grace would spurn her without blinking an eye. Or insist on taking his son's place, the old *roué*.

"Very well, if you have no questions? No? Then we just need a fair copy written, and you and Aldridge can sign before witnesses." Rede pitched his voice to carry a little further. "Aldridge? If you have finished eavesdropping, how about joining us and writing out the new copy of this contract?"

Rebecca Mary Winstanley. So said the contract, his copy of which currently resided in the case of legal papers he carried with him always. Rebecca. Becky, at least when they were private, though she would continue to use the name 'Rose Darling' in public.

He'd asked the loan of two carriages, one for him and Becky, and one for Sarah and the maid they'd borrowed from Anne. They would be one night on the road, and he did not intend Becky to spend it looking after Sarah.

Indeed, why wait for an inn, when one had a commodious carriage?

With many miles of journey ahead of them, they had plenty of time to explore one another, and he was enjoying a long appetiser to the main event when the carriage drew to a halt not a half hour out of Longford.

Becky tucked her exposed breast back into her bodice, and wrapped a shawl around her shoulders to cover the loosened stays, while he buttoned the side of his fall that she'd half released.

Just in time, as a knock on the door revealed a tearful Sarah.

"Mama, Pansy has been sick all down my dress," the child complained.

Becky apologised as she helped the little girl to wash in a nearby stream and change into fresh clothes. Aldridge made sure the travel-sick maid was supplied with a bucket. Did Rede know the maid was subject to travel-sickness? Aldridge dismissed the thought as unworthy.

Becky attempted to persuade Sarah back into the carriage, but the little girl burst into tears again.

"Bring her in with us," Aldridge suggested.

Becky looked stricken, and he reassured her, "Do not worry, Becky. We have two whole years. We can wait another afternoon."

After two hours in the carriage, he called for his horse and rode the rest of the way to the inn where he'd booked a suite for the night. His spirits, somewhat depressed by domesticity, lifted as he reflected that the little girl would be tired and go early to bed.

He had dinner served in their suite, but went down to the tap room afterwards to let Becky put her daughter to bed, the exhausted maid asleep on a pallet in the child's room. "If you are tired," he said, "we can wait till we reach London."

She lowered her lashes. "Give me one hour, my lord. I will be in bed when you return," she murmured, and just like that he was hard as nails again. Not long now.

He found a table in a corner and worked his way through the day's satchel of mail. It included a letter from his friend Overton—one that had clearly followed him for several weeks, from London to the various houses he'd visited and back to London before ending in the satchel of duchy business. It was just a brief black-bordered note saying Baroness Overton and her baby had died.

Poor Overton. He had been full of dreams when they parted—for the promised heir, for mending his marriage which was, Aldridge gathered, not a happy one. All dust now. Aldridge started a letter in return, but he could not find the words to express his sadness for his friend.

His mind drifted to the woman upstairs. He would write to Overton tomorrow.

At one hour to the minute, he returned up the stairs. The suite was silent and dark. He lit a candle from one in the hall sconce, and let himself into the bedchamber he'd reserved for them. "Becky, I am here," he said.

No reply. She must be tired, after spending the day keeping little Sarah amused. He put the candle down on the bedside table and stripped naked, muttering to himself as his fingers fumbled over buttons and laces.

He'd wake her with kisses, then... his mind full of images of what came next, he had one knee on the bed and one hand already reaching for the blanket when a tousled dark head emerged, confused cornflower blue eyes blinking at him. "What are you doing in my Mama's bed?" asked little Sarah.

Chapter Six

The Marquis of Aldridge assured Becky he hadn't minded spending the night in Sarah's bed rather than his own, that the maid barely disturbed him at all when she woke vomiting again in the early hours of the morning, and of course, the girl should travel no further. He would pay for her accommodation until she recovered, and her transport home to Longford, and Becky was to take Sarah in the carriage with her and think no more about it.

He rode.

Several times in the course of the morning, he passed the carriage, not looking, his face set and distant, though when he caught her watching, he smiled, a wicked gleam that lifted her spirits. Perhaps he was not angry. Perhaps he was just thinking.

When they stopped for something to eat, he was his usual affable, charming self, flirting with the maid who brought their meal, teasing Becky about insisting Sarah eat her meat before her pudding, telling stories about journeys he'd made when he was a boy.

As they finished, one of the grooms presented himself in the private parlour. "If you please, Mrs Darling, if Miss Sarah comes with me, I can show her the kittens they have in the kitchen."

Becky gave her permission, and then, as the door closed behind Sarah and the groom, looked suspiciously at Aldridge.

"Yes," he said. "I arranged it."

"You knew they had kittens?"

"Or puppies, or foals, or some other small, furry distraction. We have little time, Becky. I just wanted to give you something to think about between now and London."

She stepped towards him, expecting an embrace, but he held up his hand. "No. Stay there, or I will have you right on this table, and you do not want your daughter walking in on that. But I do want to tell you precisely what I have been planning for tonight as I rode."

He reached out and skimmed her shape from neck to waist, without touching.

"First, we will settle Miss Sarah in nursery, and she may have a dozen maids to keep her company and do her bidding, but prepare her, Becky, for the fact that you will be otherwise occupied."

Becky nodded.

"Then," his lips curved in that same wicked smile. He took a step backwards and breathed in deeply, letting his eyes follow the same curves he'd shaped as he breathed out slowly.

"A bath first, I think, one large enough for two, my dear, waiting, piping hot and perfumed. You will stand by the fire, Becky, where it is warm, and I will be your maid. Or perhaps not quite, for would a maid, as she loosened and removed your stays, brush your arms with feather-light touches? Would she gently and tenderly caress your lovely thighs as she rolled down your stockings, running her fingertips up, oh, so softly, almost, but not quite, to your most secret treasures?. Would she, when she lifted your chemise, cup your beautiful breasts and run a thumb over your nipples?"

She could feel them contract and harden under his intent gaze.

"They tighten and pebble. Is it the cold, Becky, that makes them so hard? Let us have you up and into the bath, then.

"Now, your turn. I have gazed upon your glories. Lie back and soak up the heat, and I shall disrobe for you. Will you be pleased with what you see, I wonder? Ah..." she was about to speak, but he put his finger just above her lips, still not touching. "Yes, you saw me before, by the light of one candle. But my room shall have many candles, Becky.

"Where were we? Ah, yes, you are lying in the bath, all relaxed in the hot, perfumed water, waiting for me to serve at your pleasure. Picture me at your feet, dear Becky, soaping my hands. We will order your own soap, the softest, finest soap money can buy, and you shall choose the perfumes to scent it with, but tonight, we shall use mine: bergamot, almond, a touch of wintergreen.

"What shall I wash first, I wonder. These?" He reached out again, this time shaping her breasts, his hands a bare inch from the dress that now felt tighter against her skin.

Step by step, he described how he would bring her to completion in the bath, and then what they would do afterward, "on the rug by the fire, dear Becky, this first time, if you will allow," and then how they would sleep and wake again, for another encounter he had also planned, and described in detail.

By the time the servant returned with Sarah, Becky's eyes were glazed and her thighs slick with arousal.

If it was revenge, it was a good one. She'd spent the rest of the trip in high suspense, struggling to respond to her daughter, grateful when Sarah fell asleep for part of the afternoon and she could spend the time imagining the night to come. Aldridge seemed as interested in her response as his own, which was outside her experience.

Still: make her burn, would he? She'd done her best to serve him likewise at every post change along the way, stroking her hands down his arms when he lifted her from the carriage, whispering suggested amendments to his erotic plans when they were in company and he could not respond, leaning towards him so her breasts lifted in her loosened dress, licking her finger and sucking it into her mouth, lifting her skirt so he (and only he) could see her ankles. Only Sarah's presence, she was sure, prevented him from following her into the carriage when, his body screening her from view, she brushed her thumb up his fall and wondered out loud whether her mouth was big enough.

By the time they arrived in the mews behind Haverford House, she was beyond worrying about propriety. Aldridge assured her the heir's wing was quite separate, he did what he wished there, and his servants were paid to make no comment and pass no judgement. And, in any case, the duke and duchess were not in London.

"You will stay here till we find the right house," he insisted. "And no one will say a word." Because no one of any importance would know, she thought. But he didn't say that, and certainly, when he escorted her through the private entrance to the left side of the massive house, the servants were everything polite and deferential. In short order, she and Sarah had been introduced to the maids assigned to look after the little girl, and whisked up to a freshly-aired nursery.

Becky gave Sarah her bath, by which time a maid had set out a nursery dinner.

"Do you eat with me, Mama?" Sarah asked.

"No, my love. But I will stay while you eat, and see you to bed. And you will have Jenny and Clara and Mary to keep you company and look after you in the morning."

The maids all nodded, beaming smiles, and Sarah nodded gravely back, her mouth full of bread and jam.

Poor darling. At seven, well accustomed to being left with a maid, or even on her own, while Becky tended to the desires of whatever male had them in keeping. Becky forced a cheerful smile.

Becky heard Sarah's prayers and told her a story, then bent to kiss her goodnight. "G'night, Mama," Sarah murmured, not even opening her eyes.

"Now, don't ye fret, ma'am," one of the maids said, benevolently. Clara. Becky was fairly certain this one was Clara. "We will look after the little miss, we will."

They looked kind, and Sarah had reacted well to them. And Becky had kept Aldridge waiting for nearly two hours. It was time.

A servant waited to escort Becky through the house. She followed in his wake, hands bunched and twisting in the shawl she'd donned against the chill of the long halls. What if she didn't live up to his expectations? He, after all, had bedded some of the most famous harlots in England, amateur and professional. Surely they knew far more than she?

He said this would be about her pleasure as much as his... and when he was kissing her, or detailing his plans, she believed him. But she had believed men before and been disappointed. Whatever he chose to do, she could not object.

And for the first time ever, she would not be able to hide her real self from what someone did to the Rose of Frampton. When he asked leave to call her Becky, she had been pleased to be known. Now, she wondered if that had been a mistake. Rose had been the one who sold her body; not Becky. And that was about to change.

The servant showed her into a comfortable sitting room in what must surely be the master suite of this huge complex of rooms.

Dinner settings for two had been laid on a small table, and a deep steaming bath waited in front of the fire, with large cans of hot water keeping hot on the hearth to rinse and refill.

Despite her nerves, she smiled. The stage was set for Scene One of Aldridge's fantasy.

Aldridge suddenly appeared, leaning against the frame of a side door, a darkened study behind him. She'd seen how hard he worked, disappearing into Lord Chirbury's study for hours each day to deal with whatever business had followed him by courier. Even on their trip, he had worked part of the time; in her carriage the first day, and at the inn this morning.

He was still wearing pantaloons and a shirt, but he'd stripped off his jacket and cravat, and his waistcoat was unbuttoned.

"Did she settle?" he asked. How typical, that his first words were of her child. Defending her heart from this rogue was not going to be easy.

"I left one of the maids telling her a story. She knows she will not see me until tomorrow. She will not make a fuss."

He lifted one brow, giving her a slow, smouldering smile that set her temperature soaring. "Possibly not until afternoon," he said, holding out his hand. "Come. I will show you around." He pushed away from the doorpost, and led her to the door on the other side of the sitting room.

She took two steps into the bedchamber and stopped. Every surface was red or gold, ornately painted or upholstered. Except for the gilt-framed mirrors glittering on each wall and—she craned to check—on the ceiling of the enormous bed. Huge though the room was, the bed dominated. She couldn't help herself; she started to laugh.

"What?" Aldridge was frowning, but it was really too funny.

"Your cousin was right," she managed to say, before going off into another peal of laughter.

It took him a moment to fathom her meaning, then his ready sense of humour melted his irritation. "A fornicatorium, is it? I will show you just how right you are, my sweet."

He gestured to a door with his free hand. "Your dressing room. You can investigate later. Dinner now, Becky? Or bath?"

His face was calm, as if the answer meant nothing, but when she whispered "Bath" through a suddenly dry throat, his intent eyes gleamed and his lips curved in triumph.

"Bath it is."

Being undressed by Aldridge was every bit the sweet torture he had promised. By the time she reclined in the bath, she was yearning for more. And he knew it, the fiend. "Patience makes the reward sweeter, my lovely," he told her, stepping away so he stood just out of reach and in the plain glare of the many candles.

The waistcoat first. Already unbuttoned, it shrugged easily off his shoulders and was tossed to a chair. "Shirt, stockings or pantaloons?" Aldridge asked.

"Stockings," Becky decided. He propped one foot on the bath while he rolled his stocking down, giving her a close view of his fall. She should have chosen pantaloons. Could he read her mind? His grin suggested he knew exactly what she was thinking.

He pulled the stocking off, revealing a long elegant foot, the toenails carefully kept. The man was too perfect. If there were justice in the world, he would have knobbly knees or thin calves. She was glad he didn't. The second stocking went the way of the first, both tossed after the waistcoat.

"Shirt or pantaloons, Becky." The slow tease was affecting Aldridge, too, his voice soft and husky.

"Shirt," she chose, and he slipped his braces off his shoulders, then ran one hand down into his pantaloons, slowly untucking his shirt tails. She watched the hand moving under the fabric, and trembled. Once the tails were no longer wrapped under him, he tugged the shirt loose, then lifted it slowly over his head, revealing the muscled chest beneath an inch at a time. He stood, then, displaying himself with unconscious arrogance, confident of her answer when he asked, "Do you like what you see, my sweet?"

"You do not sit at a desk all day," Becky observed.

"I fence. I box. I ride." That quick Aldridge grin again. "Different types of riding."

"Pan..." She had to stop and swallow and try again. "Pantaloons."

He went slowly, turning his back as he inched the pantaloons down, lifting first one leg and then the other to work them over his feet. Again he stopped, his back to her, and she was content to admire the broad shoulders, the tight planes of his buttocks, the sculpted thighs.

Then he turned. "Do you like what you see, Becky?" he asked again.

Becky shook her head in slow wonder. Nine years of old men, fat men, men who acted and smelt like swine. They were far away. This part of her new life, at least, would not be unpleasant.

He'd mistaken her head shake. She smiled to chase away the slight indignant frown, her smile broadening as her mouth dried again.

"I was right about my mouth, my lord," she teased, and was rewarded with a shout of laughter and a splash as he vaulted into the bath to join her.

"Becky, my darling," he said, as he soaped his hands ready for the next step in the evening's entertainment, "I see I can count on you never to bore me."

And Becky, as she lay back waiting for Aldridge to serve at her pleasure, devoutly hoped that would prove to be true.

Part Two
1810

Chapter Seven

1810, London

As soon as Hugh Overton managed to unstick his eyes and crawl out from whatever was weighing him down, he would search out another drink. He'd been keeping the world's largest hangover at bay for nearly a fortnight, and he wasn't going to stop now.

Meanwhile, he lay still, trying to sort through his memories and match them to sparse sensory information to decide where he was. Aldridge. That's right. And the bet.

He cautiously opened one sticky eye. The room was dim, a matter for gratitude, but light enough to confirm he was in Aldridge's private sitting room in the heir's wing at Haverford House, lying on the enormous fainting couch. And the weight holding his legs in place was a sleeping woman sprawled across his thighs. The untidy mass of brown hair didn't identify her—at least half of the women he'd bedded in Town had brown hair.

'J' something. Joselyn? Johanne? Or was that the other one? There must be two women; the details of the bet were surfacing more clearly in his mind.

Hugh shifted his hips, attempting to slide one leg out from under the woman, whoever she was. She stirred, then sat up in one motion, already talking before she was fully upright. Hugh, who had not yet dared move his head, was all admiration at her resilience.

"Devil take it, I fell asleep. What time is it? Lord Overton, do you know the time? Is it morning? It must be morning. Look at the light!"

As she spoke, she collected pieces of apparel from around the room, a dress, a stocking, another stocking—this one clocked in a different colour. She dropped it back on the floor where she'd found it, and kept searching. "Overton? The time?"

Hugh had been paying attention to her naked curves, not her words. "I beg your pardon, ma'am," he said, unwilling to hazard a guess at the lady's name. "I appear to be without my watch."

She huffed her displeasure through her nose, and marched over to the table, where his watch lay in a heap of other bits and pieces—his coin purse and, undoubtedly, his cuff links and tie pin.

"10 of the clock," the woman said, then, raising her voice, "Jessamine? It is 10 o'clock. We must hurry."

Jessamine. That was it. So this must be the other one. Damned if he could remember her name, though he had rather pleasant memories bombarding him in vignettes of the evening before.

It would be polite to help, with the lady clearly anxious to be on her way. He pulled himself up, wincing at the stab of pain. While he sat on the edge of the bed, waiting for the room to stop spinning, and dinner from the night before to return to his stomach, another woman appeared in the doorway to Aldridge's bedchamber.

This one was fetchingly wrapped in a sheet, trailing behind her. "Lillian? Did you say 10 o'clock? Oh, merciful Heavens, what if I am not home before Bally?"

That name rang a bell. Bally. The Earl of Ballingcroft. This fair lady must be his countess, then. Hugh managed to stand and bow, politely.

"Bally is unlikely to leave Baroness Farliegh's bed before noon, my dear," her friend advised. "Which was, if you remember, rather the point of you being here."

The Countess of Ballingcroft tossed her dishevelled head. "Sauce for the gander, Lillian." But her moment of defiance dissolved back into worry. "But I can't be seen leaving Aldridge's house."

"You will not, my dear. Trust me for that." The drawl belonged to Aldridge, leaning against the doorway to his study. Fully and immaculately attired, apart from his jacket, he looked as if he'd been up for hours. Based on Hugh's prior nights of raking and mayhem with the Merry Marquis, he probably had.

"You look disgusting, Aldridge," he said.

"Feeling a bit under the weather, Overton? Here." Aldridge crossed to the array of decanters and poured a good inch of golden nectar, which he brought to Hugh.

"Now, ladies. My coach has been waiting in the mews this past hour, and we can have you out of here the back way and in your own back doors in no time. Here, Mrs Barlow, is this stocking yours? How on Earth did it get up there?"

"But people will know," Lady Ballingcroft wailed.

"The coach is unmarked, Jessamine, and the same as a thousand others," Mrs Barlow reassured her friend. "No one will know where you have been."

"And when word reaches your straying husband that you arrived home long after dawn, all you do is smile and say you were out with your friend," Aldridge instructed.

Lady Ballingcroft, who had dropped the sheet and was shimmying into the shift Aldridge handed her, stopped in mid-shimmy at the thought, then resumed and emerged, clothed and beaming.

"And as long as I say nothing more, he will be left to imagine it all!"

Mrs Barlow nodded. "And if he insists you tell him where you went, you will say that you and I shared a delightful evening together." She waggled her eyebrows at Aldridge. "Which is no lie. Aldridge, darling, will you do me up?"

Aldridge performed the office, and Hugh assisted Lady Ballingcroft.

"We can do our hair back at my apartment, darling," Mrs Barlow said to her friend, "and then I will send you home in my carriage. And let Bally make what he will of that."

Lady Ballingcroft was now quite happy and, with a kiss for Hugh and another for Aldridge, left the room on Mrs Barlow's arm. "And Bally will never know he has been Aldridged?"

"He will suspect, my dear, when you start practicing the new tricks you have learned. Did I not tell you?"

"I had no idea." Lady Ballingcroft's awe made Hugh smile long after they descended the stairs and moved out of earshot.

Aldridge came back shaking his head. "What a fool Ballingcroft is, Overton. And what a surprise he will have when next he approaches his wife, and she expects to participate in the act."

"The man should be thanking us for his Aldridging," Hugh observed. "I take it that means being cuckolded by Aldridge."

"'Aldridging,' indeed. When did I become a verb, Overton? How Rose will laugh when I tell her. Although I imagine she has already heard."

"You tell your mistress about your amorous adventures?" Hugh asked. He hadn't kept a mistress in years, in part, because the opera dancer he'd spent a small fortune on before he joined the army would have hurled every vase and ornament in the place at his head, if he'd done such a thing. Yes, and then demanded he replace them.

Aldridge just laughed. "Speaking of which, we must be up and about, my lad. I've arranged to encounter today's two ladies in Green Park."

Hugh groaned. "Mercy, Aldridge. Can't you just leave me to sleep? I'll play my part tonight, but..."

Aldridge shook his head. "Can't be done, Overton. I have another engagement tonight."

"Well, take me on this other engagement then. Surely we can find a couple of light-heeled ladies..."

"This is not that kind of an engagement, Overton. I'm taking a little girl and her friends to Astley's Amphitheatre. It's her 10th birthday, and I promised. Ah. Martin, thank you." Aldridge took the mug his valet handed him. "Here, Overton, it set you right yesterday."

"It's noxious," Hugh complained, but downed the evil liquid, because Aldridge was correct. It had cured his hangover yesterday.

"It was thinking of Astley's that gave me the idea, actually. Have you ever done it on horseback, Overton?"

Hugh's head was suddenly full of erotic images. "Never. Is it even possible?"

"Oh, yes. With co-operation. We did agree to two different ladies and two different positions a day, and no repeats."

"Yes. For a week. I think Hackenburg intended us to find four different ladies between the two of us."

Aldridge's lazy smile showed his supreme indifference to Hackenburg's intentions. "He didn't specify."

"Twenty-eight conquests would better prove the morals of the ladies of the *ton* are no better than the morals of the gentleman," Overton suggested.

"Fourteen in pairs, each willing to take on two comers, proves it better. And only four more to go. Thank you, Martin. Leave it to me, now. I'll get the baron cleaned up." The servant had set up a bath, filled it, and laid out linen towels and a new bar of soap.

"I'll do my best not to let you down, Aldridge. Only one more day to go?"

Later that afternoon, Aldridge waited on the edge of one of the riding paths in Green Park for Overton to join him. His most recent companion, cross because Aldridge refused to spend the evening with her, had called for her carriage and left, and their other temporary *innamorata* would also make her own way home, once she and Overton finished their amorous encounter and emerged from cover.

Neither of them would wish to be seen with the Merry Marquis, for fear of being outed as having—Aldridge couldn't repress the grin—'Aldridged' their husbands.

Not that he did as much Aldridging as he used to. He wished he hadn't started the silly wager. However, people had money riding on him now, and he'd given his word to Overton. He'd see the week out.

Aldridge had engineered the situation to give Overton something to do. Hugh Baron Overton was celibate and sober for eleven months of the year, off in Lancashire being a good baron. But for three years running, when the anniversary of his wife's death approached, he'd come to London. Aldridge considered it a solemn duty to keep the man drunk and well-satisfied.

Unfortunately, the anniversary was today, and so was Sarah's birthday. When he'd promised, two months ago, to take her to

Astley's, if she were good, he'd forgotten about his commitment to Hugh Overton.

Well, with luck, the man would be worn out and would sleep.

But when Overton followed Lady Stenworth from the bushes, he looked anything but tired.

The two men made courteous and respectful farewells to the lady, Overton's speech and gait barely affected by the brandy he had been putting away steadily since he woke.

Both had been careful not to crush the lady's riding habit or disturb her coiffure, and only a certain glow betrayed how she had spent the afternoon. That, and the womanly musk trailing in the air after she trotted on her way.

"The split skirt is a marvellous invention," Overton observed. He took a swallow from a hip flask, then offered it to Aldridge, who refused. Becky wouldn't turn a hair if he tupped every woman in London in front of her town-house, provided Sarah didn't see. But she'd have his hide if he turned up drunk to collect her daughter.

Ah, Becky. He'd be pleased when these few weeks of excess were over and he could get back to the routine he had been perfecting for the past three years—several nights a week in Becky's bed, an occasional affair with a lady of the *ton* who caught his interest, or an assignation with a former lover for old time's sake.

Once, he had been less discriminating. Maybe he was getting old, but copulation, however he varied which bits connected where and how, was hollow without spending some time with—actually liking—the women he bedded.

"Go on, Aldridge. It's your brandy." Overton was holding out the flask again.

"Not for me, Overton. Birthday party. Remember?"

Overton dropped his head and sighed, then looked up. "Can I come, Aldridge? I haven't been to Astley's in years." He took another drink.

"You wouldn't enjoy it, Overton. Pack of little girls."

Overton insisted. "I like little girls. Have two of my own, you know." He drooped again. The man wasn't going to cry, was he? "Well, of my wife's, anyway." He shook his head slowly and sadly. "Poor Polyphemia. I should never have married her, you know."

Aldridge thought Overton had finished, but he had merely paused for yet another swallow of brandy—his fourth in as many minutes. He continued, enunciating each word. "Her last one died. Did you know? Of course you did. Died three years ago. My wife and her baby."

Odd, Overton always said 'her' baby.

Aldridge filed the information. He was going to give in and let Overton join the party. He knew it. Becky would kill him.

"I'll think about it," he growled. "But first we have to get you sober. And cleaned up. Can't go visiting a real lady smelling like that."

Chapter Eight

Becky waited by the window for Aldridge to arrive. He would come to her first, and then they would collect Sarah from the separate apartment he had established a year ago for her and her governess, and finally they would go to the homes of each of the other children whose parents accepted Sarah as a fit friend for their daughters.

She had no idea how Aldridge had worked that particular miracle, but she was grateful.

Meeting Aldridge at Sarah's apartment would make more sense, but Aldridge preferred to greet her in a manner that was inappropriate under the nose of her daughter and her daughter's servants. He was always careful to protect Sarah from her mother's role in his life.

So, she had walked from her daughter's rooms to her own town-house already changed for the evening. The clothes she kept here— her Rose wardrobe—were too frivolous, too obvious, for a night out with children, the cut and draping designed to accentuate her physical assets.

Tonight, she wore a neat walking dress in Aldridge's favourite powder blue, long-sleeved and high-necked, trimmed with piping and embroidery in navy blue to match the redingote that waited in the hall.

His note said he would be here at five o'clock. Becky checked the rococo mantelpiece clock for the hundredth time since she'd arrived, then laughed at her own eagerness.

Waiting was the lot of a mistress, and she was luckier than most. She could spend most of her time as 'the widow Winstanley,' living quietly with her daughter, two streets from the infamous Rose of Frampton. Aldridge's impeccable good manners meant that, except for a couple of occasions when he was deeply troubled, he always sent a message before he arrived on her doorstep.

Now, no more than three or four times a week, and then, only when he was in London. In the first heady days of their contract, he'd barely let her leave his side, spending every night with her when he was in Town, and taking her with him to the country estates. She'd fancied herself in love: an exhilarating mixture of sexual attraction, gratitude, response to his charm, and the pleasant experience of being heard and treated with courtesy.

But the shine wore off. His charm and humour hid ruthless self-interest. He had a deep, but patchy, sense of honour. He would cheerfully cuckold a man he knew, but never broke a promise. He wouldn't force a woman against her will, but would throw all his considerable resources into suborning her wishes.

When he first took another lover, then told her about it in detail, she did her best to be philosophical. What they had was a contract, not a love affair.

Her heart proved to be dented, not broken. When the scars healed, she was no longer in love with him. Fond, but not in love.

She enjoyed his company, and missed him when he was off on duchy business, or out making mayhem in the *ton*. She'd learned more about sex in three years with Aldridge, than in three years in a brothel and six with other men. But he was also good company out of bed, an entertaining conversationalist, happiest when his mistress had opinions and made him work hard to defend his.

The deep melancholy he kept so well disguised called to the mother in her, and she would trust him with most things in her life. Though not with a sister, if she had one, and not with her daughter, if Sarah were a few years older.

She wasn't at all sure she could trust him with the news she was going to have to tell him soon.

That was him now; an unmarked carriage with nothing to distinguish it from a thousand others turning unobtrusively into the street. Aldridge was as careful with her daughter's reputation as Becky was herself, and would not let the scandal sheets learn the connection between Rose's house and the one where Mrs and Miss Winstanley lived.

Though, they must know, surely? Scandalmongers of all classes watched him closely. But he wielded the considerable power of the Haverford duchy, and no one ever publicly hinted that Aldridge's mistress had a double life.

He was early. She crossed to the sideboard where she kept his favourite brandy, and had poured him a glass by the time his steps sounded in the hall. Two sets of steps? Who did Aldridge have with him?

The other man was as tall as Aldridge, but dark to his fair. He must once have been stunningly handsome, one side of his face still carved by a master. Subtle curves and strong planes combined in a harmonious whole, speaking of strength and, in the lines at the corners of his eyes, suffering.

On the other side, dozens of scars pitted and ridged the skin, as if it had been torn and chewed by an animal—an animal with jaws of flame, by the tell-tale burn puckers. Thankfully, whatever it was had missed his eye, now glaring at her.

"Well?" he demanded. Shaken by his voice, rich and mellow despite the curt syllable, she realised she had been staring. How rude. But for some reason, she didn't apologise as she should, but instead blurted, "I am glad whatever injured you spared your eye."

He looked startled, and suddenly friendlier. "Thank you. I am glad too."

That voice! He could read a linen inventory, and she would listen for hours.

"An unusual approach to an introduction," Aldridge observed. Becky collected herself and smiled at her protector. "No one is more important than the man who keeps you," a mentor had once told her. "When he is present, see no one else, except as it reflects well on him."

Becky's attention had been entirely misdirected. She had presented her cheek to Aldridge for his kiss, given him the expected squeal in return for his squeeze, and returned the kiss, all without being aware of anything but Aldridge's guest.

"A more traditional introduction would be welcome," she said.

"My dear, you have heard me speak of my friend, Hugh, Baron Overton."

Yes. From the description in the gossip magazine on the desk in her sitting room, she had guessed it must be he. *Lord O., who, despite his gruesome scars, seems set to bag the full haul of heads, or should we say tails, he and the M.M. need to win their bet.* Another heartless aristocrat tomcatting his way through life without thought of the suffering he left behind.

But why was he here, in her house, bristling at being presented to Aldridge's mistress as if she were a lady? She turned to Aldridge, her raised brow signalling the question.

"Overton is coming to Astley's with us," Aldridge said. She knew that mulish expression in his eye. He felt he was in the wrong, and expected her to make a fuss. He wouldn't back down, and he'd feel better if they could fight over it.

Instead, she turned to Overton. "Lord Overton, I must assume Lord Aldridge would not have brought you here if you were not sober, trustworthy, and aware that my daughter's future depends on no one making the connection between her mother and Lord Aldridge's mistress. Since my lord clearly trusts you, I will, too."

And, her tone said, *I will find a way to destroy you if Aldridge is wrong.*

Aldridge's kept woman had the carriage of a queen, and when she lectured him, eyes flashing, all Overton could do was mutter, "Yes, ma'am." Satisfied with his answer, she poured him a brandy, having already handed one to Aldridge.

He'd heard Aldridge's mistress was beautiful, though few had met her. But beautiful didn't come close. What on earth was the man doing with other women when he had this one in his keeping?

What was her name, anyway? He hadn't really been listening, had half-thought Aldridge was playing one of his japes. A mistress who couldn't be called Rose, which all the men in town knew to be her name, but had to be called some other name, and treated like a lady in front of her daughter? Surely, it must be a joke?

Apparently, it was true.

While Overton was wool-gathering, Aldridge teased Rose about the present he had in the carriage for the little girl.

He'd dragged Hugh to the shop to pick it up: a doll as beautiful as a princess, and a wardrobe to match. Inspired, Hugh had ordered two. Dark hair for Sophrania, fair hair for Emmaline. They would be ready in a few days, the woman assured him. Good enough. His annual month of freedom would be over in a week. A few days would leave him just enough time to ride home.

Aldridge, though, was assuring Rose he had a basket full of kittens, or a pair of puppies, or a pet bear cub. She just laughed at him, telling him that the care and feeding of such a menagerie would be to his cost, and not hers.

Hugh couldn't reconcile Rose's speech, the cut of her garments, her grace, her manners, with the way she earned her keep. She was unlike any light-skirt he'd ever known.

She threw him off balance, and Aldridge did too, presenting him as if she were not a harlot and he not a peer of the realm.

She acted as if she were a lady, but she was a whore as much as any brassy painted strumpet who offered her wares to all comers in a bawdy house or the street. However much she might ape her betters in this tasteful parlour, whatever Aldridge said.

"What am I supposed to call you?" he asked, and could have bitten his tongue. He was never this graceless.

"Mrs Winstanley," Aldridge said, looking over his shoulder, "and if you choose not to behave, Overton, you can leave right now."

"Mrs Winstanley," Hugh said.

Aldridge nodded, satisfied, and turned back to the woman. "Do you not think Sarah would like a pony?" he asked, clearly wanting to continue his game.

From behind his back, Hugh glared at this female who did not know her place.

Hugh enjoyed the visit to Astley's. Not so much the performance as the reactions of the little girls. Their excitement was contagious, cheering the riders, gasping at the trick riders, and laughing at the clowns.

One of the riders could be a twin of Mrs Winstanley, with the same cornflower blue eyes, the same even features and porcelain skin. Red hair, rather than dark, but otherwise, uncanny. She showed a lot more skin than Aldridge's mistress, and her legs set Hugh fantasising about what he could do with the woman's acrobatic skills.

Mrs Winstanley, whom he treated with punctilious courtesy, in imitation of Aldridge, looked like a virtuous woman. He wondered if her legs were as long and shapely as the rider's. He would bet ten guineas that Aldridge had taught her some acrobatic tricks.

He caught himself, embarrassed to be thinking such things in the presence of innocent children.

Damn Mrs Winstanley. He would not feel guilty about his lust. True, she'd successfully played the lady all evening, giving him no excuse for his inflamed longings. But why should he not imagine bedding a woman who sold her body?

He definitely needed another brandy. Two. No, three.

After the show, they went for a birthday supper at Merrick's—the highlight, a tower of iced cupcakes decorated with pink sugar flowers—and then home, dropping the guests one at a time, shedding carriages from the convoy, until the coach with Hugh, Aldridge, Mrs Winstanley, and little Sarah was the only one left.

It dropped them at the little girl's apartment, and the grooms then took it home to Haverford House, a few streets away.

Aldridge, eyes bright and grinning like a fool, instructed Sarah to shut her eyes and guided her into the parlour where he had left his present.

"Keep them closed, keep them closed," he said, as he retrieved two wrapped parcels, and propped them on the sofa in front of her.

"Now, Sarah," he said, kneeling at her side, and the little girl opened her eyes.

Beautifully mannered, as she had been all evening, Sarah curtseyed her appreciation, then hugged him and kissed his cheek. "Thank you, Uncle Lord Aldridge."

"Open them, Princess," he urged. "They're yours. I chose them myself, but the lady in the shop wrapped them. Do you like the ribbon? She said you would keep it for your hair, so I chose two different colours."

Anyone would think the child was Aldridge's own. Just look at him, watching anxiously as Sarah carefully untied the ribbon and unfolded the fabric Aldridge had chosen for the wrapping.

The child's calm self-possession fractured in the face of the doll and her wardrobe.

"Oh, I love her! Look, Mama! Look how beautiful she is. Look at all her clothes!"

Hugh looked. The mother, bending over her daughter, exclaiming over the doll's articulated arms and legs, and its wardrobe. And the child, her mother in miniature. Identical heart-shaped faces; identical dark hair, tied back but with tiny curls left loose around their foreheads; identical porcelain skin and cornflower blue eyes fringed with dark lashes. So beautiful.

So intent, eyes full of love for her daughter, like statues of the Madonna he had seen in Catholic Italy, before he sold out.

God, he needed a drink.

"Aldridge?" Aldridge was smiling fondly at his mistress and her child. "Aldridge, is there any brandy in the house?"

"Not here, Overton," Aldridge snapped. "Just wait a bit, can't you?"

Of course he could. It didn't bother him at all to see this kept woman, this harlot, bent lovingly over her daughter. It didn't bother him that she stood up to him—a head taller, a man, and an aristocrat—to protect her daughter. When his wife, damn her, had ignored her daughters, regarded them as disposable pawns in her campaign to be the mother of a peer. It didn't bother him at all. It didn't.

"I'll meet you back at Haverford House," he said. "Miss Winstanley, my felicitations on your birth anniversary. Mrs Winstanley, my thanks for a pleasant evening. Aldridge."

"Overton?" Aldridge stopped him in the hall.

"I have to go, Aldridge. I can't stay here and watch you playing at happy families with your whore. I just can't."

Aldridge bristled. "Keep a civil tongue, Overton."

"Your friend, then. Your dear, intimate friend." He didn't try to keep the sneer from his voice.

"Prig," Aldridge said, but without much heat. "Go, then."

Overton took his hat and coat from the waiting maid, and let himself out the door. He carried with him the wounded look in Mrs Winstanley's eyes. Would he have spoken so, had he realised she'd followed her lover—her keeper—to the hall? He tried to shrug off his sudden pang of shame. He'd only said what was true. How dare she be hurt!

Hadn't they passed a tavern two streets back? Surely they had.

Whatever they sold, he was drinking it.

Chapter Nine

"Go after him," Becky said.

Aldridge hesitated. He'd planned to walk Becky home to the town-house and spend the night. But Overton was in a bad way. Aldridge had seen the stricken look in his eyes.

"Go after him," Becky said again. "He is heart sick, Aldridge. He needs his friend."

Overton 'needed' a swift boot to the rear, the way he talked about Becky. Though, it wasn't like him to be cruel. The man was surprisingly prudish, given his amorous exploits, but Aldridge had never doubted his essential kindness. Something was very wrong with him tonight.

"Go," Becky insisted. "I'll stay here tonight with Sarah. And I'll be here, or at the town-house, when you've finished your disgusting bet, sobered him up, and sent him home."

"You heard about the bet?" He winced a little at the word 'disgusting'. He couldn't disagree.

"It is in the papers, Aldridge," she said. "Go after your friend, my dear. I don't know what is haunting him, but go to him."

She was right. He couldn't leave Overton alone, tonight of all nights.

Aldridge, always circumspect in Sarah's presence, contented himself with pressing her hand as he kissed her cheek.

"Thank you, Becky. You're a wonderful woman." Then, to Sarah, "Goodnight, Princess. I'll see you soon."

"Goodnight, Uncle Lord Aldridge. Go and look after the sad man."

He saluted Sarah's cheek, too, and gave the long plait of dark hair an affectionate tug. She was more like her mother every day.

As he'd expected, Overton had made it no farther than the tavern a couple of streets over. "What are you drinking?" Aldridge asked, sliding onto the bench beside him.

"Don't know," Overton said, sinking another from the line before him. Three gone, five to go.

Aldridge had a sniff. Gin. Probably illegally distilled on the premises. Rot gut, certainly.

"Let's go home and get into my brandy." Aldridge suggested, putting his hand over the poison. Overton knocked it out of the way and downed another, roaring like an aggrieved bear when Aldridge sent the last four crashing to the floor, juniper fumes rising from the spreading puddles.

Aldridge knew he wouldn't move. If anyone tried to carry him, he'd fight every inch of the way. Best to let him drink here, then drag him out unconscious. But at least Aldridge could make sure he drank decent brandy. Even if he didn't appreciate it, Aldridge would. The tavern keeper, who had come at the noise, was happy enough to accept a gold guinea for his trouble and a bottle of his finest.

Overton was touchingly grateful. "You're a good friend, Aldridge. You stick by a man. Share the best. Good friend."

Aldridge poured a glass of the brandy the innkeeper brought and inhaled the bouquet. Much better. He handed the glass to Overton, who took a revoltingly large swallow.

"She's beautiful, Aldridge."

Aldridge didn't have to ask who; everyone who met Becky had the same reaction.

"Very beautiful." He poured himself a brandy. Where was Overton going with this? His comment about sharing had better not be related.

"Loves her daughter, doesn't she?"

"She does, Overton. That little girl means everything to her. And I would kill to protect either of them."

Overton waved off the implied threat, shaking his head. "Not going to hurt them. Secret. You told me." He lifted his glass again, this time sipping rather than gulping. "Good stuff, Aldridge. I needed a drink."

Aldridge refilled the glass. If his oldest friend in the world needed to talk, the least Aldridge could do was listen.

"Polyphemia didn't."

Aldridge must have looked blank, because Overton explained. "My wife. Polyphemia. She didn't love her daughters. She died, you know."

Three years ago this very night. "Yes. I know." To his shame, he'd not gone to Lancashire when he heard, reluctant to leave Becky and knowing he couldn't take his newly acquired mistress to visit his newly bereaved friend.

Overton was following his own train of thought. "She didn't want to marry me, you know. Said I was ugly. But Pankhurst didn't leave her anything and no one else offered. So she traded her proven fertility for my title and money."

"Is that so?" What else could a person say to such a revelation?

"Wouldn't let me bed her, except in the dark. Wouldn't let me bed her at all that last year. Except the one time... But she was with child, of course."

"Was she?"

"Mmm. Needed me to think I was the father."

Aldridge tried to fend off further revelations. "Shall we go back to Haverford House, Overton?"

"I did, too. So happy, Aldridge. Thought I couldn't, you see."

Couldn't what? "I've heard from a lot of women that you can, Overton."

"I can plough well enough. I like ploughing. But I can't sow. No Overton heir. No Overton bastards, even. Lying bitch. Lying whore. I wanted to believe her, Aldridge. I thought the doctors were wrong. 'Look,' I told them. 'I got my wife with child.'"

Overton would regret these revelations in the morning. Aldridge regretted them now. He filled the man's glass again. Perhaps he would pass out and stop talking.

Not just yet, though. He cradled the brandy, staring into it as if his wife's image were floating on top.

"I was in London. You remember, Aldridge. You were here, too. 'Plenty of time', she said. 'Go to London. You can be back before the baby is born,' she said. 'Women's business.' Lying bitch."

He said nothing more for several minutes, just sat and swirled his brandy meditatively. Aldridge relaxed. Perhaps the soul-baring was over.

But no such luck. When Overton spoke again, in a quiet voice that carried no further than Aldridge's ears, the drunken slur was gone, as if his memories had burned the alcohol out of his brain. "I went home early, when you and I argued. Anyway, I missed the girls. And I was worried about my wife. She seemed—she was huge when I left, and Crawford's wife had just had twins.

"Besides, we had children to think of. Not just the new baby, but Pankhurst's girls. And if we could have one baby, perhaps there would be others. I wanted to mend the marriage. Well, build a marriage, really. What we had was a contract. But we could do better than that, couldn't we?"

"Mm hmm," Aldridge mumbled, hoping the noncommittal sound conveyed sympathy and support, and didn't sound too much like a whimper. He topped up the man's glass.

"The midwife was with her when I returned home, and things were not going well. I rode for the doctor, of course."

"Of course."

"A six-month baby, she told the doctor. I saw the midwife shaking her head, but I didn't understand."

So, Overton's baroness had tried to tuck a cuckoo into the Overton nest. Aldridge made another noncommittal sound.

Tears rolled disregarded down Overton's cheeks.

"Something was wrong. The baby was in the wrong position, or too big. They told me to stay downstairs, but she was fighting this battle for me. I had to be there."

"You did," Aldridge agreed, desperately wishing something would stop Overton mid-confession.

Overton gave no sign of hearing. "She was screaming with pain. Cursing me. Cursing some other man, too. John something. I didn't understand, didn't really listen. She was half out of her head.

"Then the doctor and the midwife... something changed. They managed to move the baby. They said it would soon be over. I tried to reassure her. I don't remember what I said exactly. Something about her being brave, and we'd soon have our son or daughter. I told her I was grateful.

"She screamed at me. Everyone in the house must have heard her. In the village, likely. I should be grateful, she said. Did I know how hard it was finding someone as tall as me to give her a boy since I was only half a man? And it had better be a boy, because she wasn't going through all that again.

"It was a little girl, Aldridge. I didn't care. The doctor put her in my arms. I loved her the minute I saw her. If she had lived, I would have loved her as my own."

"She died?" Stupid thing to say. He knew the baby had died, and the mother, too. But the woman's betrayal cast a new light on why Overton never talked about them.

"No. Not then," Overton said. "Polyphemia didn't either. She tore, and she bled. It took them a long time to stop the bleeding, but they did it. Everyone heard, though, Aldridge. The doctor. The midwife. The servants. They knew what she'd done. The whole household knew. Even if she'd said nothing... I've seen six-month babies. I am not as big a fool as my cheating wife clearly thought."

He emptied his glass and held it out for Aldridge to pour another. "Grace... I named her, because Polyphemia wouldn't. Wouldn't even look at her. Grace was born at term, and nine months before she was born, I was at sea on my way back from Jamaica."

"Ah," was the best Aldridge could do.

"What was I to do? Divorce her? I had the evidence. But then what would become of the girls? I said nothing. I didn't even speak to her—didn't go to her room. When she wouldn't feed Grace, I found a wet nurse. When she wouldn't see Sophie and Emma, I made excuses, told them she was tired, but she'd send for them soon."

Overton lapsed into silence again, sipping his brandy. Aldridge knew it wasn't over, though. The deaths of his wife and child sent Overton into a bottle for weeks every year. And Aldridge was now going to have to sit and listen to how they died, and keep making ineffectual noises. Perhaps the roof would collapse, or the tavern would catch fire.

After several minutes, Overton took up the tale again, calm voice adding another layer of horror to the bitter tale. "Three days later, she called for the baby. I was glad. I thought perhaps we could work it out. We could have, couldn't we Aldridge? We could have tried, at least, for the girls? If she'd waited?"

Aldridge tried not to shake his head. Unlikely. In his experience, a treacherous bitch remained a treacherous bitch, no matter how much she swore reform.

Overton wasn't paying attention, staring blankly at his glass. Suddenly, he thumped it down on the table and, in a wail that attracted the attention of everyone in the tavern, asked, "Why did she have to take Grace? Why?"

Overton rose with his voice, emphasising the last anguished question by shaking Aldridge's lapels, then collapsed again, huddled beside his friend, weeping.

Aldridge patted him awkwardly, glaring at the rest of the patrons until they turned back to their own affairs. Overton was going to hate himself in the morning. If he remembered. May the gods of drink and debauchery wipe it from his memory. Aldridge was only sorry he was too sober to forget. He took a long draught of brandy.

"She drowned, Aldridge. She and Grace both. Walked through the house, down the stairs, across the lawn, and down to the lake. And just kept walking. No one stopped her. No one even saw her until it was too late."

Perhaps another sip of brandy would loosen the tightness in Aldridge's throat. It was worse than he expected. Far worse.

"I'm so sorry, Overton." How inadequate that sounded in the face of such grief.

Overton misunderstood. "Why? You aren't John." He frowned, staring at nothing, clearly thinking this over. His tale told, the illusion of sobriety was fast abandoning him. "Might have been. You'd swive any man's wife. But she never met you. Wouldn't mind raising your son, though. I like you, Aldridge." He wouldn't in the morning, when he realised how much Aldridge now knew.

"You should marry again, Overton. Have a couple of sons for the barony."

Overton snorted. "Weren't you listening, Aldridge? I can't. The doctors told me, and I've tested it often enough." He giggled. "Throughout His Majesty's kingdom, on two continents and assorted islands. Tall, short, fair, dark, fat, thin. I've ploughed them all." He shook his head, the melancholy settling over him again. "She was right. My damned, lying, cheating wife was right. I'm half a man, Aldridge. And the last of the Overtons. When I'm gone, the King gets the lot."

And with that, he suddenly put his head on the table, and went to sleep.

He slept through the removal to, and from, the carriage, and the subsequent transfer to a guest bed in the heir's wing. Aldridge set a servant to watch him, to make sure he didn't choke on his own vomit in the night, then returned to his own suite.

But there was no rest for Aldridge here tonight. He tossed and turned for a while, but his friend's calm voice kept echoing in his head, retelling the horrors of betrayal and loss. After a while, he dressed again, and told the sleepy footman on duty in the front hall, "If I am needed, I will be at Mrs Darling's house." Becky would comfort him. He needed Becky tonight.

Becky was alarmed to be shaken awake from a deep sleep.

"Sarah?" She sat bolt upright.

The maid shook her head. "Not the little miss. She is sound asleep, the lamb. It's the Master. Lord Aldridge. He's at your other house, ma'am."

Becky was already out of bed, hurrying any-old-how into the clothes she had laid out to wear in the morning. What could be wrong? She'd thought he would be occupied with his friend for another few days, and had planned to spend them here with Sarah.

In scant minutes, she was downstairs and outside, surprised to find the street empty except for the two burly footmen who waited to escort her and her maid.

"His lordship said 'twould take too long to put the carriage to, ma'am," one of them apologised. "Said 'twould be faster to walk."

True. It was just two streets away, but what could be so urgent? Concern propelled her through the dark streets, her escort hurrying to keep up.

In her own front parlour, Aldridge stood when she entered, his brow creased even as he smiled. Around his eyes she could see the tiny wrinkles that only appeared when he was deeply distressed. "I am a brute to drag you out in the night like this," he said.

And yet here you are, she thought, but didn't say. His attempt at a sheepish smile was a failure, but the flaws in his usual elegance told their own story. His hair stood on end from tugging, his cravat was loosely knotted, his waistcoat unbuttoned, and his shirt cuffs left loose. "Never mind, my love," she told him. "Tell me what you need."

"Just you, Becky. Just you. Come up to bed."

He was, by turns, wild and tender, and she responded, as she always did. The only reference he made to whatever had brought him here was a wish that the week were over and Overton back in the North Country. "Three more days, and I'll load him into his carriage. His retainers will have him sober long before he gets home."

Three days. She could wait three days to tell Aldridge her problem.

Chapter Ten

In the end, it was closer to three weeks. Aldridge said goodbye to his friend, then went off to Margate, summoned by His Grace, the Duke of Haverford to explain the scandal that had erupted at a Society masquerade ball the night after Astley's. The gossip rags were relatively circumspect, aware of the Duke's reach. But the mother of one of Sarah's friends, Mrs Harrowmead, was an eyewitness and poured it all into the ears of the assembled mothers when they walked with the girls in the park.

"There was a queue. Can you believe it? Aldridge and Overton turned up hoping to find volunteers and had an excessive number of applicants for the last two... encounters. So they decided to conduct interviews. All very discreet, nothing stated plainly, but the word travelled right through the house, and—I swear to you, my dears, I saw it with my own eyes—the ladies formed a queue in the hall outside the study, and went in one at a time."

"But... their husbands?" protested one of the other women, leaning forward so she didn't miss a word, her eyes wide and avid.

"They were mostly widows, dear. One or two ladies whose husbands do not seem to mind—you know the sort—but Major Lord Vincent came and dragged his wife away; literally dragged her, and she screaming that he deserved to be Aldridged. Darlings, I did not know where to look." Mrs Harrowmead's shudder of horror would not have shamed Mrs Siddons.

"Dreadful!" the other women agreed, with great delight.

"But that wasn't the worst. After they had chosen the... successful ladies, they went back to dancing. I think they must have arranged to meet them later, do you not agree? They were but an hour in the study, and they must have interviewed at least nine ladies. I did not see the whole, for Edward disapproved heartily when he noticed I was watching, and took me off to dance."

"Then Lord Ballingcroft arrived, looking for Overton."

Mrs Harrowmead paused for dramatic effect.

"He challenged him to a duel, and Overton planted him a facer right in the middle of the Douglas Reel!"

The response was suitably shocked, both at Overton's disregard of etiquette, and at Mrs Harrowmead's use of schoolboy slang. She'd not have heard that from her husband. A careless younger brother, perhaps?

"Then Ballingcroft pulled a sword out of his cane, and Aldridge—I did not perfectly see how, but Aldridge took it from him, and, my loves, he told Lord Ballingcroft that he did not deserve Lady Ballingcroft, and if the lady ever did stray, Lord Ballingcroft would have brought it on himself, for he was an unfaithful husband and a poor..." here the lady blushed. "Um. Lord Aldridge implied that Lord Ballingcroft was inadequate in..."

"Bed sport," supplied one of the other women, bluntly.

"Then what happened?" asked Becky, who had seen Aldridge's black eye when he called on his way to Margate.

"A brawl, Mrs Winstanley," Mrs Harrowmead said. "Lord Ballingcroft hit Lord Aldridge, and Lord Overton hit Lord Ballingcroft, and some other gentlemen joined in, and even some ladies, and Edward took me home." The lady was clearly disappointed. "And Lord Ballingcroft is at home with a broken jaw, or so they say. So there will be no duel."

"But the newssheet said..." the lady who had spoken of bed sport was clearly intrigued. "How did they manage it?" And she quoted the gossip column entry from memory. "'Lord O. and the M.M., despite the unfortunate incident, apparently found time to complete the game bag required to win the bet with Mr H.' When did they find time? And the energy?"

Becky thought to herself that this lady's husband would be wise to keep her away from Aldridge. Her own experience with Aldridge suggested several plausible answers, but she didn't enlighten the company. Mrs Winstanley would have no idea about such scandalous goings-on.

Time to collect Sarah from the skipping game by the pond and make their way home.

Aldridge, as always when he had been with his father, returned jittery and bitter. No point in talking to him until he could think straight. All he wanted was the comfort of Becky's body, and for days, she barely left the town-house's great bed, as he expended his nervous energy and slowly regained his poise.

Becky kept putting off the conversation they must have, until one morning when they lay half asleep in the aftermath of a particularly energetic bout of morning bed sport.

Aldridge, who was propped on one elbow idly tracing patterns on her belly with one finger, commented, "You've put on a bit of round, my love." He circled his finger around her navel. "Eating well?"

"No more than usual," Becky said. "It isn't that."

He paid no attention, tracing up her torso to cup one breast. "Here, too. I'm not complaining. I like it."

"It isn't food, Aldridge."

He was occupied teasing one nipple back to erect attention with his finger. "Looks good enough to taste."

"Aldridge, I need you to listen."

He looked up, his laughing eyes meeting hers. "What is it, my darling Mrs Darling? A problem? Tell me, and I'll fix it." Then he curled in to touch her nipple with his tongue.

Becky twisted out of his reach. They were going to discuss this now, before she lost her nerve again. Aldridge was the most indulgent of protectors, but she had no idea how he would react.

"Please, Aldridge."

He sat up then, propping himself against some of the pillows that littered the bed. His eyes were still dancing, but he composed the rest of his face.

"Very well, my dear. What is it? Have you run through your allowance? Do you want to break our contract and run off with the Prince of Wales? Are you about to confess to being a spy for Napoleon?"

"I am with child." There. It was said.

His eyes went still and wide.

"With child," he repeated.

She nodded.

"How?"

"The usual way," she snapped back before she could catch the words on her tongue. Yes, he always took precautions and so did she, but everyone knew precautions didn't always work. Why was it that a wanted child was a credit to a man's virility, and an unwanted one the fault of its mother?

He quirked a smile at her, though it didn't reach his eyes. "Ah, yes, and quite a few unusual ways, as I recall. But it gives us a problem, does it not?"

'Us.' Thank God. Becky thought she'd hidden her sigh of relief, but Aldridge knew her too well.

"Did you think I would cast you into the streets, Becky? Shame on you."

Perhaps he didn't realise. "I won't be able to fulfil all the second year of our contract," she said, shifting uneasily.

"You want to end the contract?" He was trying for his bland look, the empty face behind which he hid what he thought and felt, but she was not fooled. His nostrils twitched as he suppressed a flare, his lips thinned before he deliberately relaxed them, and he took a deep breath to relax his jaw. Whatever he felt about her news, he felt it deeply.

"You won't want me when I'm huge, Aldridge. With Sarah, I was as big as an elephant, and so ugly."

"Ugly? With your belly rounded by my child?" Suddenly, his face flared into an expression of yearning he quickly masked, but not before she'd seen it. "My child," he said again, and leaned forward to touch her belly lightly, like fragile glass.

He met her eyes. "You will be more beautiful to me than ever, Becky, and I'll have you know, there are ways we can enjoy one another, even if you are as huge as an elephant." Then, as if her belly were a magnet drawing his attention, back they went to the rounded curve. "My child," he repeated.

After a while, he spoke again. "My other children... I didn't know Antonia even existed until she was six, and... I'm part of her life now, of course, but her parents don't... The relationship will always be uneasy, I think. And the other two—I found husbands for their mothers within their own class, and I send them a present at Christmas. Well, you know that. You're the one who told me to make it a present for the whole family, to save jealousy."

"Aldridge." She tried to invest the word with all the comfort she could. He'd spoken before of his children, but always with such cheerful insouciance, she'd had no idea he felt their lack.

"And now another one." That was said in a tone of mournful acceptance. Then, briskly, "Well, we'll have to make sure he has a good start in life, and his mother is free to give him all he needs. But Becky, will you let me be his godfather, at least?"

"Of course, Aldridge." She laid her hand over his where it cupped her belly, then teased him, to try to lighten the moment. "Or hers."

He pulled her to him, so she was nestled in his arms, her head under his chin. "What do you want, my love? A new identity with a trust fund to keep you in comfort? I know it isn't to stay here with me; you told me last year that you'd not renew the contract at the end of this term."

"Sarah will be eleven when this contract term ends," she reminded him. She shouldn't be apologetic, but he sounded so forlorn. "I can't give her a normal life as your mistress, or this new baby, either."

"I know. I know. I even agree with you, my love. I wish... I wish I were not the next Haverford. Then I could marry you, and we could go on being comfortable."

"If I were your wife, Aldridge, I would object to your lovers. And then you would not be comfortable at all."

He gave a bark of laughter. "True. But I do love you, Becky, dear."

"You are fond of me, Aldridge, and I am fond of you. But we do not love one another. Which is a very good thing, no doubt."

For a moment, he let his mood slip. Serious and intent, he said, "I will leave it as long as I can, but one day, I will choose a wife for her lineage and the advantage she offers the duchy. The poor lady. I will be a dreadful husband, I expect, though better than His Grace, I hope."

"You do yourself an injustice, my dear," Becky said. "You will be kind to your wife, I know, and will treat her with respect. And I hope and pray you find a woman you can love, and who will love you as you deserve. That is my dream for you, Aldridge—marriage to a woman who will absorb, and complete, and fulfil you."

Aldridge's short laugh rejected the notion, though his eyes were wistful.

"And what is your dream for yourself, Becky?" he asked.

"Oh, I shall be satisfied with a little cottage, somewhere in a country town, where I can be a widow, and no one will know my past."

Aldridge pulled back to look into her eyes. "Satisfied, perhaps, but what is your dream? Come; pretend I am a magical creature with the power to grant wishes. What are your three wishes, Becky?"

She decided to play along. "Three wishes. Let me see. Marriage of the sort I wish for you. That is my first wish: to be married to a man I love and who loves me."

"Marriage and love. What is your second wish?"

"This is silly, Aldridge. No one will marry a woman with my history."

"Tell me anyway," he coaxed. "Wish two."

"A husband who will be a true father to my children, who will care for them as I do, and treat them as his own. It isn't going to happen, Aldridge. I've been a whore since I was fifteen."

"You are a unique and special woman, and any man would be lucky to win you as his wife. Wish number three."

She flapped her hands in a gesture of dismissal. "Might as well wish for him to be a peer, then. A commoner is no more likely to marry me than a lord of the realm. Find me a peer to marry, oh, granter of wishes."

He tucked her back under his chin again. "Marriage, love for you and your children, and social position. That's what you're really asking for, is it not?"

"It is just a dream, my dear. Best to focus on what we can achieve, do you not think? Will you help me find my little cottage, Aldridge?"

"I will help you find a place, my Becky. Somewhere you and Sarah and my child can be safe." His hands were roaming again, exploring her curves. "I cannot believe I didn't notice. You are fuller here and here, and more rounded down here. Lie back, Becky. I want to kiss my child." He tipped her backwards, followed her down, and spent several minutes murmuring to her belly. Then kisses became licks and nips, and tended lower.

Becky shifted to accommodate him, content to let the conversation drop. Aldridge had given his word, and he never broke a promise.

Chapter Eleven

It was worse this time. Twice before, Hugh had run away to London to escape the anniversary of his wife's suicide, and spent the time drinking and raking with Aldridge. This time, the sour taste of three weeks of excess lingered, even after five weeks under his own roof.

Physical exercise—productive, necessary work—helped. He'd thrown himself into the harvest. This was the last farm, and they'd scythed and cocked more than half the tenant's grain today.

Hugh stopped at the end of the row. How much progress had they made? The sun would be down soon; they had perhaps another hour of light.

"Reckon we'll finish this field tonight, my lord," said Beckham, whose barley crop they were getting in. Hugh nodded as he took a tankard of ale from the man's wife. "I reckon we will, Beckham," he agreed.

He downed half the tankard in a huge swallow, relishing the sensation of the liquid seeping into his parched flesh. They'd done well. They'd finish scything tomorrow, and then they'd join the teams who'd already begun collecting and stacking sheaves from previous days, dried enough for the next stage in the harvest.

The weather looked like it would hold dry for another week. They could count it a good year.

With another couple of swallows, he finished the tankard and returned it to Mrs Beckham with his thanks.

"Come on then, men," he said, picking up his scythe again. "Let's finish this field."

On the first anniversary, he and Aldridge had met by chance at an inn a day outside Town, and Aldridge's flirtation with a servant girl had led to an invitation for her to bring a friend and join them. Hugh had bedded a scant handful of women since the shrapnel burst that scarred him, and none but his reluctant wife in four years. He enjoyed himself thoroughly.

But on the ride to London, when Aldridge laughingly teased him about the girl's admiration of his performance, he attributed her compliments to his lavish payment. "Look at me, Aldridge. Who would want this monster in her bed if she had a choice?" That was a direct quote from Polyphemia—one of the many things she'd screamed at him that last, awful day.

Aldridge laughed. "A few scars is nothing, Hugh. You're just as pretty as you once were on the other side and, in any case, it is men that are shallow about good looks. Women'll look past that, if you pleasure them well." Then he proposed proving his case by introducing Hugh to some of the women he knew in London. "You haven't lost the skill you had when we were lads, Hugh. That girl had the glow. You gave her a night she'll never forget. Get a reputation for that in London, and your bed need never be empty."

He was right. Hugh went home the first year sated and satisfied. He rode up to London the second year looking forward to his holiday rather than backward to his guilt and grief, eager to renew his acquaintance with at least some of the widows he had enjoyed the year before.

The second year was even wilder. In certain circles, the story of the scarred baron's three weeks had made the rounds, and Hugh found himself propositioned endlessly. Though three of the five widows he'd known the previous year were now married again, and one was out of town, he had no difficulty finding a bed partner.

His conscience troubled him when he discovered some of the ladies who approached him had living, if neglectful, husbands. He couldn't understand being so casual about a solemn vow, made before God. He consoled himself that he wasn't party to the vows strangers made. And he only tupped women whose husbands were unfaithful. He wasn't doing to another man what the unknown John had done to him.

Still, he was saddened by it, and besmirched, too. Riding home that second year, he decided he'd show more discretion in future, avoid the worst of the debauchery.

This year had started like the second, but halfway through the second week, in an idle conversation about the morals of the ladies of the *ton*, Aldridge claimed he'd known whores with fewer lovers. They were at White's, and already well down the brandy decanter, or perhaps they would not have accepted Hackenburg's now-infamous bet: two ladies each in every 24-hour period, in two different sexual positions, with no repeats for a week.

At the time, drunk as they all were, the bet had seemed like fun. When they left to plan their approach, Aldridge's suggestion—swapping partners partway through the day would make winning easier—sounded logical. They'd swapped partners before, especially in their youth when, it sometimes seemed, they'd sampled half the female population of England, Wales, and lower Scotland.

But the execution of their plan left him feeling dirty and despicable.

Was it the cold-blooded plotting? The fast succession? The feeling the ladies they'd played clicket with were interchangeable body parts instead of real people? The undeniable fact, emphasised by that damnable queue on the last night, that the *ton* was riddled with ladies who were little more than whores? No, worse than whores, for at least a girl selling her body up against the wall in Covent Garden knew no better, and did it so she could eat.

The Ballingcrofts broke his heart. An adultery virgin, Aldridge had called Lady Ballingcroft, and laughed. Hugh had looked into Lord Ballingcroft's wounded eyes and seen himself. Stupid bastard. He'd promised before God to honour Lady Ballingcroft and protect her, not to drive her into the arms of other men. Hugh's self-hatred had fuelled the punch that broke the idiot's jaw.

Word was, on that last day in London, Lady Ballingcroft was hovering over her wounded lord and smothering him in kindness, so perhaps some good would come from it.

In all three weeks, he'd met only one woman who epitomised the qualities he thought of as ladylike: demure, graceful, dignified, discreet. What an upside-down world, when Aldridge's kept woman was more of a lady than the peeresses and their friends who trooped through Aldridge's disgusting tupping palace.

The exquisite Mrs Winstanley had haunted him since he'd returned home. He could barely remember the faces and forms of the women he'd actually bedded. But Mrs Winstanley, who had given him no cause for his fevered longings, welcomed him in his dreams, capturing him between the soft thighs of the Astley rider; offering her soft curves, porcelain skin, and silken hair; leaving him awake, hard, and lonely, night after night.

She was not for sharing. He'd hinted to Aldridge before he was sober enough to think better of it. Aldridge had donned the ducal mantle he never wore with his friends, and frozen the thought in its tracks with a terse, "No."

Hugh scythed two rows of barley and was back where he started, half a row ahead of the other workers. Stretching a kink out of his back, he watched them approach. They would soon be done for the day. It would be a good harvest.

A familiar voice echoed his thought. "It looks a good harvest."

Aldridge? What on earth was he doing here? Looking, from the top of his exquisite beaver to the toes of his highly polished boots, as if quietly hacking in Hyde Park, not a speck of dust or a thread out of place.

"They said up at the house you were down here. Can I help?"

"Dressed like that?" Hugh laughed, and Aldridge examined his coated arms with a smile.

"I would, of course, take my jacket off."

He could do it, too. They had worked side by side before, on holiday from school and rejoicing in their youth and strength. And they'd basked in the appreciation of the village girls at the harvest dance afterwards.

"Thank you, Aldridge, but we're nearly done."

The tenant had finished his row and was stretching at the end of it, keeping one eye on his lord. "Beckham, I'm going to take my guest up to the house. It's been a good day's work."

"That it has, m'lord," the tenant agreed. "And we'll have her finished this half hour, never you mind."

Aldridge hadn't visited Overton Park since those long-ago school days. Still Hugh asked no questions. He sluiced his head with water from one of the buckets under a tree by the fence, shook it to disperse the worst of the water and pulled on his coat. His horse had been saddled and bridled for him while he'd been washing.

Mounting, Hugh called to Aldridge, "Race?"

The Park was twenty minutes away across country, and Hugh's horse had been resting all day. Aldridge's horse was one of Hugh's, too; clearly the Park's stable had mounted him for the short ride to Beckham's field.

Aldridge's only reply was to nudge his mount into full flight and, with a whoop, Hugh was after him. With evenly matched riders and horses, they thundered neck and neck into the courtyard and pulled to a stop in front of the stables.

The Marquis of Aldridge had arrived shortly after noon, Hugh's valet told him while he had his bath and dressed for dinner. The marquis had read in the library for a while, visited Miss Sophrania and Miss Emmaline in the schoolroom, then called for a horse and directions to Beckham's farm.

Aldridge in his daughters' schoolroom? Whatever for? Not that he minded, of course. Even if they were not gently-born virgins, a species Aldridge avoided like the plague, at 10 and 8, they were safe from the man's incessant pursuit of women.

The Astley's exhibition had shown an unexpected side to his friend. Aldridge mediating a quarrel between two girls, putting out a protective arm when a carriage came too close, sharing the birthday cakes in a way that gave each child precisely the same number of sugar roses. The little girls all treated him like a favourite uncle, and Aldridge was respectful, tender, and protective.

Even so, Hugh went downstairs to dinner still trying to think of a reason why Aldridge would want to visit Sophie and Em.

Aldridge was a few minutes behind him, immaculately dressed in a dark blue coat, grey breeches, and a silver and blue waistcoat, flamboyantly embroidered. A sapphire-and-diamond pin studded his intricately tied cravat, echoing the sapphire-and-diamond buckles on his shoes.

"You are welcome, Aldridge, of course," Hugh began, "but I must admit, I wonder why I am being honoured with your presence."

How ungracious that sounded. Aldridge couldn't be blamed for Hugh's fevered dreams of Mrs Winstanley, after all. The man had been his host in London for three years running, and was, besides, his last surviving school friend. Hugh's last surviving friend, in truth. The men he'd known in the army were all gone, killed in the continuing war with Napoleon. And he didn't mix much with the neighbours, three of whom were called John. Not, perhaps, *the* John—it was a very common name—but still.

Aldridge did not take offence. "I do have something I wish to discuss with you, Overton, but it can wait until after dinner." Not in front of the servants, then.

Usually, Hugh ate his meal in the study, to avoid the solitary splendour of the dining room. It was nice to have company, someone with whom to discuss the harvest, the war, the rioting in Manchester, and the health of the King's youngest daughter.

But after the second remove, Hugh dismissed the serving footmen. If privacy Aldridge wanted, privacy he would have. He slid Aldridge the port and watched his friend focus too much attention on pouring himself a glass. Aldridge sat back, holding the tumbler with both hands and stared down into it, uncharacteristically silent.

"Well?" Hugh asked.

Aldridge took a slow sip before replying. "How much do you remember about our talk in the tavern after Astley's?"

Bits and pieces. Surely he hadn't told Aldridge everything? He was afraid he had, but why would Aldridge raise this now?

"Why?"

Aldridge answered with another question. "How much does it matter to you that the title will go to the King when you die?"

"And the land," Hugh said, gloomily. Clearly he had told all and Aldridge remembered the lot. "My uncle and my cousin renewed the fee tail; the land goes with the title."

Aldridge said nothing, waiting for an answer to his question.

"Damn you, Aldridge. I can't change it. I've tried. The lawyers say breaking the fee tail might take a hundred years and cost more than I could ever pay. I've had them hunt every little twig of the family tree. Nothing. I am the last of the Overtons."

The wound was always raw. The Overtons had never been prolific breeders, but they'd held this land and served these people since Charles II had rewarded a faithful ancestor at the Restoration. And Hugh would be the last.

Aldridge couldn't possibly understand, with his younger brother and cousins and second cousins and, for all Hugh knew, sixth and seventh cousins. And who knew how many by-blows to prove he could do his duty by the title when the scab-scratching louse finally settled down.

"But you would change it if you could."

Hugh clenched his jaw to keep from cursing his response, but Aldridge hadn't finished.

"I have an idea that might answer your need. Just might, mind you. It's a gamble, but I promise you'll not be worse off, and you might just win the heir you want."

Hugh's cynical snort was propelled by ten years of broken hopes. "So what have you got? A gypsy remedy? I've tried them all. It won't be prayer and fasting, not from you. I know: you've a pregnant lover to offload." He choked on the joke when he saw Aldridge's face.

"No."

A flat and uncompromising no. He'd not give his name to any bitch who'd whore herself to the likes of Aldridge. "No, Aldridge. No. I'll not do it."

"Hear me out, Overton. Will you do that for me? It will be your choice in the end, but hear me out."

Hugh refilled his glass, hand shaking slightly. Aldridge had only one woman he wanted. But in her proper place—set up in a house in the nearest town, where he could sink himself into her softness when not doing his duty to his people and his stepdaughters.

He pushed the port decanter back towards Aldridge, and Aldridge shot out a hand to stop it tipping. Hugh had no choice. He could hardly turn the man out of his house, and Aldridge wouldn't go until he'd had his say.

Aldridge took a meditative sip of his port, then studied it as if the words he needed were written on the ruby surface.

Hugh wasn't going to say anything. Aldridge wanted to talk? Let him talk.

And eventually he did. "My mistress is with child."

"Mrs Winstanley?" Hugh was horrified.

That surge of hope was just his cock talking. It didn't rule him. Aldridge couldn't know... Or did he? Had he guessed? Did he hope to use Hugh's reaction to offload his leavings on Hugh and his daughters?

His daughters. "Do you think I would let a woman like her anywhere near my daughters? How dare you suggest I should give them a harlot as a mother!" He was on his feet, shouting. "A doxy's bastard as Overton? Over my dead body!"

"Well, obviously," Aldridge drawled, and something in the tone penetrated Hugh's fury. People who didn't know him said Aldridge never lost his temper. Hugh had been at school with him during the years he'd struggled to contain the volcanic anger that, when it flared, consumed everything in its path. Hugh knew that drawl. He knew the white lines around the lips and the glitter in the eyes.

"Your dead body is rather the point." Aldridge was on his feet, too, leaning forward over the table, his voice quieter than ever, his eyes chips of brown glass. "And sooner, rather than later, if you continue to insult Mrs Winstanley."

He pushed away from the table, throwing his energy into pacing the room punching his fist into his other hand. Hugh, his own anger high, would have preferred the punch directed at him, though a small voice cautioned that Aldridge would undoubtedly win in a fair fight. Hugh was fit, but Aldridge boxed with Jackson three times a week, fenced with a master every day, and fought scoundrels in low dives for the sheer joy of battle.

Might as well live dangerously. "How can I insult a whore?" he asked.

Aldridge stopped in his tracks, clenching and unclenching his fists.

"This was a mistake," he said at last. "You have always been a bit of a prig, Overton. And a hypocrite. You'll swive anyone who offers, but you've another rule for the rest of the universe. I'll leave in the morning."

He crossed to the door, but stopped with his hand on the latch, and met Hugh's eyes. "You know nothing about what brought her to the life she's led; a life she has survived with dignity and grace. She shows more honour in her least action than most women of the *ton* can muster once in a lifetime. Brave. Honest. Clever. A devoted mother. I'm leaving because you don't deserve her. You aren't fit to kiss the hem of her robe."

Hugh opened his mouth to ask Aldridge why he didn't marry this paragon himself, but before he could speak, Aldridge laughed with a decide lack of humour.

"God, she would have sent that governess of yours packing the first time she raised a finger to your little Emmaline."

He was only just in time to arrest Aldridge's exit.

"Wait. Aldridge, the governess hits Emma? What are you talking about? What have you seen! You know what I think about hitting children." He and Aldridge had made a pact at school to never beat a child the way they'd been beaten themselves. They'd been sleeping on their stomachs at the time, after an escapade had come to the attention of the masters.

"Ask your daughter. My concern is my own child." Aldridge put his hand on the door, then heaved a sigh and turned back. "Look, Overton. Open your eyes. The woman favours the older girl, who does her best to step between the governess and the little one. Little Emmaline has bruised knuckles, sits awkwardly, and flinches when the governess looks at her. And she's a hard-eyed, grasping, bitter, old bitch, that one. I've seen her like before."

His narrowed eyes looked into a childhood populated by the succession of nursery tyrants he'd described many times, before he returned to his grievance, sneering, "But perhaps you don't care. She isn't yours, after all."

"But..." Overton was quickly reviewing every visit he'd made to the schoolroom, every time the girls had been presented to him in the parlour or his study. Little Em had been quieter since the new governess had arrived, a month before his London trip. Sophie had taken to answering for her, and Hugh couldn't remember when he'd last heard Em's sweet little chuckle. Em's cheek was bruised just last week. An accident while playing, the governess said. The governess. She'd been all that was civil to him, even charming. But the other servants didn't like her, and—yes—he'd noticed the girls' reserve, even after several months.

Aldridge, damn him, was right. The clues were there, and Hugh had been too deeply buried in his own misery to notice.

"I care." And he'd be checking with the housekeeper, who would tell him the truth if he asked a direct question. And with the girls. He sighed. It had taken him months to find a governess who would live all the way out here. Now he'd have to find another.

Aldridge was leaning against the wall by the door, his arms crossed on his chest and his head tilted to one side.

"Damn it, Aldridge, how can I marry someone with a secret like this? We'd be living on a powder keg, waiting for someone to find out... If she marries into the peerage, Society will tear her to pieces, and me and my daughters with her. And your child. Set her up as a widow somewhere."

Aldridge nodded. "I can do that. It's what she's asked of me, actually. But she deserves better, Overton. She deserves to be treasured, to grow old in the protection of a husband, with her children and grandchildren around her."

"Marry her yourself, then," Hugh scoffed.

To his surprise, he caught a hint of longing, before Aldridge answered thoughtfully, "I wish I could. I'd have to leave England, of course..." One side of his mouth quirked in a half-grin. "...but I could fake my death so Jonathan could have Haverford." He laughed at the shock on Overton's face. "Yes, I've plotted it all out. I don't love Becky, and she doesn't love me. But we're fond of one another, and marriages have been built on less.

"Still, she won't have me. She says I will make some poor woman a terrible husband, and she's right, of course. I cannot imagine sticking to only one woman, and Becky—well, she is a faithful soul. Believes in the sanctity of marriage."

He crossed back to the table and picked up his abandoned drink.

"And she says I would hate her after a while, if I left Haverford for her. I suppose that's true, too. I've trained to be Haverford my whole life. I don't know who I would be, if not Aldridge, the heir."

"Make her your marchioness, then," Overton suggested. "Your duchess, one day. She'll stomach your infidelities for that kind of title."

"You're wrong, Overton. In any case, what you said about Society? I can think of ways to bury her past, if she marries into the lower levels of the peerage, but a duchess? When I choose a bride, the harpies and the gossip rags will dig until they've uncovered every wart and fart." He shook his head again.

"It could be a daughter. The baby, I mean." Hugh was surprised to find he was considering the outrageous proposition.

Aldridge obviously understood. "I still have to present the idea to Becky," he warned. "She didn't much take to you, Overton."

Chapter Twelve

Once Overton had agreed, Aldridge was keen to get back to London, but had to wait for his friend to fire the governess and arrange his absence. Overton fetched his old nurse from the cottage he had given her for her old age, put her in charge of the girls, and told them they could have a holiday till he returned.

Finally, they were ready, or Aldridge was. The luggage coach had left at first light, but Overton insisted on waiting till his daughters were awake.

Aldridge stood with the horses, watching Overton say farewell.

"I will bring a new governess with me," Overton said.

Little Emmaline reached for her sister's hand, and Sophriana said, "But not a pinchy-pokey governess, Papa? A nice governess?" Overton dropped to his knees and took both girls into his arms. "A kind, gentle governess," he promised, and the look he shared with Aldridge made it a knight's vow. "And perhaps another playmate, my dears. Would you like that?"

The girls agreed, cautiously, that they would. Prompted, they curtseyed polite farewells to Aldridge, kissed Overton, and waved. They were still standing on the steps, waving, when the two riders paused at the top of the hill and looked back.

They loved their stepfather, and he loved them. If Becky would agree to the marriage; if Overton didn't stuff it up with his starched notions; Aldridge's child would be safe, secure, and loved.

During the ride to London, they honed their strategy. They'd use the separation between the Winstanley and Darling identities, and Aldridge would marshal his army of female relatives and friends to the support of the new Baroness Overton.

Overton pointed out that many people knew, or at least suspected, that Becky Winstanley and Rose Darling were the same woman. "We need her to be seen in two places at once," he said.

"Or two of her in the same place," Aldridge agreed. "Pity Sarah isn't a little older. She is going to look just like her mother in a few years."

"The Astley rider." Overton seemed to think that meant something.

"What has an Astley rider to do with anything?"

But when Overton explained he'd seen a mirror image of Becky at Astley's, Aldridge could see the advantage. If they could find her, Overton's fiancée, Mrs Winstanley, and Aldridge's mistress, Mrs Darling, could meet face-to-face in front of the largest grouping of high society the plotters could find.

By the time they reached London, they had gone over their plans a dozen times. All they needed now was Becky's agreement.

"No." Becky didn't even pause to think. Baron Overton? "Have you run mad, Aldridge? No, I will not marry Lord Overton."

"Hear me out, Becky," Aldridge pleaded. At least he'd had the grace to see her alone, leaving the baron in the parlour to entertain himself.

"What could you possibly say, Aldridge? Overton is a drunkard and a womaniser. He would be a worse husband than you!"

"Not usually, Becky. He has a bit of a blowout when he comes down to London, but I'm probably to blame for that."

"Huh!" she said. "So he is weak-willed, too. Anyway, he despises me. It would never work, Aldridge."

Aldridge, his half-smile more exasperated than amused, rubbed one hand over his head, ruining his valet's careless tousling.

"I swear, I've already had this conversation! The two of you are perfect for one another. Yes, Becky, he judged and condemned you without a hearing, just as you have done him. But he was big enough to admit he might be wrong and agree to at least get to know you."

Infuriating man! How could he put her in such a position?

"You persuaded him, you mean. And what does 'get to know you' mean?"

"Conversations. Walks in the park. Visits to a museum, if you like. He will treat you with respect, Becky, I promise. He is deciding whether to court you."

"Hah! I saw the way he looked at me. He called me a whore, Aldridge! How can you make promises on his behalf?" She paced the room, her skirts swinging with each stride. The man was a dunderhead. Could he not see?

"I have his promise, Becky, and he is a man of his word." Aldridge added fuel to her anger by staying calm.

"I cannot risk Sarah. I cannot." Her deepest fear and her trump card.

"Hugh has two daughters who need a mother, Becky. The older is Sarah's age. You lose nothing, risk nothing, if you give the man a hearing. Is it not worth the chance to give all three girls a complete family?"

She argued some more, but he had a counter for every point. In the end, she said: "Very well. I will talk to him. But do not expect me to change my mind."

Aldridge went off to the study she kept for him, to wade into the ducal post that followed him everywhere, leaving Becky to see Lord Overton on her own. He was sober and on his best behaviour.

"Black, oolong, or green tea, my lord?" she asked.

"Oolong, please. No milk, thank you."

She poured his cup and presented it to him, returning the sugar basin to the tray when he refused. She poured the same for herself—oolong with no milk or sugar.

"You prefer the oolong?" he asked.

Did he think she drank it just to imitate him? "I do, my lord."

"Your daughter... I trust Miss Winstanley is in good health?"

"Yes, thank you."

"She appeared happy with her doll."

"She was, my lord."

"I bought dolls for my girls." Overton was twisting his tea bowl round and round in the palms of his large hands. Capable hands, they looked. Well-manicured and clean, but a little worn, with calluses and healing abrasions from recent physical work. "They were happy too. With the dolls, I mean."

"I am sure they liked them. Would you care for cake, my lord?"

"No, thank you. This is very good tea."

Becky nodded. Only the best for Aldridge and, by extension, any household he supported.

Overton cast about for something else to say. "May I say, your dress is very charming?"

It was a morning gown in her signature powder blue; one of the Winstanley gowns, thank goodness. She would not have been able to face this interview in a Rose of Frampton gown. High-necked and long-sleeved, it armoured her against unwanted attention, and the high waist disguised her swelling belly.

"Thank you." She should make a bit more of an effort. "My *modiste* tells me these slight puffs are all the rage in Paris," she offered.

"Ah. Very nice." Overton lapsed into silence again, exploring the room with his eyes, as if another conversational topic might be hiding in a corner or on top of the bookshelf.

"I see you are reading about roses?" he managed. He must have excellent eyesight. The catalogue she'd been exploring was across the room.

"A dream of mine, my lord. I have no garden here in London, but I would dearly love to grow roses." As she warmed to the topic, she forgot her self-consciousness in her enthusiasm, explaining the difference between the English roses and new double Scotch roses just now appearing on the market. He did his polite best to keep up, poor man, until she took pity.

"My lord, I am sure you have no more interest than I in the latest Paris fashions, and very likely, less interest in the best plant food for roses. Shall we discuss this ridiculous scheme my Lord Aldridge has cooked up?"

That got his attention. While she talked of planting roses with a nail and a bone in the hole, he had been staring into his cup, but he jerked his head up, his eyes wide. "Are you so set against it, then?"

"Gloves off, my lord?" She returned his nod with a brisk one of her own. "Very well. I will not marry where I am despised. And I cannot imagine what Lord Aldridge has said or done to convince you to consider it. You think me a whore, and you are right. I have sold my body since I was ten-and-five. I spent three years in a brothel, and have been passed from protector to protector ever since.

"And I tell you this, my lord. You look down on me, but the women of Society?" She gripped her gown in white-knuckled fists, the better to keep her hands from sweeping the tea service off the table in a satisfying crash. "The 'ladies' you and Aldridge lie with? Who will abandon all that is moral and right—risk their reputations, their families, and their health for a bit of frivolity? For a GAME?" The word echoed in the room as she took a deep breath, trying to still her shaking.

When she could trust her voice again, she said, "They have a choice. You and Aldridge have a choice. I was given none. I have done what I must to survive." She glared at Overton, trembling with grief and anger.

"I..." Overton hunched one shoulder slightly as if to shelter from her words. "I cannot argue, Mrs Winstanley. You have seen me at my worst, and you are right. I have no right to condemn you for behaviour I have been willing to exploit, and I have no idea what drove you to this way of life.

"Aldridge would not tell me about your past. He said that was up to you. But he is a powerful advocate for you. He believes you would be a good wife for me and a good mother for my stepchildren."

Becky, despite her misgivings, had to admit Overton was a powerfully appealing advocate for his own case. He seemed sincere. And she had found him attractive from that first night, the scarred side of his face just adding to the charm of the other. "I do not understand why you would even consider it, my lord. The baby I am carrying might be a son. Have you thought of that? He would disinherit any sons of your own who came after. Unless you repudiated him."

"Did Aldridge not tell you?" Overton shifted in his seat and picked at his cuff. "I cannot sire a child. Your baby, if he is a boy, will be the next Overton. If not, the title becomes extinct. I have no relatives, you see.”

She took a turn around the room. This would be much easier if he had remained the disdainful, half-drunk, leering buffoon of a few weeks ago. Sober and respectful, he was temptation personified. But it would never work. “I would expect fidelity, my lord. And sobriety.”

“So would I,” he responded.

Fair enough. Most of the barques of frailty she knew lightened the gloom of their lives with drink or opium. Or laudanum, which combined the two. She had started down that track in the brothel; had nearly died of an overdose. She still shuddered at the memories of the withdrawal, and the cravings she fought afterward. “I do not drink, my lord, and keep my promises. If ever I marry, I will be true to my vows.” She could not resist emphasising the final ‘I’.

“So will I,” said the baron.

Becky sank back into her chair again. “I must do what is right for my daughter.”

“If you marry me, she will also be my daughter.”

“Aldridge says you have a stepdaughter the same age as my Sarah. Ten years.”

That was one of the ways Aldridge had persuaded her to at least consider Overton’s offer: that he was a good father to his two stepdaughters.

“My Sophie is nearly eleven, and Emma is eight. They would welcome another sister.”

If only it could be! Sarah, with sisters and a father, and a safe future as the acknowledged daughter of a baron. But Sarah would not be safe, would she? “You tempt me. But no, my lord. The answer must be no.”

“Is it because I am scarred?” he asked.

“No!” Indignant, she slammed the palm of her hand on the table between them and leapt to her feet. “I am not that shallow!”

“My wife could not bear to look at me. The face is bad enough, but it continues down almost to the knee.”

His matter-of-fact tone tore at her heart and dragged the truth from her. “It is not your scars, my lord, but mine.” The rasp in her voice came from a painfully stiff throat, but she forced the words out.

"I have lived a life you cannot imagine and my soul is sick from it. I am afraid, Lord Overton; afraid I will come to love you and your daughters and then you will cast me out."

She paced the room like a caged animal, faster and faster, as if she could escape her past, were she only swift enough. But there was no escape, and it was cruel to tempt her so. She flung the words at him. "When my history becomes known, and surely it will, and Society takes up against me, you will cast me out, if only to protect your daughters."

He caught her then, stopped her in her stride with a hand on each shoulder. His dark eyes sought the raw wounds he and Aldridge were making of her scars. "I've set a plan with Aldridge to establish you safely, and I promise you this. Whatever comes, I will stand by you and your children. If you and I agree to wed, I will never abandon you."

He was taller than Aldridge, and broader. She felt tiny next to him. But his hands were gentle and his eyes kind and sincere. Could she trust him? The quiet anonymous life of a middle-class widow would be safe, but the dream she had outlined to Aldridge was ahead of her, if she dared reach for it. Perhaps even love. He would be easy to love, this battered warrior who sheltered orphans and was prepared to change his mind when he was wrong.

"I will think about it," she conceded, and he smiled, the unscarred side of his face glowing with pleasure.

"As will I."

Chapter Thirteen

After they agreed to consider a future together, Mrs Winstanley took him to see Sarah, with Aldridge trailing along.

"Do you feel better now, Lord Overton?" the little girl asked, politely.

Hugh had no wish to discuss their last meeting. "I am, thank you." What could he say to give her mind another direction? "How is your doll, Miss Winstanley?" he asked.

Her eyes lit, but she retained her reserve. "Very well, thank you, Sir."

"My daughters liked the ones I bought them in the same shop." And talked about them and showed them off to anyone who would listen. Surely this grave child would take the bait? "I chose one with dark hair for Sophie, and fair hair for Emma. Sophie's doll is named Frances, and Em's is Charlotte."

Sarah admitted her doll was called Anne, and—at a suggestion from her mother—went to fetch the toy and its wardrobe. After half an hour sitting on the carpet in the parlour, displaying all the doll's treasures, Sarah had thawed only slightly, largely because 'Uncle Lord Aldridge' was down on the carpet with them.

If Hugh made little progress with the daughter, he had, at least, pleased the mother. When he left after the proper thirty minutes, she gave him the warmest smile he'd yet seen.

"We are invited to Mrs Winstanley's for the evening," Aldridge told him, when they met to dress for dinner at Haverford House. "Miss Winstanley's actually, but Becky is moving to stay with her daughter." He exaggerated his sad face, pushing out his lips and drooping his mouth and his eyes. "She says she cannot lie with one man while she is contemplating marrying another."

Hugh forbore to comment. Or to punch Aldridge, as the man deserved.

"She is still under contract," Aldridge complained. Hugh rethought the punch, then saw Aldridge's lip twitch in a half-smile. The man used to needle the masters at school just so—to relieve boredom, satisfy curiosity, or out of sheer devilry.

"Poking the bear, Aldridge?"

Aldridge just laughed.

Hugh's admiration for Mrs Winstanley grew in the course of the evening.

Aldridge's claim that she came from the gentry was borne out. She showed it in a thousand ways. Gentle manners and speech could be learned, of course, but she was natural, and at ease, and never made a slip.

She showed a keen mind, too, and was clearly well read, discussing with equal ease the impact of enclosure on the good health of farming workers, Walter Scott's new narrative poem, and the war on the Peninsula.

They left early, but not before Mrs Winstanley had accepted his invitation to go driving the next day.

Becky and Sarah were waiting when Lord Overton arrived at two o'clock, just as he had promised. Becky paused on the doorstep. He had borrowed a curricle from Aldridge; she recognised the horses. It would be a tight fit for the three of them.

Sarah had no such qualms, and was already down in the street, renewing her acquaintance with Prince and Brown Beauty, chattering away to the groom Lord Overton had also borrowed, another old acquaintance.

"We'll tuck Sarah between us where she will be warm, and out of the wind," Lord Overton said, correctly interpreting her concern. "Neither of you are large. We will fit."

It was a tight fit, and at first Sarah shrunk away from Lord Overton. Soon, though, she was telling him everything she knew about the horses, as they made their way through the streets to the park, the groom up behind.

With his focus divided between Sarah and the horses, Becky was free to watch him, and to wonder what life would be like as his wife. If he continued to be kind and respectful, if he were not putting on an act, if this plan of Aldridge's worked...

By the end of the drive, Sarah and Lord Overton were friends, and he cemented the friendship by producing sugar cubes for her to feed the horses. She went to her governess and the schoolroom in full charity with him.

Lord Overton stood in the hall, smiling, watching her skip up the stairs.

"Do you intend to charm me by charming my daughter, Lord Overton?" Becky challenged.

He turned, laughing. "Is it working, Mrs Winstanley?" Then, serious again, "But no, I wanted to charm her, as you call it, for her own sake. Is she always so quiet and good?"

"She does not take easily to strangers," Becky said. Sarah had reason to be wary, and Becky would do well to remember it. Still, Lord Overton's attempt to win Sarah's favour was more to his credit than not.

He returned for dinner that night, and it became the pattern for their days: an outing in the afternoon, dinner in the evening, and afterwards, cards, chess, or reading together. And they talked. Lord Overton had read many of the same books she enjoyed. He agreed with her views on enclosure. She did not share his confidence in the military genius of General Wellesley, but acknowledged that his own background as an army officer gave him the edge in judging such a thing.

She asked about his estate, and about his daughters, who would be her daughters, too. Perhaps. If she dared...

And at night in her bed, she wondered whether his shoulders were as broad, his hips as slender, as they looked.

Surprised to discover that Mrs Winstanley and Sarah had never been to the Royal Menagerie at the Tower, Hugh arranged a visit. It was not a success. Though others visiting the Royal beasts seemed not to care they were kept in small dirty cages, both mother and child grew quieter and quieter. When a boy poked a stick through the bars of a cage to rouse a lethargic leopard, Sarah turned swimming, pleading eyes to Hugh.

"Here. Leave the animal alone," Hugh told the boy, who made a rude gesture but desisted.

Hugh moved his ladies on, and asked the keeper for directions to the room where the monkeys were kept.

"Had to be removed, didn't they," the keeper told him. "Attacked a boy. Mauled him something awful."

"Probably," Becky suggested tartly, as they left the Tower, "because the boy attacked the poor monkeys."

Hugh consoled them with ices at Gunter's, including one for the silent governess who played propriety. Uncle Lord Aldridge took her to Gunter's, Sarah confided, but he'd never taken them to the park, or to the Tower.

"You didn't like the Tower, Sarah," he pointed out.

"No," she agreed. "But I liked that you took me. Some of the other girls have been."

He delivered them home, wondering about the little girl's life. He forgot for hours at a time that Mrs Winstanley was a kept woman. He only knew that he wanted her.

He was light-headed in her presence, his blood being otherwise occupied, and he grew adept at keeping furniture, or his silk hat, or his folded overcoat in a strategic position to avoid letting her know what an advantage she had. When he was alone in one of Aldridge's spare bedchambers at night, he let the memory of her fill his senses, and imagined the touch and the taste of her. Her skin was pale, protected from the sun, but it would be paler yet on her breasts and her thighs. Pale, and tender, and soft.

The silk of her hair would cling to his fingers as he spread it out on his pillow. Yes, and while he was paying due worship to her lovely breasts, he would find the silk of her other hair, too, and what it guarded. He wanted to taste the sweet honey of her desire more than he wanted to breathe, to bring her to glorious completion, to find his balance again between her warm thighs.

The fantasy was unwise. It didn't make the days easier to bear, the momentary satisfaction giving way to a profound hollow only she could fill. Was she using some ancient concubine's art to ensnare with lust?

No.

He must forget that she'd been Aldridge's kept woman or he wouldn't be able to go through with it. And marrying Mrs Winstanley had become his most ardent desire.

When Lord Overton asked if she would call him by his first name, he was sitting on her parlour carpet, eating a picnic lunch, their expedition to the park being aborted because of rain.

He leant towards her, his eyes warm but his smile a little uncertain.

"It not being consistent with a lord's dignity to feed pastries to dolls on the carpet, we had better dispense with all this 'my lord' business, do you not think? Will you call me Hugh, Mrs Winstanley?"

She studied her hands, fiddling with a ribbon on her gown. "If you will call me Becky, Hugh."

Later, when she and Sarah had seen Hugh out the door, Sarah said, "May I ask you a question, Mama?"

"Of course, darling."

"Is Lord Overton going to be my new uncle? Doesn't Uncle Lord Aldridge love us anymore?"

This was a conversation for the parlour. Becky held out her hand and led Sarah into the room, closing the door firmly behind them.

"Come and sit with me, darling."

How to explain? With Sarah cuddled against her side on the couch, she started with Sarah's question about Aldridge.

"Sarah, Lord Aldridge hasn't stopped loving us." Did Aldridge love her? It didn't matter. Aldridge did love Sarah, she was sure of that, lavishing on the little girl the affection he could not give his own lost children. "You will always be special to him. But we cannot stay with him forever. I told you we would be moving to the country one day."

"Then why do we need another uncle?" Sarah asked. "I thought it was going to be just you and me."

"Lord Overton would not be your uncle, my darling. But would you not like him for a papa?"

Sarah frowned, but did not reply.

"You like Lord Overton, do you not? Would you mind very much if our house in the country were his house? If I married Lord Overton?"

Sarah pulled away far enough to look up. Tears drowned her eyes and dripped down her cheeks. "Married, Mama? Forever?"

Not if Sarah were against it. Becky swallowed against a huge lump in her throat. Until she faced giving him up, she had not realised her growing desire for Lord Overton and this marriage.

She started to shake her head, but Sarah threw herself against Becky's shoulder, speaking around great hiccupping sobs. "Oh, Mama, that would be wonderful. He will never, never leave us, will he, Mama? If he marries us, he will stay forever? No more uncles?"

"No more uncles, my dearest. Forever." Becky was crying too. "No more uncles."

That evening was one week to the day since Aldridge first suggested the marriage to Becky. She was waiting in the parlour when Hugh arrived for dinner. "I think we can make a bargain," she told him. "If you still wish it, Hugh."

Chapter Fourteen

Aldridge was delighted. He suggested a special licence, and an encounter as soon as possible with the woman from Astley's.

"Have you spoken with your cousin and your other relatives about supporting Becky while we run the charade?" Hugh asked.

"Your mother might," Becky offered.

"The Duchess of Haverford?" Hugh asked, cautiously, as if Aldridge had a choice of mothers.

"She said she would support me to a new life when my contract with Aldridge was over."

Aldridge's eyebrows shot up. "Mama said that?"

"She..." Becky blushed. "She might not approve of me marrying a baron. She certainly warned me not to attempt to marry you. But she did say she would help me and Sarah when we were ready."

"If she accepts you as Baroness Overton, the rest of Society will follow her lead." Aldridge had shaken off the surprise and was considering the agreement between his mother and his mistress with his usual equanimity. Hugh was still wondering how the two had met.

"I think we should call on her," Aldridge continued. "And Rede is in town, too. We can ask Anne. She liked you, Becky. I'm sure she'll help. And my half-brother's wife, Prue. Rede's cousin, Susan. My own cousins. Yes, we'll do very nicely."

Hugh shook his head. "That's a lot of people to share our secret."

"I don't intend to tell them our secret, Overton. Mama knows, and Anne. And Prue, probably, because it's the sort of thing she knows. But they can all be trusted. All I need to tell the others is that my friend Hugh is marrying a widow who has not been much in society, and I'd appreciate their support."

Becky insisted they talk to the key players before the planned encounter on Rotten Row between the Merry Marquis, the baron, and their respective ladies. Hugh could see the point.

"It won't take long, will it?" he said.

His lands and his daughters needed him. And he needed his new bride. Love was no more part of this second marriage than in his first—but at least he liked Becky, and she seemed to like him. And desire... he had plenty of that! They would deal well together, and he was keen to get started.

While Aldridge visited his Mama to explain what they wanted, Hugh went cap, and purse, in hand to Doctor's Commons to arrange a special licence.

It took longer than he'd hoped, and a lucky encounter with a friend from university, to be admitted to the Archbishop's presence, but two days later, he had his licence. It was in his pocket, and Becky at his side, when they waited on Her Grace, summoned by a scented note delivered by the hand of a liveried footman.

Hugh had been in the heir's wing many times, and at Haverford, the family seat, when he was a boy. He had never entered Haverford House by the main door. Designed to impress, the approach sat back from the road, admittance through a gatekeeper. They were paraded through the paved courtyard by another liveried servant to the stairs between pillars that stretched three stories to the pediment above.

Inside, the ducal glory continued; a marbled entrance chamber the height of the house that would make a ballroom in any lesser mansion, with majestic flights of stairs rising on either side and curving to meet, only to split again in a symphony of wood and stone. Grenford ancestors were everywhere, twice as large as life, painted on canvas and moulded from stone, cold eyes examining petitioners and finding them all unworthy.

Aldridge met them in the entrance chamber, and led them up the first flight of stairs and down a sumptuously carpeted hall that was elegantly papered above richly carved panels. Four men could have walked arm-in-arm down the middle, never touching the furniture and art lining both walls, between highly-polished doors.

Busts on marble pedestals alternated with delicate gilded tables and seats upholstered in the Haverford green, scarlet and gold, many embroidered with the unicorn and phoenix from the Haverford coat of arms. The art in gilded frames that hung both walls showed more Grenford ancestors, interspersed with favourite animals, scenes from the Bible, and retellings of Greek legends. The ornately painted ceiling boasted flowers, leaves, and decorative swirls, the many colours highlighted in gilding.

Here and there, an open door gave them a view into one large chamber after another, each room richer than the last. At intervals, curtained arches led to more halls, more stairs.

Hugh was openly gawping, and Becky drew closer to him, as if for protection.

"A bit over the top, don't you think?" he whispered to her, and was rewarded with a quick, nervous, smile.

The duchess received them in a sitting room that, if rich and elegant, was at least more human in scale.

She offered a cheek to Aldridge for a kiss, and a hand to Hugh. Becky held back.

"Come, my dear," she coaxed. "Mrs Winstanley, is it not? Soon to be Baroness Overton. You shall kiss me, my dear, and I shall be godmother to your child, since I cannot claim the closer title."

Hugh relaxed, then. Her Grace would champion them for her grandchild's sake. He took the offered chair, and Aldridge leant against the mantelpiece. The duchess ignored them both to focus on Becky.

She insisted on Becky sitting beside her.

"Are you keeping well, my dear? Are you eating?"

"Yes, Your Grace." Becky's voice was so quiet Hugh had to lean forward to hear.

"You must eat several times a day, dear. More as the baby takes up more room..." she trailed off as Becky blushed scarlet. "And when do you expect the little one to arrive?"

"At Yuletide, Ma'am. Or perhaps early January."

"What of sleep, Mrs Winstanley? Are you able to rest in the afternoons?" She turned to Hugh. "An afternoon rest is most efficacious for women who are increasing, Lord Overton. I will expect you to keep her in bed in the afternoon."

"Yes, Ma'am," Hugh replied, blushing in his turn.

The Duchess silenced her sniggering son with a raised eyebrow. "I suppose you have a plan, Aldridge, for convincing the *ton* that Mrs Winstanley and Lady Overton are two different people?"

Aldridge explained about the woman from Astley's.

"Will she keep her silence if the gossip rags guess she had a part in it? They pay, I am told. And is she willing to continue playing the part?"

"We intend a tragic accident, Mama. The horse will bolt, The Rose of Frampton will fall, and the Marquis of Aldridge will attend her funeral and wear a black armband for a full year."

Aldridge's mother pursed her lips. "Six months for a mistress, I think, my love. One would not wish to be thought excessive. And promise the girl a yearly payment if she is silent."

"I beg your pardon, Your Grace," Hugh ventured, "but might that not encourage her to seek an increase?"

"Blackmail, you mean?" Her Grace raised an elegant eyebrow. "Aldridge, you will make it clear that any attempt to seek an increase will be met with... considerable ducal displeasure. My godchild's mother is not to be inconvenienced or embarrassed."

She patted Becky's hand. "Now, my dear, what do you have to wear for your wedding? And may I ask... would you allow me to stand witness, Mrs Winstanley? I would be so delighted."

After that, things moved with blinding speed, although not as fast as the Duchess first suggested. Becky demurred at marrying immediately, without Sarah present, so Aldridge was dispatched to collect her. Becky was swept off into the Duchess's chambers, and Hugh was sent to the heir's wing, where Aldridge's valet waited to dress him for his wedding.

Two hours later, Hugh joined a cleric and a resplendent Aldridge in the Haverford House Chapel. Hugh had chosen formal court dress and had been pleased with his coat of cream silk velvet, grey breeches and a dark blue waistcoat, richly embroidered in powder blue and silver. Until he stood next to Aldridge.

Aldridge had also found time to change into formal attire. His coat and breeches—of a midnight-blue silk velvet, with a deep band of embroidery on each side and on the cuffs—fitted him as if sewn to his broad shoulders and muscular thighs. Snow-white lace foamed at his neck and cuffs, matching his pure white stockings with silver clocking. His waistcoat put Hugh's in the shade, near-painted in a riotous multi-colour pattern on a salmon pink ground to match the roses in the coat's embroidery.

Hugh glared at the roses, suspecting that particular sartorial choice was another poke at him. He would ignore it. In a very short time, Becky would be Lady Overton, and within a week, the whole of London would know the Rose of Frampton was dead and gone.

A few minutes of nervous waiting, and the Duchess arrived, hand in hand with Sarah. Sarah's stately glide showed her consciousness of her cream dress flounced in lace, the sash exactly the shade of her eyes, her dark curls confined by a ribbon the same colour.

"You look beautiful, Sarah," Hugh told her, and Aldridge crouched down to rub his finger across her nose. "Beautiful," he agreed. "And so grown up, Princess."

Sarah beamed, but Hugh barely noticed. Becky was standing at the other end of the short aisle. The Duchess had dressed her in silver lace over a pale peach silk, and she was breath-taking. The dress was full from the high waist, but hugged the lower curves of her breasts. Above, a breath of silk trimmed the bodice in a narrow flounce that continued across both shoulders, a frame for the sweet slope of her creamy chest and throat.

He dragged his eyes up the slope to her face. Through the lace veil that covered her face, he met her eyes, pale and serious. "Soon be done," he whispered, smiling just for her. She placed her hands in his, and managed a shaky smile in return.

With blinding speed, the wedding was over. Becky was Baroness Overton, his wedded wife in the eyes of God, his to have and to hold, from this day forward, 'till death us do part'.

"I have ordered a light collation," the Duchess told the newly-wed couple, after they signed the register and thanked the cleric.

Becky looked around. "Where is Sarah?"

"Aldridge has her. They have gone ahead," said Her Grace.

Hugh and Becky found out why moments later, when they entered the parlour, to be showered with rice and seeds from behind the door. A giggling Sarah was sitting high on Aldridge's shoulder.

Hugh reached out for her. "Will you give your new papa a kiss, Sarah?" he asked. She allowed herself to be lifted down, and gave him a shy peck on the cheek, but retreated to her mother's side as soon as he set her on her feet.

Aldridge bowed as though to the queen herself. "Lady Overton," he said, which was entirely correct, though the twinkle in his eye didn't escape Hugh's notice. Aldridge knew full well, Hugh would punch him if he tried to kiss the bride.

Aldridge soon had Sarah giggling again, tempting her with bites from the many selections the Duchess thought suitable for a light snack after a wedding, and describing the delights that awaited her at Lord and Lady Chirbury's house, where she would spend the night with Lady Daisy. Her excitement at the prospect overcame whatever concerns she had about Hugh's entry into her life.

"Will you and Becky stay in the heir's wing tonight?" Aldridge asked Hugh.

Never, Hugh wanted to shout. Spend his first night with his new wife in the Haverford House heir's wing? Where he'd bedded more women than he wanted to remember, and Aldridge had swived an entire army? They would go to the apartment. Or a hotel.

But the duchess spoke before he could answer.

"I have arranged guest chambers for the Overtons, Aldridge, and tomorrow they will return to the apartment Lady Overton shares with her daughter."

His daughter, too, now. Becky was sitting with Sarah, showing her the ring with which he'd sealed his promises. He'd scoured London to find one with a stone that matched Becky's eyes, a blue Irish topaz, set with pearls, in a gold setting of hearts and doves.

Sarah's fingertip traced the gemstones. "It is so pretty, Mama."

Very pretty, the two dark heads, so alike.

"Your papa chose well." She blushed when she said *papa*, and looked more beautiful than ever. How long would the duchess expect them to stay and be polite before she would let them escape to these promised guest chambers?

Mercifully, it was no more than an interminable hour before Aldridge took pity. "Now, Mama, we must leave the newlyweds to themselves. Hugh has barely eaten a bite of this lovely tea, and Becky even less. Send them off to their suite and let them sort themselves out."

The duchess looked at them doubtfully. "I'd like to invite you to come down to dinner, only Haverford will be here, and he might be... I'm not sure..."

"Send up a collation, Mama," Aldridge advised, giving Hugh a broad wink behind his mother's back.

Sarah clung a little when Becky said goodnight.

Aldridge had expected it, and planned a surprise to ease the moment. "Princess, say goodnight to Mama and Papa. I have a surprise for you, and we must not keep the horses waiting."

Sarah narrowed her eyes at him, exactly as Becky did when he promised to surprise her, and she wasn't sure she'd like it. His heart lurched.

"Quickly, now," he commanded, forcing a grin.

Sarah's eyes lit. "I know! You are taking me to Lady Daisy's! In the curricle, Uncle Lord Aldridge? With Prince and Brown Beauty?"

"In the curricle," Aldridge confirmed, and she tucked her hand into his.

"Goodnight, Mama," she said. "I will see you tomorrow."

The temptation of the treat carried her downstairs, and through greeting the horses she loved.

Tucked up beside him with a rug to protect her from the September chill, she turned sober again.

"What is it, sweetling? Are you worried about your new papa? He is a good man, Sarah, else I would not let you go to him."

To his dismay, she began to cry.

Aldridge pulled the horses to a stop and sent the groom to their heads. If the whole of London wished to look on, let them. He took the little girl in his arms.

"Princess? What is it? How can I fix it?"

She burrowed into his shoulder, but shook her head. "You cannot. It is too late." The words were muffled by his coat, but he heard them clearly enough. Too late for what?

"Tell me, Sarah?" he coaxed.

She pulled her head away enough to meet his eyes, her own brimming with tears. The violence of her hug had knocked her bonnet off her head, and he freed one hand to untie the ribbon that threatened to choke her. When he brushed her chin with his hand, it seemed to spur her into speech. "Why could you not keep us, Uncle Lord Aldridge? Do you not love us anymore?"

Ah.

"I love you very much, Sarah. I will always love you."

He tucked her back under his chin, rubbing his cheek against the silk of her hair, so like her mother's.

"Lord Overton will keep you safe, you and your mother, in a way I cannot, Princess."

"But you are a Great Man, Uncle Lord Aldridge. You can do anything," the child protested.

Not this. For his mother's sake, for the sake of the duchy, even for the sake of Becky and Sarah, he could not have done what the child wanted. And now it was too late. Hugh and Becky were married.

"I will make you two promises, Sarah. First, I will always love you. For my whole life, you will be my Princess Sarah, and I shall be your Uncle Lord Aldridge"

"But I am going far away and will not see you," Sarah protested.

"Then you shall write to me, and I to you. That is my second promise, Sarah. Lord Overton is my friend, and he will be a good papa for you and a good husband for your mother. But if he makes you unhappy, either one of you, send for me, and I will come. I will always come, Princess, and I will take you away. I promise."

"Come. Let me dry your eyes and tie your bonnet. Lady Daisy will be waiting."

His promises seemed to reassure her. She trotted into Chirbury House willingly enough, and Rede and Anne escorted them up to the nursery floor. Sarah greeted her friend with smiles and hugs. Aldridge and his cousin watched from the door as Daisy showed off the treasures of the playroom, and Sarah, at Anne's prompting, described her mother's wedding.

She would be content enough for tonight, and Becky and Hugh would soothe her fears in the coming weeks.

He had been planning to dine at his club, but it lacked appeal.

"Blue-devilled, cousin?" Rede asked. The man was too perceptive by half.

Tonight, though, he could not, would not, be the Merry Marquis. Or perhaps he would. After all, legend had it, he always pleased himself.

"Anne?" he asked, "Do you think I might stay for nursery tea?" Anne agreed with the friendliest smile his disapproving cousin-by-marriage had ever given.

Chapter Fifteen

"I could fit my entire town-house in here," said Becky, in a small awed voice that echoed in the palatial suite.

"And a fair part of Overton Park into the space left over," Hugh told her. "The Grenford family don't do things by halves, do they?"

She smiled, clearly cheered by the casual attitude he'd assumed for her benefit. They walked through the suite together, exploring the two bedchambers off a central sitting room, each with an adjoining dressing room. Most of the furniture was in the modern style: turned and gilded legs, damask upholstery in shades of green, inlays of marquetry in a dozen different woods with highlights of ivory and jet.

The draperies were also green, brocade on the windows and figured velvet for the hangings on the huge beds, the only old-fashioned note. Undoubtedly, the beds had stayed because they were too big to shift without cutting into pieces. Even so, they were dwarfed in the huge rooms.

Becky's night attire had been laid out on one bed —a fetchingly virginal nightrail in white linen with a bodice of sheer muslin trimmed with lace and ribbons a deep flounce of lace at the hem. His cock twitched. She wouldn't need that.

Wait. Yes. Yes, she would, for he'd take great pleasure in removing it. His smile must have hinted at his thoughts, because Becky blushed.

His bag had been unpacked in the other chamber. They'd see about that.

"Your chamber or mine? And I warn you now, Becky, we will not have separate chambers at Overton Park. I intend we shall spend every night in the same bed." No repeat of the debacle of his first marriage.

"You choose," she said, so he instructed the servants to move his things to Becky's room.

The servants fussed around, putting out food and drink, making sure the fire was stoked, plumping cushions, until Hugh chased them all out of the suite, and he and Becky were alone at last.

She stood in the middle of the vast expanse, lost and alone, till he crossed to her and took both her hands.

"Do you want something to eat?"

She shook her head. "You go ahead, Hugh. I am not hungry."

"I am not hungry for food."

She smiled and nodded, looking up at him from under her lashes, her colour rising again. Who knew that a woman of her experience could be shy? No. He had to stop thinking that way. This was Becky. Rebecca Overton. His wife. His baroness.

She followed without comment when he led her by hand through to their bedchamber.

There he hesitated. "Becky, it is still daylight, but if I pull the curtains…"

"No need, Hugh. Unless… I am not too large and ugly yet, Hugh, truly."

He shook his head, grimacing. "I was thinking of my scars. They're not pretty, my dear. My first wife…"

She put her finger on his lips. "Shall we agree, husband, that our pasts will not enter our bedchamber? You gained those scars fighting for king and country. They are nothing to be ashamed of."

He kissed the finger, then sucked it into his mouth, and she took a sharp breath. "Hugh." A breathy gasp. A trained response?

No. He mustn't think like that. She was right; no pasts in their bedchamber.

He took her into his arms then, and kissed her as he had wished all week, burying all doubts and questions in sheer sensation.

When his hands fumbled at her sash, she drew away. "You first, Hugh. I want to see. Keep still." He shook his head, but made no further protest, not moving while she tugged off his coat and unbuttoned his waistcoat. She slipped her hands under the edges and ran them up his chest to his shoulders, pushing the waistcoat so it slipped backwards.

She could feel his warmth through the fine linen of his shirt, and her own heat rose. His breath shortened, but he continued to obey her command to keep still, letting her slide the waistcoat off, then circle him, pulling the shirt from his waistband.

She ran her hands up under the fabric, revelling in the feel of his hot, bare skin, but when she started to gather the material to lift the shirt off, Hugh trapped her wrists against his firm torso, caging her in a gentle, but inexorable, grip. He swooped in for another searing kiss.

This time, it was Hugh who drew back, reluctantly, pulling her lower lip gently between his teeth and echoing her sigh.

"Turnabout is fair play, Becky. My shirt stays until your gown goes."

She nodded, turning obediently so he could undo the sash. "You will need scissors, Hugh. The gown was a little large, and Her Grace's maid sewed it to fit after I put it on."

In a rosewood box on a side table they found a vanity set with a set of sharp-bladed scissors. The maid had used fine, almost-invisible seaming to shape the cloth over Becky's breasts, but Hugh quickly found the long tacks that reduced the diameter of the gown at the sides, and sundered them with eager snips.

She trembled when he drew the gown over her head, his hands brushing her sides and her arms. He threw the expensive garment over the back of a chair, never taking his eyes from hers, and reached for her stays, but she stepped back.

"The shirt," she croaked.

He obeyed, standing still while she slipped the braces over his shoulders then pulled the shirt gently, tenderly, until it slid from the pantaloons and she could lift it up and over his head.

She was prepared, or she would have gasped. As with his face, smooth skin on one side contrasted with seared and puckered scars on the other. Show no disgust. Nothing but polite interest. In truth, she was not disgusted, but compassion would not be welcomed, either. He would take it for pity.

His eyes were wary, the lust banked embers for the moment.

"Your breeches?" she suggested.

"Your stays first."

Fastened loosely at the base to accommodate her spreading belly, they were so tightly tied at the top that he cursed and retrieved the scissors to cut the laces. He tossed the stays after the gown, and stood for a moment, stroking her breasts through the chemise, running his thumbs over the hard nubs of her responding nipples.

"The breeches," she insisted.

"You do it." His body quivered slightly, like a hound waiting the command to course the hare.

Her own hands fumbling, she undid the buttons on one side, very conscious of the fabric that strained over the evidence of his arousal. Her own breath was shuddering in her throat as she undid the other side. His fall dropped, and what was underneath sprang free, straining upwards, hard and ready. She swallowed.

Her passage was readying for him: heat, swelling, liquid. Almost, she touched the proud jut, but she diverted her hands to unbutton the waist so the breeches dropped. He kicked them off, not looking down.

The scars covered his left side from his cheek to his knee, pitting and knotting his shoulder and upper arm, his torso, hip and thigh. Becky traced them with both hands, her fingers exploring the ridges and hollows.

"A cannon shot. Is that right?"

"Yes. A ball designed to break apart on impact. I was lucky to survive."

"I am lucky you survived, Hugh. Very lucky." Her exploring hands had reached his hip. She let one drift around to cup his firm buttock, and the other cross to brush against his shaft.

"They don't disgust you?"

Focused as she was on his arousal and hers, she took a moment to understand him. "The scars? No. They do not. Your one-eyed soldier there? Decidedly not!"

Hugh caught Becky to him again, another insistent kiss, his hard length pressed into the swell of her belly, then demanded, "The chemise."

He helped her draw the garment over her head and sent it after her stays and gown. He sank to his knees then, smoothing reverent palms over the swell of her belly.

"Beautiful," he said. One hand tended lower, and she pressed against it urgently as he slid practiced fingers in exactly the right places. "Beautiful," he said again.

Then he surged to his feet, and lifted her in his arms, carrying her to the bed. "We will take our time, Becky." His calm voice was at odds with his wild, intent eyes. "With my body, I thee worship." The words of the vow he had made scant hours ago.

"Worship me quickly, Hugh. We'll go slowly next time."

Afterward, as they lay in one another's arms, she returned to the topic of his injury, tracing the scars that decorated one hip.

"Is that what... Is that why..."

"Why I can't father children? No, nothing so heroic. I had mumps." He'd never talked about it before, but somehow, it was natural to tell her.

"A confounded illness I should have had in childhood. Dear Lord, it hurt. My cods swelled up like pumpkins. My throat too, and under my arms. But my cods were the worst. I wanted to die. But slowly everything went back to normal. The doctors said I'd never be able to... rise to the occasion again. And if I could, I would certainly never be a father."

Becky snuggled closer, one hand tucked under his shoulder, and the other running soothingly back and forth across his hip.

"I was 21; well 22, by then. I bought my commission, and went off to kill myself for king and country. I can't tell you how grateful I was when the little fellow first poked his head up again."

"He's doing so now," his wife observed, chuckling. His wife. The first time had been a little rushed; they had not even removed their stockings! This time, he would make sure he took his time. Ladies first. That lesson had served him well all these many years.

"Shall I show you worship, Lady Overton? Shall I pay due reverence to every inch of my wife's beautiful body?"

"It means 'worthy,'" Becky said. "I find you worthy to be my wife." At his quizzical look, she flushed slightly. "My father's scholarly interest was the medieval church. Sometimes he would set bits from the ancient prayer books for my Latin translation exercises."

"With my body, I find you worthy," Hugh agreed. He found her breasts worthy for quite some minutes, then shifted to find her thighs worthy, and then her nether lips and the sweet bud between them, until she stiffened, her high-pitched, wordless cry becoming a long ululation. She lay limp, exhausted, but as he entered her and began to move, she roused again to return thrust for thrust.

Later, much later, while they ate a cold supper, still cuddling, feeding one another a bit at a time, he finished the story.

"I never expected to be baron. My family are not prolific, but my grandfather had two sons, and my father the younger. I am an only child, but my uncle had two sons and a daughter. Then, five deaths in the family in one year, and suddenly, I am Baron Overton."

"So you married," she prompted.

"I hoped the doctors were wrong, though none of my mistresses had 'taken,' but to increase my chances, I married a widow who already had children. She had a daughter, and she was with child again." He was silent, then. Had Aldridge told her how Polyphemia had died? Probably not; he seemed to have kept his counsel about everything else. It wasn't important. No pasts, she said. He did not need to tell her.

"I was married four years. With all the women I have bedded since my illness, four years of marriage, and more women in the three years since, my seed has not taken root once." He felt inside the loose robe she had donned to cup her rounded belly. "This is my one chance to give the barony a future. Thank you." The kiss of gratitude he gave her deepened, and they abandoned their supper.

Chapter Sixteen

They were married on Friday, and spent Saturday quietly at home in the apartment with Sarah, except for a walk in the park in the afternoon, where several of Hugh's friends were delighted to be presented to the new Lady Overton.

Sarah was cautious at first, but by late afternoon, sat on the parlour rug with him, laughing as they played at spillikins. Becky, who had begun to fall in love with him during their week of courtship, tumbled a little deeper as she watched him with her daughter. Particularly after last night.

Aldridge had been kind, courteous, and skilled. Hugh was those things, but also grateful. He treated her with respect, and not just in bed. He took her out in public and proudly introduced her to the wives of his friends. He needed her—not just the baby, but her, Becky, as chatelaine and mother to his children, to reassure him when he felt ugly or off-balance, to give him an heir to save the title.

The vows they'd exchanged thrilled her. To love and to cherish, forsaking all other as long as they both shall live. She repeated them silently to herself over and over through the day. And 'Rebecca, Lady Overton.'

She reminded herself again and again, love was not part of their bargain. He would give her and Sarah a home and respectability. She would give his daughters a mother and him the child in her womb. If she were foolish enough to fall in love with him, she would not burden him with that knowledge.

Aldridge had given Becky the deed to her daughter's apartment to her as a wedding present. "I promised you the town-house," he apologised, "but questions would be asked if you owned the town-house where The Rose of Frampton lived." The solicitor that Aldridge hired secured the apartment and a substantial sum of money to her name, persuading Hugh, at Aldridge's direction, that her marriage settlement should give her the atypical right to continue to own property.

On Saturday evening, Lord and Lady Overton went to a dinner party at the home of the Earl and Countess of Chirbury, where Anne (as she insisted they called her) introduced Becky as 'a friend of mine from the Southwest counties. Her daughter and mine are of an age.'

On Sunday, they attended church at St George's, in company with the Chirburys. The Duchess of Haverford herself greeted them outside, showing her public approval of the new wife of her son's best friend, even presenting Lady Overton to His Grace, who was making one of his rare appearances at Sunday services.

Aldridge was not at church, but in the park, riding with his *chère amie*, as a husband scornfully pointed out to a wife who thought she saw a resemblance between the new Baroness Overton and the Merry Marquis's Rose.

Later that day, Aldridge and his mistress strolled in the pleasure gardens at Vauxhall, in plain view of half the *ton*, and Lord and Lady Overton attended a musical afternoon at the home of Mrs Wakefield, a *protegée* of the Duchess of Haverford.

On Monday, the Overtons, after a quiet day at home, joined the Chirburys in their box at the opera. Aldridge, in his own private box with the infamous Rose of Frampton, caused something of a stir when he and his mistress passionately embraced halfway through the second act, then left the theatre abruptly.

By now, a number of people had noticed the resemblance between Lady Overton and Rose Darling, but that they were two separate women was beyond doubt.

On Tuesday, the Duchess of Haverford held a ball, and Society held its collective breath to see the Merry Marquis meet a lady who looked so like his mistress. They were disappointed. Beyond a certain possessiveness in the way the baron put his hand over the one his wife nestled in the crook of his arm, and the laughing bow with which Aldridge acknowledged what nearby onlookers whispered was a refusal to dance, the three were clearly well acquainted and on good terms. And the baroness did not dance that evening, so nothing could be made of her not dancing with Aldridge.

On Wednesday, they met again, this time in Hyde Park. It was, of course, scandalous of Aldridge to bring his mistress there at all, especially at the most fashionable time of the afternoon. But what else could one expect of Aldridge, and didn't Mrs Darling ride well? She moved as if she and the horse were one.

She wore a riding dress in her signature powder blue, cut close to her curves, with a deep scooping neckline. A jaunty top hat with a veil perched on her pile of dark curls, and the dress was draped to show neat boots that hugged shapely ankles.

Lady Overton, by contrast, wore an afternoon dress and redingote in shades of rich deep red. She had been wearing jewel colours all week: red, deep blue, a rich emerald green. There was, beyond a doubt, a surface resemblance between her and Aldridge's doxy, but Lady Overton was every inch a lady.

Aldridge tipped his hat to his friend and his friend's wife as he rode past, and onlookers noticed that the lady did not seem to be offended when the mistress grinned cheerfully and waved a hand. Not at all high in the instep, Lady Overton. A good sort. Society was inclined to approve of anyone so clearly sponsored by its *grandes dames*, and Baron Overton was well regarded (except his occasional excesses, which most blamed on Aldridge) but Lady Overton was fast winning supporters on her own modest and charming merits.

What happened next, nobody quite knew. Something spooked Mrs Darling's horse; that much was obvious. It bolted. Bolted so suddenly and so fast that Aldridge, whose attention had been on the Overtons, was seconds late in responding.

In moments, horse and rider disappeared into the trees, with Aldridge in hot pursuit. The park erupted in a collective gasp when a low branch swept Mrs Darling from the horse.

The Overtons were among the first on the scene, and Lord Overton persuaded the distraught Marquis to allow the still, broken body to be lifted into the Overton carriage. Aldridge insisted on taking his mistress to Haverford House, and servants were sent running for any doctor who could be found.

Three of them arrived in quick succession, and together they examined the body and pronounced it dead. If they thought the injuries inconsistent with a fall from a horse, none of them mentioned it, even to one another.

Naturally, no one at a nearby workhouse hospital linked the disappearance of a body with the death of the Marquis of Aldridge's mistress. Why would they? What had a low street prostitute, beaten to death by a client, to do with goings on in the upper echelons of Society?

The following day, the Overtons left for their estates in Lancashire. Aldridge, reportedly deeply affected by the death of his mistress, did not come to see them leave.

Two days later, Aldridge walked behind the coffin at a small private funeral. His half-brother, David Wakefield, was the only other mourner. Afterwards, Aldridge thanked him for coming. "It's the least I could do," David said. "After all, I found her for you. Poor girl. That coffin is the most luxury she has ever known."

Elsewhere, at the same time, Christiana O'Blair, formerly an equestrienne in the employ of Astley's Amphitheatre, stood at the rail of a ship with the horse trainer who was her husband. The docks of London disappeared into the fog.

"Don't you go missing that high life, Chrissie," said the husband.

Chrissie tossed her head. "It were fun for a few days, Charlie, but it ain't me. All that gossiping and such, and the screechy music, and that there Marquis? Spoilt, he is. Thinks he's God's gift to women, and so he does."

"If he tried it on, Chrissie, I'm going straight back to London to knock his head off."

Chrissie made a face, poking her lips out in distaste. "Nah. That's not to say he wouldn't have, if you know what I mean. But I'm a married woman, Charlie, and so I told him. And if any of that was in the plan, then it was no deal, I told him."

"It's a rum deal, and that's a fact."

Chrissie looked alarmed. "You won't say nothing, though, Charlie? You promised."

Charlie laughed. "And lose the money his nibs is going to pay us right and tight every year? Not likely. With what he gave you, and what we've saved, we're going to have us a stud farm and horse training school, Chrissie, my love. And in a land with no Marquises and such sniffing 'round another man's woman. No. He's got what he wanted, and you and me, we're going to get what we want, and no mistake."

Chapter Seventeen

3 months later, Lancashire
Becky knew from whence the letter came before she took it from the salver. The Haverford seal embossed the heavy wax, and the Duke of Haverford had franked it. She held it to her nose for a moment; she had a better sense of smell when pregnant, but would have recognised this scent even without the extra boost of her condition.

She levered herself to her feet to go to her desk, refusing help offered by the hovering butler. She still had four or five weeks to go, according to the local midwife and the very expensive *accoucheur* Hugh had brought up from Liverpool, but she felt enormous. Surely she hadn't been this big and awkward with Sarah?

The servants would have wrapped her in cotton wool if they could. Hugh, too. She smiled at the thought of her attentive husband. She was so happy, so very, very blessed. It was a heady thing to be treated as a lady, a person worthy of respect.

And Hugh, who would be home from his week in Liverpool this very day, he seemed content too. It was simple enough to keep a man satisfied. All she had to do was make sure his house was comfortable, his daughters cared for, and his needs met. And this letter would help, she was sure.

Her letter opener made short work of the seal. She unfolded the letter carefully, and laughed. No economies for Her Grace, the Duchess of Haverford. Three sheets were covered with her small, elegant hand. Becky scanned them quickly. Most comprised instructions, admonitions, and suggestions about her pregnancy.

Several lines brought her up to date with news on Aldridge, who was—so the duchess said—well and about his usual activities. 'And still wearing that ridiculous arm-band, my dear Rebecca, which I cannot like, though whether that is in memory of his mistress or because of the sympathy it wins from woman, I would not like to venture a guess.' Becky snorted. She did not have to guess.

Ah. Here is what she sought. She read quickly, her smile broadening. But this was perfect! Hugh would be so pleased, and so would the girls. And Miss Wilson, Sarah's governess, who had come as a favour to Becky and Aldridge but was anxious to begin her promised retirement before the first snow.

She began a reply. She wouldn't send it until she had spoken to Hugh, but needn't waste time.

A footfall behind her announced her husband an instant before his hand came over her shoulder and snatched up the letter.

"Hugh!" she turned awkwardly in the chair. Her husband's stormy face unsettled her. "Hugh? Is something wrong?"

The storm faded quickly. His frown turned to puzzlement, and he nibbled at his upper lip as he read the first page of the letter, then turned to the signature. "The Duchess of Haverford?"

"Who did you think?" Becky knew perfectly well what he thought. How could he? She had given him no reason to doubt her!

"I... uh..." He shuffled the pages, shifting uncomfortably. He covered his embarrassment with a glare. "Why is the Duchess writing to you? Does she mention Aldridge?"

It hadn't occurred to Becky until this moment that they never talked about Aldridge. Never. And what a large oversight that was. He was supposed to be Hugh's best friend, and had, in his own way, been a good friend to her, but in this house, he had ceased to exist.

"She says he is still wearing a black armband and enjoying sympathy, presumably, mostly from women," she told Hugh, trying to keep the hurt and anger from her voice.

"That sounds like Aldridge." He looked down at the letter.

Becky took a deep breath and let it out slowly. Calm. Stay calm. "I wrote to the duchess to ask if she would find us a governess,

Hugh. Miss Wilson only came for a short time, and it has already been three months."

"Oh." His face flushed, and he shifted again from foot to foot, avoiding her eyes. Good. He should be embarrassed to think so ill of her. "I… can we start again, Becky? Can I go out and come in again and just pretend this never happened?"

They should talk about it. She shouldn't let him just brush it away. But she could not stay cross while he smiled at her, begging with his eyes. She smiled back and nodded, and he tiptoed to the door with ostentatiously large steps, trying to make her chuckle. Which she did, just to please him.

Moments later, he poked his head around the door again. "Becky, my love, I'm home."

"Hugh, how lovely. You're early."

"I finished early, and could not wait to see my lovely wife."

He'd crossed and was now kneeling beside her, his hand tipping her forward for a kiss. She poured all the love she was afraid to confess into that connection between them, opening her lips to his tender invasion, sucking gently on his tongue and sliding hers to explore his mouth in her turn.

"And what are you doing here, Becky?" he asked, when they paused, both short of breath. "Writing letters?"

"I have heard from the Duchess of Haverstock," she told him, playing along. "Hugh, she has found us the perfect governess! All the accomplishments we were looking for, and just think, Hugh, she has a daughter almost the same age as Emma! I have been so concerned; I tell Sarah and Sophie that they must include her, but she struggles to keep up, and they do forget. Besides, three is an awkward number. However kind the older girls might be, Emma keeps getting left out, and they are not always kind, Hugh." She was babbling. She knew she was babbling. But his face—the unscarred side—had gone cold and still. What had she done wrong?

"It is unusual for a governess to be a widow," he said, his voice even and expressionless.

"She is not a widow," Becky admitted.

The frown was back. Hugh picked up the letter again, and this time scanned until he found the passage about the governess. "Becky, you cannot hire this woman. I forbid it."

The cold in Hugh's voice crept into her own. "What is your objection, Hugh?"

Let him state it bluntly.

"You can ask? Becky, she's from a seminary for fallen women! She has had a child out of wedlock! What is the duchess thinking? A woman like her isn't fit to have charge of children! No decent person would even let her into their house, let alone near their family."

Dear God. All this time she had thought he accepted her, respected her. All this time, he thought... The cold seeped through her, touching her heart and turning it to a lump of ice.

"You did." Becky let the words fall uncompromisingly, stopping him in mid-speech.

"Becky. No. I didn't mean... Becky, you're different." Hugh looked bewildered. The benighted, stupid, arrogant lummox. "You didn't want to... I mean, I'm sure you felt you had no choice."

"*Felt* I had no choice? *Felt?*" The cold flashed to heat so fast, the burn scorched through her veins. She was out of her chair more quickly than she had moved in weeks, stalking towards him so fiercely, he stepped back and fell, rather than sat, on the sofa behind him.

"You are absolutely right, Hugh. I *felt* I had no choice. Is that what you think? That if I had just tried harder, I would not have fallen, and you would not have been forced to compromise your integrity to allow me in the same house as your children?"

"Becky, you are being ridiculous." Hugh tried to sound stern. "This is not about you. And you should not allow yourself to become so emotional. Think of the baby."

"The baby. Yes. Because this is about the baby. Of course. How could I forget?" Tears rose to her eyes, and she fought them back. Hugh would take them as further evidence she was overly emotional.

She paced the room, trying to slow her breathing, ignoring Hugh's struggle to find something to say.

"Hugh, I have never told you how I came to be Aldridge's mistress."

"I don't want to know," Hugh said quickly. "I want to forget it. I hate thinking that you were his before you were mine, that he was just the last in I don't know how many. I cannot bear to think of it. Can we not just pretend it never happened?" He held his hands out to her again, but his eyes were still angry in a stony mask.

She almost stopped. For her entire adult life, obeying the man who kept her had been her only choice. If Hugh wanted to pretend she had come to him an innocent, was that a bad thing?

But he hadn't finished. "I don't want to ever hear you speak Aldridge's name again," he said.

The rage flared incandescent again. "Aldridge," she said, as though casting a curse. "He was my protector, Hugh. My buyer. Do you know what that means? Do you know how it feels? To be an object to be purchased, a body to be kept in a corner in case the owner might want to take it out and use it?"

"Silence!" Hugh roared. "Stop it! I don't want to hear it, I say!"

She shouted over him. "You have to hear it. You have to, Hugh. I cannot live knowing you despise me. I cannot, I cannot." It was no good. She couldn't hold the tears inside any longer, and they flooded down her face, ripping deep, wrenching sobs from some hidden wound inside her soul.

Suddenly, Hugh's arms were around her and he guided her to the sofa.

He cradled her in his arms as he patted her on the back murmuring, "It's all right," but it wasn't. It wasn't all right. And "There, there," which meant nothing, but was somehow comforting. And "Don't cry, my dear wife," but she couldn't stop. And "I don't despise you, Becky. I don't. I admire you," but it wasn't her he admired, and that was the problem. He admired a vision of Becky he had made in his imagination, and he didn't want the real one. She cried still harder, and he kept patting and murmuring.

She struggled to stop. Such crying couldn't be good for the baby. And, at last, she managed to bring herself under control, with only an occasional shuddering sob still escaping, however hard she tried to suppress it. Hugh's anger had vanished, and his eyes held nothing but concern as he tipped her chin up to examine her face.

"Is that better?" he asked, the smug, male statement nearly setting her off again.

"I have to tell you, Hugh. And you have to listen." She was determined. For three months, she had been living in a fool's paradise, believing the feeling between them was growing respect, even affection. If he wouldn't face all she had been, it was a mirage.

Hugh shook his head, and her heart sank, but he wasn't denying her. "If it is that important to you, Becky. But first, let me get you a cup of tea."

He brought the tea trolley himself, and with it a bowl of warm water and a flannel to wash her face.

"Becky, this isn't necessary. I... I have come to terms with what you were. You don't need to... I know you must have... I daresay you thought you loved the man who..."

"I was raped," she said, baldly, stopping him mid-sentence. "I was 15, Hugh. By just a few days. The three sons of my father's employer... they took turns to rape me while the other two held me down and gagged my screams."

There were no tears now. She had cried for that poor, brutalised child more often than she could remember. Yes, and for what came after.

"The youngest son was just a year older than I, and the only person who was ever kind to me. After my mother died, I was so lonely. My father was librarian to... the Master, I'll call him. And tutor, sometimes, to his sons, when they needed extra help with their studies.

"We lived in our own apartments above the Master's library. After Mother died, Father left me there alone, most of the time, except when he needed my help in the library. I was allowed in the garden and our apartments and the library. But I wasn't to go into the rest of the house.

"Benjamin used to talk to me sometimes, in the library or the garden, and I started looking for him. I was a child, Hugh, starving for company.

"He told me to meet him in the far corner of the garden, and all three of them were waiting for me. Ben went first."

Hugh swore, quietly. While she had been talking, he sat beside her and lifted her onto his lap, resting her head on the shoulder still wet from her earlier tears

"He said he was sorry. But that it was my own fault. I shouldn't have accepted the invitation."

"What did your father do?"

"When I told him? He accused me of leading them on, enticing them. It is always the woman's fault, Hugh. But it isn't true. I did nothing. I would have done nothing. I was not to blame."

Her voice rose as she struggled to convince him, and he coaxed her head back to his shoulder again. "I believe you. I do, Becky. You're right. Men blame women, when it is the animal within themselves they should blame."

"My father threw me out. He said I was a whore and no daughter of his. The Master's sons came after me, laughing. They would have used me again, had they caught me, but I knew a way behind the stables and under the wall, and I ran until my feet were bleeding worse than my..."

"Ah, Becky." Her eyes were dry, but his were not. "Becky, my poor girl. Who saved you, Becky? Was it Aldridge?"

"No one. I have run away many times, Hugh, and there has never been a handsome prince or knight errant. That first time, I was found by a bawd and her bullies, who locked me up until I stopped trying to run away. I did stop, after a while. You can get used to most things. Take enough gin, and you don't even feel it after a while.

"Most whores spend their earnings on drink or laudanum, did you know that, Hugh? Because being used by man after man, all day and all night, just a convenience for them to rub themselves on... it hurts, Hugh. It hurts more than you can imagine."

"Becky." It was a broken plea, almost a sob, but she had no mercy left.

"Do you think we all want to be whores? Some of them were forced, as I was. Some believed a man's honeyed words for a day, or a week, or months, before he left them to go off and ruin some other poor lass. Some say their man was true, but he died and no one believed the vows they'd made in secret. Who am I to say they were wrong? They ended as I did, for all of that.

"And yes, some thought making a living on their backs would be the easiest option, or they had no other way to eat.

"I even met some who liked what we did. Women have appetites too. And some women... I have met people who will use others, many others, to satisfy their appetites."

She tipped her head to see his eyes. "Do you know what we call them, most of them? Do you, Hugh?"

"Light-heeled?" he suggested, clearly choosing the gentlest insult he could think of.

She shook her head. "Men. We call them men!" She almost spat it at him, and he flinched as if she'd slapped him.

Did his conscience bother him? Good. Her anger and grief still high, she could spare him no pity. In the next moment, a tear escaped and ran down his cheek, and she almost stopped. But if she did not finish her story now, she might never again have the courage.

She hid her head again in the crook of his neck. She didn't want to see his face when she told him what happened next.

"I took too much laudanum. It was... I do not know. It must have been stronger than I expected. I do not remember what happened next, but I was told later... one of my customers bought me from the abbess. I was cheap, I suppose, because they expected me to die.

"He took me to a doctor and paid to have me nursed back to health."

Hugh said nothing. His jaw was rigid, and tears streamed down his cheeks.

"When I was well enough, he moved me to a little cottage on the grounds of his house, far enough away that his wife, who was an invalid, was not offended by the sight of me. He visited me there most days. I should be grateful to him, I expect. He did save my life, and he did stop me taking the drink and the drugs."

"But he also used you," Hugh said, quietly.

Becky grimaced, the memories cascading around her. The sheltering confusion of laudanum was gone. Later, she learned the knack of separating her mind from what was being done to her body, but back then, she was sober for the first time in years, and without defences.

"He used me," she confirmed. "He kept the door locked and set a servant to watch it, afraid I would run away. To where? I had no heart for it. He was so angry when he found I was with child. He cursed the doctor for not purging the brat when I was first removed from the brothel. He said I was a poor investment, and... well, never mind."

Hugh was finding this hard enough. He did not need to know she had been forced to pleasure the old man with her hands and mouth since, he said, he couldn't bear to touch her when she was so bloated and ugly, but he'd paid and would have his use of her.

"He died. Shortly after Sarah was born, he died. And his son sold me to another protector."

"Sold you? But... how could he sell you?" Hugh sounded more indignant than unbelieving, but she explained anyway. "I do not know what else to call it, Hugh. He found another protector, told me I could choose that man, the brothel, or the street. And later, I found he had taken a considerable sum of money for the transaction. My new protector made me give Sarah to a wet nurse, so she would not disturb his pleasure, and he would not tell me where she was."

Many times, she had been tempted to turn back to the mindlessness, the dreamtime security of drink and laudanum. But her baby was out there somewhere. She was determined to get her back. Fortunately, her new protector was indulgent, in his own way, free with his gifts, and—once he was sure of her—happy for his mistress to go visiting and shopping when he had no need of her.

Becky soon discovered where Sarah was kept, and she began to plan a future free of men and their demands.

"I knew I would never be free unless I started using the men who would use me. I chose my next protector, and the one after that. I insisted on keeping Sarah with me, and a nursemaid to look after her when I..."

"I began to save, mostly jewellery I was given, but some of my pin money. Then..." She fell silent, still angry with herself for choosing Perringworth. He had seemed the best choice at the time: gentry rather than merchant class, apparently wealthy, and willing to give her a house of her own, albeit in a village some distance from Bristol.

"Was that when you... fell in with Aldridge?" Hugh asked. He sounded apprehensive.

Becky shook her head. "No. In fact... the man I chose... the man I thought would be my last protector was my worst mistake of all. Bad things have happened to me, Hugh, but almost never by my choice. Perry was my choice, and he cheated me of everything I'd saved, then offered me to his creditor. Not just me, Sarah, too. If Aldridge hadn't happened along, Perry's creditor would have put us back in a brothel to pay off his debt. Smite, they called him. He already had a buyer for Sarah."

Hugh was swearing again, low, long, and vicious.

"Aldridge rescued me from Smite's men, then he went to London and paid for Sarah so Smite would not come after her. I owe him, Hugh. Even if Perry had not stolen everything, I could never have afforded to pay Smite, but Aldridge did it without thinking, and without... we had no agreement. He could have demanded anything, and I would have given it gladly, to save Sarah. He never once made demands."

"It would have been nothing to him, you know. He is so rich, I doubt he noticed."

"That is immaterial. He saved Sarah, Hugh, and he did not have to. Then, after I agreed to be his mistress, he set her up in her own house, and did everything he could to protect her from what I was. I will owe him forever. I know you do not like it, but I cannot change how I feel. He saved Sarah."

"You love him." Hugh looked suddenly much older, all the strength drained from the muscles of his face.

"Love him?" Becky was surprised. Hadn't Hugh been listening? "Hugh, he used me, too, the same as the others. He is a kind man, and so rich being generous is no trouble. He was my rescuer, and I was grateful. But he became my protector. Do you not understand? I was under an obligation to him. I had a contract with him. I was not free to choose him. I owe him for saving me and Sarah, especially Sarah, but I do not love him. I am fond of him, perhaps, but I do not love him. He was to be my last protector."

Hugh set her gently back on the couch and stood. Whatever powerful emotion racked him, it was too strong to take sitting down. He strode back and forth, his face working, then suddenly knelt before her and took both her hands in his. He lifted them to his mouth and kissed them.

"Thank you, Becky," he said. "You were right. I needed to hear. I did not realise…" He seized her shoulders and pulled her into a violent kiss, and she met his passion with her own, not understanding what he was feeling, but moved by it nonetheless.

Then, suddenly, he pushed away. "I… I need to be alone for a time. Forgive…" And he was gone, leaving her in the wreck of her own storm, to wonder what damage she had just done to their marriage.

Chapter Eighteen

He rode all afternoon, though it felt longer. He let the horse pick the way much of the time, while his mind went over and over the horrors his wife had lived through. His wife. His gentle, kind, comfortable wife who had made his house into a home, gathered his daughters into her heart, and made him happy.

He was no better than all the rest: a user, a destroyer of women. Lady Ballingcroft's face floated before him again, and dozens of others he'd tempted with honeyed words.

Like he had Becky. Oh, he'd offered marriage, but that wasn't what she wanted, was it? "I was not free to choose," she said. He hadn't offered her freedom, he and Aldridge. Instead, she was being used again. To carry the child who would save the estate. To mother his other children and manage his household. And to comfort him with her body. He was no better than the unnamed and uncounted men who had used her before.

What was it Aldridge had said? "You aren't fit to kiss the hem of her robe." He hated that Aldridge was right. He hated Aldridge. He hated every man who had used his Becky, up to and including himself.

She wanted her freedom, to be left to her own devices, and no wonder. After all she had been through, why would she ever want to service a man again?

But he and Aldridge had barged in with their selfish plans.

He couldn't fix it; couldn't turn back time and give her the quiet village she wanted, but he could respect her wish to be left alone. He wouldn't impose himself on her again. From this day, she would be a saint in his household, to be cherished and protected, but worshipped from afar.

His mind made up, he returned home.

In the schoolroom, he was told when he asked after Lady Overton. He thought of following her there, but decided to wait until they met at dinner. He had to act normal, convince her nothing had changed.

But only one place was set, and the butler informed him Lady Overton had retired early. "Her Ladyship complains of a headache," he said.

"Ah. Yes. She was unwell earlier," Hugh replied. Was his butler glaring at him? No. Just his guilty conscience. He shouldn't have left her. He should have stayed and reassured her. He pushed his plate away. "I find I am not hungry. You can clear."

But when he arrived in their bedchamber, she was asleep, pale, except for her red-rimmed eyes and small, but for the great mound of her belly.

He wandered up to the nursery. The children were also asleep, but the governess was still awake, doing some mending by candlelight. Yes. That was decidedly a glare. Had Becky said something? No, she never complained, never criticised.

He remembered her red eyes, and their raised voices. Undoubtedly, the servants had drawn their own conclusions and taken sides. And they were right. He wished the woman a good night and went back down to his bedchamber, where he crept into bed beside his sleeping wife, not daring to touch her.

In the morning, Becky's heavy-lidded eyes suggested her sleep might have been feigned. She'd clearly had as little rest as he. "Stay in bed," Hugh advised. "You don't need to get up."

But she came downstairs, wan but composed, before he left to supervise firewood cutting on the far side of the estate. "Make sure you stay warm," she said, but there was no warmth in her voice. It wasn't cold, exactly. Lifeless and dull, as if the woman who lived inside the beautiful, brittle shell had gone away somewhere.

That evening, when Becky joined him for dinner, he ventured to discuss the duchess's letter that had set off the disastrous conversation. "The governess that the Duchess of Haverford recommended..." he began.

Her head came up, and her eyes met his for the first time that day. Alarm? Fear? Hugh put out a hand as if to an injured animal, not touching, just showing he held nothing that could harm her. "You believe she would be suitable?"

Her voice sounded rusty, as if she had injured it with all her crying the day before. "Her Grace..." she stopped, cleared her throat, and started again. "Her Grace has interviewed her, and says she is suitable."

"Will you send an acceptance? Or do you wish me to do so?"

Becky looked startled.

"I have thought about what you said. I believe you, Becky. It is wrong to blame women when the fault lies as much—no, even more—with men. I know that governesses are often treated poorly. If the duchess believes this woman can be trusted with our daughters, then I will trust her. And I will trust you to... to notice if anything is wrong."

Becky nodded, but she looked no happier. "I will write to the duchess," she said.

"Becky."

She was watching her fork push food around her plate, and he had to say her name again before she would meet his eyes.

"Becky, I just wanted to say... I need to say... I am so sorry. I... forgive me." She looked bewildered, and well she might. He barely knew what he meant himself. What he'd done to Becky was the least of what she had suffered. But he wanted her absolution for crimes against all the women he'd ever bedded, using them to meet his needs and blaming them for their lack of purity. So what if he had done the same as every man he knew. That was no excuse for being a user. A destroyer.

She was shaking her head, eyes dry and bleak. What did the gesture mean? 'I won't forgive you?' 'I don't understand?'

He couldn't stay to explain. His own eyes were filling and he couldn't weep in front of her. He had no right.

He took himself off to his study and the brandy decanter. When he was calmer, he would apologise again.

He was sorry for hurting her, for not trusting her, for manipulating her into marriage, for being a man and, therefore, a representative of the tribe that had hurt her. He was sorry for it all, and he could never make it up to her. But he would live his life trying.

For the next few weeks, he worked manfully and kept to his resolution. He asked after her health, rode into the village to find treats to tempt her failing appetite, hunted her out several times a day to make sure she was comfortable.

When he wasn't with her, he rehearsed telling her how sorry he was, but in her presence, faced with her polite reserve, the words dried up.

He gave up suggesting things they could do together in the evening, after she begged off three nights in a row, though he missed the quiet times together reading, and missed still more, making music together: he singing as she played the pianoforte.

Instead, Becky went up to bed early, and Hugh retired to his study and the brandy, creeping up after she was asleep to chastely dress in a nightshirt and tuck himself spoon-fashion behind her in the dark. A nightshirt! He hadn't realised he even owned such a piece of attire. But he felt the need to reassure her she was in no danger of being forced to endure his attentions. Indeed, when his ardour rose at the touch and smell of her, just the thought of the horrors she had been through was enough to shrivel him again.

Slowly, it dawned on him that he had fallen in love with his wife. Fallen in love with her, been severed from her, and missed her like a lost limb. It was too late now. If only he had told her! He couldn't force the words on her now, when he had hurt her so badly, and she so clearly regretted marrying him.

The house was in mourning.

Becky barely talked and never smiled, except when she was with the children. The servants crept silently about their tasks. And Hugh escaped as often as the weather allowed, which was rarer and rarer as Christmas approached.

The new governess and her daughter arrived and were installed. Patrice Goodfellow, Mrs Goodfellow under their roof. She seemed a nice enough woman; modest and polite. And the girls liked her. Soon, Emma and the Goodfellow child, little Portia, were the thickest of friends, and the schoolroom was ankle-deep in preparations for Christmas.

Becky, who had made so many plans for the holiday, lost interest. She pretended for the children's sake, and Sophie and Emma accepted her feigned enthusiasm. But Sarah was worried, hovering over her mother, answering questions for her when Becky drifted off into silence, finishing decorations her mother started, when Becky's hands fell idle.

"She will be well when the baby arrives," Hugh reassured Sarah and himself. He hoped it was true.

The only happiness left in the house centred on the schoolroom. Hugh started going there often. And, if he was careful and quiet, if she didn't see him watching, his wife sometimes smiled at things the children said. Once, even laughed. A sad little chuckle, reminding him how much he missed her happy gurgle. It had been gone for weeks. Since before he had forced her confession.

Before and After. His life had fractured into two pieces. Before, when he had been happy and thought Becky was. After, when he knew she only pretended, and he didn't know how to console her.

Chapter Nineteen

The baby was born on Christmas Day, coming into the world so quickly that the midwife was barely in the door before she was up to her elbows in the final work of the delivery.

"I have the lady now, Lord Overton. You can leave her with me," the woman said.

Hugh, proud and relieved Becky had been holding tight to his hand since the first pain struck hard an hour earlier, refused to leave the room.

"Well, stay you there, then. Her Ladyship and I will be busy enough."

"I need to push," Becky said, almost a wail.

The midwife hurried to the bottom of the bed and checked under the sheet Becky's maid had draped to preserve her modesty.

"Not quite, my lady," she advised. "Pant." And Becky panted, short hard puffs of breath until the pain crested and sank away. Her hand, clutching his hard enough to crush, had just begun to relax when the next surge hit.

"Very good, my lady," the midwife encouraged. "One more like that, and we will be ready."

One more like that and he may never have the use of his hand again, but if it helped Becky, it was a small sacrifice. Again, a moment's relaxation. Again, a powerful contraction that had Becky whimpering even as she panted. "I cannot help it. I cannot."

The midwife checked again, and rose beaming. "I see him, my lady. Push when you are ready."

And Becky did, digging her chin into her chest and using his hand to anchor herself against the mighty effort her body was making.

"That is it, Becky. I am so proud of you." He was hardly aware of what he was saying, and she ignored him completely, absorbed in the work of bringing the child into the world.

She sat half up almost before the child was fully in the midwife's hands, demanding, "What is it?"

"My lord, my lady." The midwife was beaming. "You have a beautiful, healthy little daughter."

"A girl." It was a despairing wail.

Hugh took the baby from the midwife.

"A beautiful girl. A healthy daughter, Becky. Our daughter." He was pleading with her, but it made no difference. She was shaking her head.

"But you contracted for a son. Oh, Hugh, I am so sorry. So sorry." She turned away from him then, and away from the dear, little treasure he held out for her to see.

Chapter Twenty

There was a fog. No. Heavier than a fog. A bank of clouds. A blanket, almost, covering everything. Sometimes, she could see through it a little, or hear a few words, or feel a touch. Sarah came to visit. She was sure of that. Her belly hurt. Was it the baby? No. The baby was gone. There was a grief there, somewhere just out of reach, waiting to consume her, but she wouldn't think of it. She was so hot. No, she was cold. So cold, she was sweating.

Voices. Hands washing her, changing her. Hands touching her intimately. No! She wasn't going back there!

"Hush, Becky. Hush. Don't struggle, my love." Hugh's voice. She must be dreaming, then. Hugh didn't love her. She leant into the arms that restrained her anyway.

Another man's voice. It must be a dream. Hugh would never hold her for another man. "...fever, my lord... infection... best I can do... crisis..." Becky held desperately to the belief that if Hugh were there, she was safe, and tried to ignore what was happening further down: the scraping, the vile smell.

More washing. So hot. Cooler, please... There, someone lifting her, holding a cool drink to her lips. Hugh's voice again. "Slowly, Becky, slowly."

She had been sick for two weeks, her maid told her. They had been sure she would die. The master would not leave her side, "No, not for a moment, not till the doctor said the crisis was past. Then, off he went to sleep, and that was fifteen hours ago, my lady."

She turned, but he was not in the bed he had promised they would always share. Even the last weeks before Christmas, after she had driven him away with her sordid story, he had come each night to their bed. He didn't desire her anymore, and who could blame him? But he had come to their bed each night and held her when he thought she was asleep.

But that was before she failed him, of course, before she had a girl instead of the son he needed.

The maid was speaking again, asking something. She worked back through her memory of the sounds. The baby. Did Lady Overton want to see the baby? "No. No, thank you. I think I will just sleep."

Hugh brought the baby to her later, the reminder of her failure. She turned her head away to hide her tears, but she couldn't stop her shoulders from shaking with sobs, and he left. But not for long. He took the baby away and came again to sit with her.

He was kind, always so kind. She couldn't bear to face him. Poor Hugh. How much disappointment must lurk in his eyes, stuck in this marriage to a harlot and not even a son to show for it! After a while, the feigned sleep became real, and when she woke again, he was gone.

Two of the maids were talking as they cleaned out the fireplace and re-laid the fire.

"Poor master. Losing this one, too, happen."

"The mistress? Mendin', an't she?"

"Same as t'other, the first Lady Overton. Had the bairn and was mendin'."

A bairn? Becky's mind was slow and dull. Surely Hugh had said nothing about a baby?

"But er wouldna' look at un. Not once. Cried ever so, if we brung un. Another little girl, it was."

"Jus' like this one!" said the listening maid, thrilling to the drama.

"Then," the story-telling maid slowed and deepened her voice, "one day 'er sent for t'bairn. And walked out of t'house and into the lake."

"No!"

"True as I stand here. Both of 'em drowned dead, and the master near demented."

"But why? Why did er do it?"

Yes. Why? Becky wanted to know, too. She was holding the fog back by main force, reaching for the words the maid dripped so slowly. If she had the energy for it, she would hate that other wife, the one who had told Hugh he was ugly, who had abandoned him and taken his child. But something was wrong. Hugh had told her he could not have a child.

"Feart," the gossiping maid said. Afraid, Becky wondered? Afraid of what.

"Nobbut a bit to do now, Mary. Just tha wipe the tiles while I set the fire alight. Yes, feart, I reckon. The whole house knew t' bairn wasna' the master's, and er thought he'd set her aside, happen."

Ah. Poor Hugh. History repeats. Becky listened to the retreating maids and wept for her husband's losses until she cried herself to sleep.

Becky improved so slowly that Hugh had to compare one Sunday with the next, but bit by bit, she improved. Physically, at least. When he and Mrs Goodfellow held a belated Twelfth Night party for the girls, she was not well enough to attend, though she roused sufficiently to admire the new clothes Mrs Goodfellow had sewn for their dolls, and the little wooden boxes Hugh had crafted, with the help of the estate carpenter, to hold them.

A few moments were all she could manage, and when he asked if she wanted to give the girls the shawls she had been embroidering, she shook her head. "You," she said, so he found them in the drawer of her chest. Four. She must have made an extra one in secret, after she knew Mrs Goodfellow had a child. He was not sure which colour she intended for which child, but she didn't answer when he asked, so he and Mrs Goodfellow decided, before the governess took the children back to the nursery floor.

He called the doctor back the next day. The man diagnosed an imbalance of the humours, and prescribed bleeding, which left

Becky so close to death's door that when the doctor visited again, Hugh sent him away and told him not to return.

It took more than a week before she was as well as she had been for the Twelfth Night party.

A few days later, Becky sat up for half an hour, while the children made their daily visit after tea. She smiled and asked what they had been doing, and Hugh rejoiced, but the bleakness settled over her again, as soon as they left.

A fortnight passed, and she was able to move to her couch, and then a week later, come down to his study, where she could recline on cushions and read or write letters. Though she didn't. He glanced up frequently from his work. She watched the fire, or lay with her eyes closed.

She would make an effort for the girls, so he had Mrs Goodfellow bring them to her several times a day, for short visits, sending them away again before she outran her small store of strength.

He left her only when estate business took him outside, or to spend time with their daughters, especially Sarah. She was frightened, and reassuring her broke his heart a little more every day.

Becky wouldn't look at the baby, wouldn't choose a name or comment on the names Hugh suggested. Little Isabelle Eleanor Hope Rebecca Antonia Overton was baptised in the presence of her father, three of the servants standing in as proxy godparents, since Aldridge, his mother, and the Countess of Chirbury could not be expected to brave the bitter winter weather to make their way so far north.

"Isabelle for your mother," Hugh told Becky. He'd had to consult his copy of the marriage licence to find the name, because Becky didn't answer when he asked her, just shook her head and looked bewildered, as if his words made no sense.

He gave up trying to persuade Becky to take the baby in her arms, afraid she would cry herself into another illness.

Belle, they called her, and beautiful she was, a dear, quiet little thing who only cried when she was hungry, and who would happily lie for hours sleeping or gazing up into the faces of her sisters, the wet nurse, the governess, or any of the nursery staff who could persuade her father to surrender her.

Holding Belle comforted Hugh, and he sat rocking her against his shoulder for an hour or more at a time, while Becky sat or lay nearby with her eyes closed, ignoring them both.

Becky ate very little, spoke even less, and only smiled when the girls came to tell her about their day. And each day her smiles grew rarer and more distant, and the bleak emptiness in her eyes spread.

He was losing her. Each day, she faded more, even as he chivvied the cook to invent some new delicacy to tempt her appetite, or rode through the snow to the village for the post in hopes of a letter to amuse her, or read aloud to the little girls with one eye on her still form. And each day he realised anew how much he had come to love her.

Then, one day in early February, he was called away to the stables where heavy snow had collapsed the roof of a lean-to. He returned to find her standing at the window, looking out at the garden. Filled with joy that she had stood and walked to the window on her own, he hurried to her side.

"Hugh." Her voice, as always nowadays, was a calm and distant monotone, all emotion leached away. She glanced sideways at him, then turned her attention to the lake, covered in thick ice on which the four children were skating, with various levels of success.

"Would you like to go out and watch, Becky? Shall I tell the maid to fetch a coat?"

Would that be enough to keep her warm? He couldn't risk her catching a chill. "And a shawl?"

She misinterpreted his frown. "Don't be cross, Hugh. I would never take the baby. I have seen you with her. I know how you love her." She smiled, a smile so sad, it dragged at his gut. "You are such a good man, Hugh. Polyphemia should have left her little daughter. She would have been safe with you." She turned back to the window. "It is no use. The ice is too thick. I will have to wait." And she made her slow and careful way back to the *chaise longue* by the fire.

Chapter Twenty-One

That day, Hugh wrote to Aldridge. "Come immediately. Any way you can. As fast as you can. Becky is threatening to kill herself and I can't..." He crossed out the last eight words, and replaced them so the last sentence read, "Becky needs you."

He wrote several copies and addressed them to all the luxurious places the Marquis of Aldridge might be holed up for the winter, with a notation on the front saying they were urgent and should be sent on. Then, Hugh settled in to watch Becky even more closely, until her rescuer arrived to save her again.

Aldridge must have been closer than Hugh expected. Three days after he sent his letters, a train of elegant sleighs coasted up the drive. Carriages, really, but with skids rather than wheels, each pulled by a pair of sturdy horses. The children, taking advantage of a break in the weather to play in the snow, stopped in their tracks and watched.

From the study window, Hugh could see three of the ornately carved and painted sleighs turn away towards the stable yard, and the remaining two continue to the front steps. He was not surprised all five sported the Haverford crest.

He excused himself to Becky, who didn't look up from the fire she was examining so intently, and sent a maid to sit with her while he went down to greet his guest. He pasted on a smile. Hugh had sent for the arrogant, self-centred, wife-stealing son-of-a-bitch. And if Becky wanted to go with him, then that was the price Hugh would pay for Becky to be well again. Even if it meant losing Belle.

Smile. He needed to smile.

One carriage was disgorging an enormous number of retainers. How had they all fit? Sitting on one another's knees? Aldridge stood at the door of the other, handing down a lady. Surely even Aldridge wouldn't bring one of his paramours here!

Then the lady lifted her head. The face under the bonnet brought his smile out in truth.

He hurried down the steps to greet her. "Your Grace. I am so glad you have come."

Then Aldridge was there, right in his face. "Overton, you scum-sucking louse! What have you done to Becky? If you've hurt her, I'll..."

"Aldridge," said Her Grace, "please do not embarrass me, my love. Lord Overton will explain all to us shortly. Now, give Cousin Agatha your hand, dear. Lord Overton." She held out her own hand for Hugh to escort her up the steps, where the butler was standing with his mouth open.

"Will you come into the parlour to warm by the fire?" Hugh asked. He settled her in a chair, took the cape she handed him, and went to find out what had happened to Aldridge and the cousin.

The butler was still hovering in the hall. Hugh gave him a few terse, low-voiced instructions about chambers and refreshments. When Becky had proved to be so good at making his house a marvellously comfortable place to live, he had let his elderly housekeeper retire. He could do with her now. Even more, he could do with his wife back, and that was the truth.

Aldridge was outside on the steps, sitting on his folded greatcoat, talking to the girls while the cousin hovered anxiously.

"May I invite you in, ma'am?" Hugh asked her, but was interrupted by Sarah, who shouted, "Papa, Uncle Lord Aldridge says Mama and I may go with him if she wants, and I won't, Papa. I can stay, Papa! Say I can stay? You said I could stay with my sisters forever and ever, and Mama too." And she turned on Aldridge, fierce as a tiger cub, and shouted at him, stamping her foot. "You go away. You just go away, nasty, old Aldridge. Mama is sick, but when she is better, we shall be all happy again, like we were before. You just go away."

Hugh reached her as she burst into tears, hissing at Aldridge as he passed, "I should break your neck." Then he was occupied with soothing all of the little girls, since the other three were weeping in sympathy, and the governess was doing nothing, torn between correcting her charge's manners and attacking the invading home-breaker on her own account.

"No need for tears, Sarah, I invited Lord Aldridge here, because he may be able to help make Mama well. You do not need to worry, girls. No one is going anywhere, unless they choose."

Sarah glared at her former favourite. "Then why did he say he had come to take Mama and me away?"

Hugh thought manners should make an appearance again, now that the tears were being blotted up. "You say 'His Lordship' or 'Lord Aldridge,' not 'he.' Why did Lord Aldridge say such a foolish thing? Because he did not precisely understand the situation. He will meet with Mama, and then I will come and tell you all about it." Somehow, it had not occurred to him that shocking Becky out of her lethargy might lose him Sarah, as well as Becky and Belle. How would he live without them?

It was a struggle, but he smiled. "Now then, the snow is soaking through my trousers, and no one is going anywhere tonight, except inside to the warmth." He stood, lifting Sarah with him and standing her on her feet. Then he chivvied them all inside, kissing each girl, including little Portia, as they passed him on their way to the back stairs.

He opened the door to the parlour, ushered Cousin Agatha through, and went in behind her, followed by Aldridge.

On the other side of the room, the Duchess of Haverford had opened the double doors into the study, and was talking to Becky.

In the past three days, he had rehearsed Becky's possible reaction a thousand times. It was both his nightmare and his dream that she would take one look at Aldridge and come back to herself. "Aldridge," he imagined her saying, "I knew you would come for me."

When he wasn't torturing himself with those visions, he accepted there might be no reaction at all, that the deep blanket through which she viewed the world would continue. Anything would be better than that.

He could never have predicted what happened: all the blood draining from the already pale cheeks; the haunted distant eyes focusing in horror; the tortured scream. "No-o-o!"

Before anyone could react, Becky was up, hurling herself across the room and through the doors with a careless disregard for furniture and the duchess, whom she brushed past as if she were not there.

Aldridge clearly thought she was coming for him, because he tried to shoulder Hugh to one side, but Becky dodged his reaching hands and flung herself at Hugh's feet, clinging to his knees as if losing grip would mean a fall into oblivion, repeating, "No. No. No. Oh, Hugh, please, don't make me go back. I know I failed. I'm so sorry, Hugh. I tried. I really tried. Let me stay. Don't send me away. Please, Hugh."

Aldridge, who had had the presence of mind to close the door on the startled eyes of the servants, now hissed in his turn, "I should break your neck, Overton."

"If you will take my recommendation, Aldridge, you will not make yourself ridiculous," said Her Grace. "Overton, you and Lady Overton might be more comfortable in the study, with the door shut."

Hugh, preoccupied with trying to comfort his wife and lift her from the death grip on his knees, was barely aware of anyone else in the room.

"Stay, Becky. I want you to stay, my love. You haven't failed; you've given me a beautiful daughter. So beautiful, but never as beautiful as her mother. Not to me, my love. Never to me. I want to see you, every day of my life, Becky. Treasure of my heart. My love. My wife. Stay, Becky. Please stay."

Unable to raise her, he was kneeling with her, brushing the hair off her wet cheeks, trying to kiss them dry as he wet them again with his own tears.

"But... Aldridge?" she asked.

"Forever and ever, Becky. You promised. We promised. To have and to hold, from this day forward..."

"Till death..." Becky whispered. She looked at him then, met his eyes deliberately for the first time since Belle was born. And her eyes were clear, focused on him. She recognised him. She yearned for him.

"I love you, Becky. I love you so much."

Becky went very still, her eyes clinging to him as her hands went limp. And then, with a sigh, she collapsed into his arms, snuggling under his chin as she had before That Day.

"Thank you, God. Thank you, God. Thank you, God." It was quiet, almost under his breath, but in his heart he was singing great, rolling paeans of glory. He lifted her; she was so light, so frail that it broke his heart anew, but then she shifted to put her arms around his neck and the joy returned.

The duchess's party was gone. He vaguely remembered her herding her companion and her son out of the room some time ago. He would need to thank her. Later. For now, his wife needed him. His wife. His Becky.

Hugh fed Becky her dinner, only a few mouthfuls, but more than she'd eaten in weeks. He had the maid cut it, so he could use just his fork, since she clung to his hand as if without that anchor, she would drift back into the darkness. He had left instructions for Aldridge and the duchess to be given his apologies if he didn't come down in time, afraid to leave her, but she surprised him again.

"Hugh, you should go and have dinner with Her Grace and... Will you tell them I am sorry? I don't think... should I come down? Will the duchess think me rude?"

He reassured her. She had been ill. She should rest. She could meet the guests tomorrow. He instructed the maid to call if he was needed, and crossed to the door, then hurried back to her bed for another clinging kiss. "I love you, Becky," he said again.

He was a little early for the meal, but he needed to go via the nursery to reassure the girls. He ran up the stairs two at a time, relief making his legs light.

He could be hopeful, but shouldn't expect the current rally to last, the Duchess of Haverford instructed him. She had sent her son to play cards with her companion, and demanded that Hugh escort her into his study, where she asked him incisive questions about Becky's illness and her treatment.

"The doctor said her humours were out of balance, and he bled her, but..."

"Stupid," Her Grace said. "Very stupid. She had just had a baby and lost who knows how much blood, and the man bled her?"

"He bled her for the fever, too," Hugh admitted. "But the second time, she was so weak. I was afraid she was dying. I wouldn't let him do it again."

"Good." The duchess nodded. "You have some sense, then. I had my doubts. Very well, Overton. You shall place yourself in my hands, and I shall tell you what you must do."

"I will not put her away," Hugh said, firmly. "Even if her mind is weak..."

"Put her away? Why would you put her away? She will recover fully, and I will help. I have seen this before, Overton. Women, after giving birth to a child, often suffer a disorder of the humours. It passes. Your wife has had a worse time of it than many, perhaps because she also had childbed fever. I sometimes think that we gentry are more prone than cottagers, because others will do our tasks if we turn our faces to the wall.

"Several of my goddaughters have had this melancholy, and I, myself, after the birth of my dear Jonathan. Also, Overton, I think there has been some cause for estrangement between you. You will tell me whether I am right, for I do not suggest it to be a busybody, but because you need to mend it for your wife's sake. A misunderstanding, of course, because she cannot bear to be parted from you. And you, it seems, love her dearly, about which I am delighted, since I hold myself in some sort responsible for the marriage.

"Whatever the cause, she has roused now, and we shall keep her with us, but be prepared to work hard and be patient."

And so they began a strict regimen designed to build up Becky's body. "Her mind will heal itself, Overton," the duchess lectured, "but she needs good food, exercise, and sleep. And you must reassure her often. You will do that, will you not?"

Her Grace descended to the kitchen, and her visit inspired the cook to new heights in preparing small, tasty meals for a flagging appetite. Becky was served something tempting to eat every couple of hours. Hugh took her walking in the snow when the sun shone, and up and down the stairs and the halls when the weather closed in. And, on the advice of the duchess, he moved back into their bedchamber.

"She thinks you have moved out because you no longer want her," Her Grace said bluntly. "And if you continue to treat her like a plaster saint, Overton, you are a great fool. She is a woman, and if her needs are blunted at the moment by her sadness, that will not last."

So, Hugh slept spoon-fashion against his wife, but he continued wearing a nightshirt and made no attempt to make love to her.

Aldridge took over the work of the estate and the factories Hugh owned, so Hugh could spend most of his time with Becky, and Aldridge and Sarah reached an understanding to restore him to 'Uncle' status, a privilege Sarah's sisters also deigned to confer.

These activities kept him mostly away from Becky, and he treated her with cautious courtesy when they could not avoid being in the same room, as if she might explode if he ventured any familiarity. "I do not understand, Overton," he said once. "Was it so bad, being with me?"

Hugh could afford to be generous. "Not so bad. She said you were kind, Aldridge, and she will always be grateful."

Aldridge shook his head as if emerging from water, his mouth twisted in disgust. "Grateful! I did not want her to be grateful!" He never mentioned it again, but his puzzled gaze followed Becky when she was not watching.

Twice a day, Hugh and Her Grace took Becky to spend time with the children, and once a day Mrs Goodfellow brought them to her. And not just to be in the same room. "She needs to do things with them," the duchess insisted. "Read them a story, teach them a sewing stitch, or help them on the pianoforte."

Becky resisted only the duchess's last change.

"Did you intend to hire a wet nurse?" Her Grace asked.

Becky paused before she answered, as if she had to come a great distance to hear the question. "No," Hugh answered for her. "She said she would feed our baby herself."

The duchess narrowed her eyes, thinking, then nodded decisively. "It has been not quite two months, and you have fed before."

Becky shook her head. The duchess said nothing more then, but must have spoken to Becky later. Hugh came back from signing correspondence to find the duchess watching benignly, and the wet nurse anxiously, as Belle suckled at Becky's breast.

At first, Belle was as angry at the change as Becky, but the duchess persisted, and Belle was put to each of Becky's breasts every two or three hours for four days.

"It is no use," Becky said. "I have no milk."

But that very afternoon, a delighted Belle came away too replete to suckle from her wet nurse, and an equally delighted duchess reported success.

Chapter Twenty-Two

Becky marked time by Before the Day Aldridge Came, and After. Before, she had been shut off from the world by thick, wavy glass. She could barely see or hear without diligent concentration. And she was too tired to concentrate. So very, very tired.

When she recognised Aldridge, the glass was suddenly much thinner, and the glare of the real world almost destroyed her. She remembered little of the encounter, just terror at the thought of being expelled from her home, then Hugh holding her and saying he loved her. She wanted to tell him that she loved him, but she couldn't make her lips move. She couldn't remember how talking worked.

After The Day, the duchess and Hugh wouldn't let her stay behind the glass. One of them was always there, making her do things. Coaxing her, scolding her, tempting her. Bit by bit, the glass faded, until she could see and hear clearly, though always at one remove.

Aunt Eleanor—that was what Becky was to call her—Aunt Eleanor made her feed the little girl. It was her primary job. The little girl was very pretty, and everyone loved her. Becky thought she should love her too, but she could not summon more than a remote interest.

Love sat somewhere on the other side of the glass. Far away, where she could not touch it. She had loved once. Sarah. Hugh.

Aldridge. Sophie. Emma. The love was still there, but she couldn't reach it.

Soon it would be spring. She would need to plan her gardens. She had promised Hugh roses, and they had been planted in October before she became ill, but other plantings would be needed when the ground warmed a little.

It worried her that Aldridge was still here. Was he waiting for her to fail, so he could take her away? But Hugh said he was waiting for his mother. Hugh said Aldridge was helping him, and that he would go when Her Grace left.

Becky hoped it would be a long time till Her Grace left, because after she went, Becky would be alone with Hugh, and she was so afraid of disappointing him.

Finally, before Becky felt ready, the duchess said they would soon have to move on to the next house in the endless round of Haverford duchy properties. Two days later, Becky stood on the steps with Hugh and the girls, saying goodbye.

Cousin Agatha—if she had another name, Becky hadn't heard it—presented a pale cheek for a kiss. The duchess enfolded Becky in a perfumed embrace and then kissed Hugh and told him to carry on with what he was doing.

Aldridge was the last.

He had been saying goodbye to the children. Now, he came and clasped Hugh's hand and shoulder. "Don't forget, Overton, I've promised you a broken neck if you mistreat her."

"And I, you, if you tease her," Hugh grumbled back. But both men were grinning, so it was just some silly male ritual.

Then Aldridge came to kiss her, and she was grateful for the glass, thin though it now was, because she didn't flinch when he hugged her and pressed a kiss to her cheek. "For you are as close to me as a brother, Overton," he told Hugh fiercely, "which makes Becky my sister."

She managed not to shake, and even to smile, as they entered the carriages, now converted for the thaw by the addition of wheels that had, apparently, travelled in one of the baggage carriages. Hugh must have sensed something, because he squeezed her hand and whispered he was proud of her.

And then they were gone, five splendid carriages in a line down the drive. And she and her family had the house to themselves again.

Little changed, except Hugh had to take up the estate and mill business Aldridge had been doing for him. He liked to have her near, and she would recline on the couch in his study while he worked, and feed the baby, or sew, or read. Sometimes, he discussed his problems with her.

She struggled to believe in the love he professed. How could he love her, when he knew where she had come from? But he continued to reassure her, not just in words, but in his care for her, in the way he organised the household around her weaknesses, rode through the snow to the village to bring her treats, sang and read aloud to keep her entertained. And with every loving word and gesture, the glass between her and the world grew thinner and thinner.

Until one day, when the little girl was feeding. The wet nurse was long gone, no longer needed. A nursemaid brought the baby to her at mealtimes, and the baby liked her meals complete and often. Today, though, she was almost full, and was playing with the nipple instead of feeding.

Becky removed it from the little girl's mouth, and then bumped it against her cheek to encourage her to take it properly.

A gurgle of laughter, and just like that, the glass thinned almost to nothing.

"Belle," she cooed. Such a good name for a beautiful little girl. Belle gurgled again, her lips spread into the most delightful grin. "Belle, Belle, Belle." With each repeat, Becky bumped Belle's cheek, and Belle gurgled. "Look, Hugh, Belle is laughing."

A sound alerted her. He was kneeling a few feet away, tears running down his cheeks. "Hugh? Hugh, my love, what is the matter? What is wrong?"

"You have never called her by her name before." He scooted closer, putting protective gentle arms around them both. "You have never called me your love before, either."

She ducked her head, suddenly shy. "I love you, Hugh. I have loved you for a long time now."

"I love you, Becky. I think I have loved you since the day we met." He lifted her chin, and touched her lips with his, pulling her closer, until they clung together and the baby between them protested.

"I was afraid I had lost you," she told him. "You didn't want me anymore. You wouldn't make love to me. You moved to another room. I was so afraid, so lonely."

"I was afraid I had lost you, Becky. After all you had been through, I was afraid I was just another man who had taken away your freedom. I couldn't bear to come to you, in case you rejected me, or—worse—pretended to want me, but hated me in your heart."

"No. Oh, no, my love. Hush, little Belle, I didn't mean to crush you. Here, kiss her, Hugh."

He kissed his little girl, then his big girl, and made them both giggle.

"It was different with you, Hugh. You promised to love, honour, and cherish me, to worship me with your body. We were not... You did not use me. You never used me. You completed me. We did not couple, we united. We became one."

He kissed her again at that, and Belle wriggled and squealed. "Has she finished her meal?"

Becky nodded, knowing what he was saying. Belle would yell the house down if she was still hungry, and the nursemaid would bring her back, and Becky didn't have to look at Hugh's fall to know what he was hungry for. The glint in his eyes spoke for him, and besides, she was hungry, too.

Hugh took Belle from her, opened the door where the nursemaid waited, handed the baby over with a final kiss, and carefully locked the door.

Then he turned back. "We became one," he agreed. "It is different, is it not? One flesh. Not just two people after pleasure, but pleasure that takes us beyond ourselves into... I don't know how to describe it."

She shook her head. She didn't have the words either, and then suddenly she did. "I have never been united with anyone before you, and you have never been united with anyone before me."

Hugh agreed. "We complete one another." He dropped his voice to that low, melodious tone that vibrated through her pelvis to her most intimate places. "At this moment, I would very much like to unite with you, Rebecca, Baroness Overton."

And Baroness Overton welcomed her baron home, as the last of the glass between her and the world disappeared entirely.

Part Three
1813

Chapter Twenty-Three

Lancashire

If Becky had been asked to pick her favourite times, she would have been hard pressed to choose, but this would be on the list: lying in her husband's arms after their passion was spent, not sleeping, not talking, just being.

She smiled against Hugh's chest. Their neighbours would be shocked that they came straight up to their bedchamber after breaking their fast, that 'going for a sleep after Church' rarely involved sleep, even if the children believed the comfortable lie.

Given that a Sunday afternoon in bed had been the Overtons' habit for close to three years, the neighbours undoubtedly did know. For what the servants knew, would sooner or later be known through the village.

"Becky, I've been thinking," Hugh said.

"Are you sure you have sufficient energy for that, my love?" she teased.

He dug his fingers into her ribs, making her wriggle and squeal. "You stole it from me, you witch, and shortly, I shall take it back, see if I don't." The thigh she brushed against his groin confirmed his energy was returning fast, and they had the whole afternoon ahead of them. Becky smiled again.

But Hugh's mind wasn't on lovemaking, whatever his body thought. "I want you to come down to London with me, once the roads are passable. We'll take the girls with us, too."

London? She propped herself up on her elbows to reach the scar that snaked through his hair and ended a bare inch above one eyebrow. "I thought we agreed you would not attend Parliament this year. You are still recovering!"

In one easy movement he reversed their positions, tipping her and rolling with her so she was caged by his body, his thighs enclosing hers and his forearms holding his weight so she wasn't crushed. "My wife tells me I'm much improved," and he captured her mouth in a passionate kiss that had her lifting her hips to meet him.

But he rolled again, bringing her back against his side.

"My accident is why we must go, Becky."

Again, she pushed back to have his whole face clearly in view. "The headaches? Are you feeling worse? Yes, we must consult a doctor! Hugh, you should have said."

"Nothing like that, my love. The headaches are nearly gone, thanks to all the powers of Heaven. And I'm fit again. But I nearly died, Becky. When the bridge went down, when I was swept away..."

Becky shuddered and pressed herself closer. She would burrow inside if she could. Thank God his foot had become caught in the stirrup. A thousand thanks that the horse had pulled him from the river. When they'd found him at first light, more than three miles downstream from the collapsed bridge, he was still hanging, attached to the wet and shivering horse by one booted foot.

Whether it was trying to protect its master, as Hugh claimed, or just unwilling to drag dead weight didn't matter. He was still alive. And she managed to keep him that way through both the head injury and the fever contracted that long, cold night.

Oddly enough, that interminable time of managing his affairs while watching by his bedside had given her confidence she had always lacked. With him unconscious, she was without his careful protection, his constant reassurance. She conferred with his land agent, even fought with his factory manager and prevailed. She needed to be strong for Hugh, for their daughters, for the household and the barony—and she found she was strong, the last of the old nightmares laid to rest at last.

"I nearly died, Becky, and it frightens me."

She frowned, then. Frightened? He was a grown man, and had been a soldier. But he was still talking. "I am frightened for you and the girls, if something happens to me before they are grown."

She worried, too. The land would go to the Crown, along with the title. Hugh's will left her the cotton mill in Liverpool. The income was down, as the long war against Napoleon drew to an end, but it would be enough for her and the girls to live on, especially since her settlement from Aldridge was untouched.

It would not be enough to establish all four girls in the life that Hugh intended for them, though. As daughters of a baron, they could expect to make marriages in the gentry. But a baron's relict with an obscure past and no landed relatives, making her income from trade, would be a far less attractive parent-in-law, in a class that married for family advantage. Only a very large marriage portion would overcome such murky roots.

"Then live, Hugh," she told him, fiercely. "You must live to see them grown and established."

He pulled her head back against his chest and kissed the top of her head. "I know, my love. I know. But we must have a plan."

"If only I had given you a son!" she mourned.

"I love our Belle, beloved," he protested. "You know that. I wouldn't change a hair of her head, let alone make a boy of her."

She shook her head, not comforted.

"So," Hugh took up the thread again, "that's why I want to talk to Aldridge."

Becky felt the blood drain from her head, and for a moment the world receded, as if sounds, sights, smells, touch, were filtered through a long, long tunnel.

"Aldridge?" Her voice came out in a squeak, and Hugh tipped her head back to see her face.

"Becky? Are you feeling ill? Becky, you look as white as a sheet. Here, my love, lie back against the pillows. What is it? Does something hurt?"

Her heart. Her heart hurt.

"What..." Her voice caught and she had to make another attempt. "Why do you want to speak to Aldridge?"

Hugh's anxious look cleared. "Not, foolish wife, what you obviously suspect! Becky, Becky, how could you think I would let that randy hell-spawn have at you?"

"You need a son, Hugh." But she could breathe again, and the vice around her chest loosened.

"Not so much I'd ask my wife to whore herself." He put a finger to her lip as she opened it to speak, obviously guessing what she was about to say. "No pasts, Becky, remember? One man for you, and one woman for me, as long as we both shall live. Here. Let me remind you."

She gave herself to him with a certain desperation, forgetting everything in the moment, but afterwards, he returned to the topic. "I thought Aldridge might be willing to stand as guardian and sponsor to the girls. If anything happens to me."

"He's a bachelor, Hugh," and one with a reputation that would not benefit their daughters.

"With Haverford's health as it is, Aldridge will be duke by the time they're ready to be presented," Hugh insisted. "He'll have to take a wife then. And his mother will support them, I'm sure. I thought I could sound out Aldridge, and you could talk to the duchess. She likes you."

Becky thought about it. Hugh made good sense. Yes. They would go to London.

Chapter Twenty-Four

The Duchess of Haverford's ball was the usual crush. Hugh managed one set with Becky, then the Earl of Chirbury asked her to dance, so Hugh retaliated by sweeping Lady Chirbury into the set. They had a number of friends here tonight, and Hugh did his duty by the wives, as Becky danced with the husbands. Aldridge had still not returned to town, so his mother said, though she'd hoped to see him tonight.

Hugh was resting between sets, halfway through the evening, when he caught a glimpse of Aldridge, half-hidden in an alcove, watching the dancers. Hugh grinned. He shouldn't tell Aldridge about Becky's bright idea from that very afternoon. Becky would be furious. He couldn't resist, though. The joke was too funny not to share with its butt.

He made his way unobtrusively around the edge of the floor.

"Overton." Aldridge greeted him with a nod, without looking. Hugh followed the direction of his gaze. A group of debutantes, all in white, none much older than Sophie and Sarah. The thought made him shudder, which drew Aldridge's attention.

"They're not that bad, surely?" Aldridge asked. "Unless you're expected to marry one, of course." He grimaced, a quick twist of the lips.

"Sophie and Sarah will be out there in three or four years," Hugh said baldly. "Antonia, too, I would remind you. All these men looking them over like horses at Tattersall's..." He shuddered again, more artistically this time.

"Three or four years?" Aldridge sounded startled. "I suppose you are right. Good God!" He turned back to his perusal. "No wonder they all look far too young for me. I could easily have been a father at seventeen or eighteen. Some of them really are young enough to be my daughters.

"I'll have to choose someone, you know. Not yet, but soon." From his tone, he might have been asked to organise his own execution.

"A duke must have a son," Hugh acknowledged.

"Yes. And a duchess, preferably." Aldridge's eyes shifted, and Hugh's widened as he picked up the new target.

"One of the Winderfield twins? Really?"

"No chance. You know my father tried to have their uncle's marriage declared invalid and his children bastards?"

The sensation of 1812 would have been the sudden reappearance and ascension to the ducal title of the long-lost second son of Charles Winderfield, sixth Duke of Winshire. Except the news was greatly overshadowed by his reputation as a robber king in the mountains of Central Asia and the large family of sons and daughters—half-Asian sons and daughters—he brought home to England with him. All seasoned warriors, men and women alike.

"He will not consider anyone from my family now. Besides, with my reputation? My well-deserved reputation? Her many cousins will separate me from my bollocks, if I so much as breathe in her direction."

"They could do it, too," Hugh acknowledged.

Aldridge's huff of laughter was not much amused. "I will need to choose a bride without male relatives." He had not taken his eyes from the woman on the far side of the room.

"None of which would stop me, if Lady Charlotte didn't despise the ground I walk upon." Aldridge said this last to himself, so quietly that Hugh had to strain to hear it.

"Good God. You're serious about her."

Aldridge shook his head. "No point in thinking it, Overton. They call her Saint Charlotte, did you know? Charity work... sworn off marriage... thinks men are oafs, and I'm the worst of them." Hugh's friend resumed a devil-may-care mask, settling it over himself like armour. "And she is not wrong, of course. Nice to see you back on your feet, Overton. How is Becky? Your daughters?"

"All well. I wanted to talk to you about them, as a matter of fact. I have a favour to ask."

"Name it," Aldridge said, carelessly. He had stepped out to scoop up two glasses of wine from a passing servant, and now handed one to Hugh.

"I nearly died last year when that bridge collapsed," Hugh said, "which would have left Becky and the girls... you know all about it, Aldridge. I don't have a son to inherit."

Aldridge stopped with his drink halfway to his lips, his eyes suddenly devoid of expression.

"No." Hugh shoved the idea away with both hands, wrinkling his nose in disgust. "Honestly, what is wrong with people? No, Aldridge, I am not asking you to bed my wife."

"I would rather you didn't." Aldridge took a healthy gulp, as if suddenly thirsty. "Neither you nor Becky would ever forgive me if I agreed." His wicked grin appeared again. "And I would be sorely tempted to agree."

That was an interesting perspective. Hugh and Becky had agreed infidelity—even negotiated infidelity in the cause of the family's future—would injure the precious bond they'd forged, but they hadn't considered how they'd feel about Aldridge afterwards. "It is not going to happen," Hugh said. "I wouldn't suggest it, and Becky wouldn't agree. Although..." The afternoon's conversation with Becky set him chortling all over again. "Becky did have another idea for achieving the same end."

"Do I want to know?"

"Probably not." Hugh could barely speak for laughing. "One of her... Becky used to know someone... She remembered this instrument the doctors used to clean out..." He slapped Aldridge on the shoulder and gripped tight, trying to control his laughter enough to finish. "He was convinced washing his insides regularly was good for him."

Aldridge frowned, clearly not seeing the picture. "Washing his insides?"

"A clyster syringe. Have you heard of it?"

A shake of the head, but Aldridge was looking suspicious, and well he might. Hugh went off into another paroxysm of laughter.

"The doctors fill it up with water, introduce the tube to the patient's posterior, up goes water, and down comes... well, you can imagine."

"Sounds uncomfortable. What on earth has that to do with you having a son?"

Hugh, doing his best not to laugh again, told him. "It occurred to Becky that the same tool could be used to deliver a man's seed into a woman's passage, without, er... bed sport."

Aldridge nodded. "I suppose there's no reason why—Blistering hell, she didn't think I...? Damn it, Overton, you're my friend, but..."

Hugh couldn't help it. The idea of the Merry Marquis, the consummate lover, Society's darling, his charms rejected, sent off alone to commune with a clyster syringe... And Aldridge's reaction just as horrified as Hugh expected. He had to laugh. Aldridge, his frown so deep his brows nearly met, was decidedly disgruntled, which only made Hugh laugh harder.

He wasn't aware of Becky coming up beside him until she slipped her arm into his, which sobered him quickly enough. "Hugh, you did not..." she said. Then, looking at Aldridge, "He did, didn't he?"

"Told me your clever little plan? Yes. Thank you, Becky, for the compliment to my progenerative powers. How delightful to be appreciated."

Becky scoffed at his cold tone. "Do not be silly, Aldridge. It is a great compliment we have paid you, seen in a certain light. Anyway, Hugh said it was a foolish idea, and you would be insulted." She glared at her husband. "So, why he told you, I do not know."

"Because he would be insulted," Hugh muttered.

One could always rely on Aldridge's sense of humour , even when the joke was on him. A smile returned to lurk in one corner of his mouth. "To put me in my place, my dear Becky, firmly in the distant past. For which I do not blame him. But poor strategy, Lord Overton, to annoy a person from whom you want a favour. You have come to ask a favour, did you not say?"

—•——⟨❀⟩——•—

Chapter Twenty-Five

When Aldridge sought her out the following afternoon, the Duchess of Haverford was resting from her exertions over the ball, by planning the next entertainment. She had her companion, her secretary, and three of the servants on the hop: writing guest lists, hunting out a fabric from the attic and a china pattern from the depths of the scullery that she was certain would go together in a Frost Fair theme; searching through her invitations to pick a date that would not clash with entertainments she wished to attend; leafing through the menus of previous parties to decide on food "that will not disgrace us, dear Aldridge, for one would not wish to do things in a harum-scarum fashion."

"May I have a moment, Mama?" Aldridge asked. "It can wait if you wish."

"Not at all, Aldridge. My dears, you all have jobs to do. I will be with my son. Aldridge, darling, shall we take a walk in the picture gallery? Very chilly, today, I am sure, but I will wrap up warm and the exercise will be good for us, do you not think? Ah, thank you, my dear." She stepped back into the cloak Aldridge took from the waiting maid, and let him settle it on her shoulders.

"Now, my dear, tell me how Mama can help."

Aldridge waited, though, until they were alone in the picture gallery, a great hall of a place thirty feet wide, twenty tall, and a hundred and twenty long. With the doors at each end shut, they could speak in private.

"Mama, Overton has asked me to look after his wife and daughters, if he dies before the girls are grown and married."

Her Grace nodded. "And you have agreed, of course, dear? I will present the girls, in any case. Or your wife, if you have done your duty by then."

Aldridge ignored his mother's increasingly less subtle insistence. He would marry when he must and not before.

"Of course I have agreed, Mama. But I am wondering if something more might be done."

The Duchess tapped her index finger against slightly pursed lips, her eyes distant.

"Something more might always be done. Have you an idea of what?"

Aldridge watched her closely. "It is not unknown for a daughter to inherit a barony."

His mother blinked slowly as she considered the idea. Her answer was slow and contemplative.

"Only the old ones, dear, and if there is no son. But Overton is a relatively new peerage. The Restoration, I believe? And if his Letters Patent allowed female inheritance, he would have said."

"Letters Patent can be changed, Mama. They did it for the first Marlborough."

"Over a century ago, Aldridge, and I have never heard of it being done again."

She fell silent, her eyes unfocused in thought. "But it does seem a pity our little Belle cannot be a baroness."

"I wondered if perhaps you asked His Grace..." Aldridge began.

The duchess shook her head. "It will not serve, Aldridge. He is not popular in the House, as you know, and the Prince Regent... well, Aldridge, suffice to say, the information I might use to persuade His Grace to support the Overtons has set the Prince Regent firmly against him."

Aldridge was aware his mother occasionally compelled his father to an action the duke was disinclined to take, by threatening to disclose something he wished to keep hidden. She used the power rarely, both because each confrontation widened the gap in their marriage, and because very few scandals were large enough to discommode the Duke of Haverford, who cared little for the opinions of others.

"What piece of information is this, Mama?"

"I cannot tell you, Aldridge. But the Prince Regent is most unhappy. How he found out the Grenfords are trespassing on his preserves, I have not been informed..."

No. Surely not. Aldridge had a sudden mental picture of the beautiful woman currently in the prince's keeping, laughing with Aldridge at corpulent elderly men who thought they could keep a young woman satisfied. Laughing with him while occupied in... No... She hadn't, had she? With his father, too?

"Really, Aldridge," his mother said. "You did not think you were being original, did you? I daresay the young lady is just securing her future, and who can blame her? You are very nice, dear. Rich, and by all accounts, virile. But you are not yet the Duke of Haverford. And you are certainly not the Prince Regent."

Aldridge felt slightly ill. One woman wanted nothing to do with him; one wanted his seed but not his body; one was happy to share him with his... no. He could not think of it.

"The Letters Patent, Mama," he said firmly. "Could we get enough support without His Grace? Or even against His Grace, if he insists?"

"I may be able to help, dear." Aldridge's mother had an encyclopaedic memory for the *ton* and all its major and minor branches, a network of contacts developed over a lifetime, and the analytical mind of a general. "Yes. That might do very nicely. And then... Yes. We will do it. Aldridge, order the carriage. We are going to make a call on the Duke of Winshire."

A call on Lady Charlotte's uncle? Was Mama serious?

"The Duke of... Winshire, Mama? He will certainly not help us and may even not receive us."

The duchess just smiled, her eyes far away as if watching something pleasant. "The carriage, Aldridge."

Chapter Twenty-Six

On the day of the final vote, Aldridge and his mother waited with Becky in the Overtons' town-house. The numbers were tight. The vote could go either way.

They had spent weeks lobbying those who would be considering the Duke of Winshire's bill to change the Letters Patent. Becky had visited the wives, mothers, and sisters of every member of the House of Lords, and many of those in the House of Commons, accompanied by Her Grace, or the Countess of Chirbury, or Winshire's niece the Dowager Marchioness of Barchester. Overton, Aldridge, and Winshire himself canvassed the menfolk. And Her Grace of Haverford directed all, keeping track of the supporters, the waverers, and the adamantly opposed.

Overton had taken his seat today, of course. His presence might convince some of the waverers, though he would abstain from the vote.

"If the bill passes, it still needs the Prince Regent's seal," Becky said.

"Winshire says he is in favour," Aldridge said.

"Even knowing he will lose the barony?" Becky asked, as she had a dozen times before.

Her Grace repeated again. "A small barony, far in the future, when Overton and His Royal Highness are both dead, compared to a large and valuable present from the Orient, here and now."

"Rugs, lamps, and furniture from His Grace of Winshire," Becky agreed. "He has been very generous. And I'm grateful, too, that His Grace of Haverford has withdrawn his opposition."

Aldridge and Her Grace exchanged glances. Aldridge had no idea what his mother had said, but His Grace had taken himself off to Margate, after telling his supporters to vote in favour or abstain.

"You and Winshire are old friends, seemingly," Aldridge said to Her Grace, expecting the comment to be ignored, as it had been every other time he'd made it these past weeks.

But Her Grace surprised him. "It is not a secret, Aldridge. Enough people must remember. We met when I was seventeen. He danced with me at my first ball, and from that moment, I had eyes only for him, and he for me.

"But he was a second son. My father accepted Haverford and rejected James... Lord James Winderfield, he was then. James, foolish man, challenged Haverford to a duel. Swords. They were both wounded, and it was thought Haverford might die. Lord James's father sent him overseas. There was a great scandal."

She paused. Aldridge thought she had finished speaking.

"James... we were told he had been killed by bandits. So I married Haverford, and I have you and Jonathan, Aldridge, dear, and you have both been a great joy to me, so no doubt it has all been for the best."

And now the rejected second son had come home and was Winshire. No wonder he and his successful rival had barely spoken to one another these past two years.

The door was flung open, and they didn't have to ask Overton for the news; it was written boldly on his face.

"We won!" Aldridge said, beaming, but Overton disagreed.

"You won," he said to the duchess, and forgot himself enough to give her a great hug. "Thank you, thank you." He then recollected himself and stepped back, shifting from foot to foot as he apologised. "I beg your pardon, Your Grace."

The duchess, though, was flushed and beaming. "Not at all, dear Overton. I quite think of you as a son, you know. Which is to my advantage, of course, since if you and Becky are my adopted children, then your daughters are my grandchildren, just as it should be. And our dear Belle will be a baroness." She smiled with great satisfaction. "Who would have guessed that, Becky, my love, when we first met?"

"Not I, Aunt Eleanor, certainly," Becky returned. She had only part of her attention on the duchess, stealing looks at Overton, who was not even pretending to listen, simply grinning at his wife like a fool.

The duchess laughed at them both. "Go and kiss your husband, child. It does my heart good to see you together."

Becky needed no further encouragement, and she and Overton were soon locked in an embrace that did Aldridge's heart no good at all. It made him maudlin. He'd need to be either drunk or properly bedded, and soon. Both, probably.

He started when his mother touched his arm. "You did a good thing, Aldridge, putting the two of them together. Overton needed her, and she needed him. You did well."

He smiled, then. Yes. Mama was right, as always. Overton and Becky were good for one another, and his daughter—his goddaughter, he corrected himself, careful even in his thoughts— would grow up heiress to a barony. And all because Becky had dared to dream, and Aldridge had made her dream come true.

Suddenly much happier, he grinned. He had a dream of his own, the same one Becky had outlined for him long ago. If he dared reach for it.

Meanwhile, the world was full of beautiful women just waiting to be pleased—or at least pleasured—and the Merry Marquis was the man for the job.

Epilogue

Home was best.

London had been a triumph, and Becky had thoroughly enjoyed the house party at Longford Court afterwards, as had the girls. The weather was glorious, the schoolroom on holiday, and the visiting families mustered nearly two score of children between them. The nursery floor was crowded to overflowing, and Lady Daisy Redepenning was promoted to a second-floor bedchamber which she shared with Sophie, Sarah and Antonia.

Indeed, Sophie and Sarah were upstairs this minute writing letters to those dear friends. And Belle had wept when parted from Lady Mary Redepenning, a spare three months her junior. But home was best. The girls had erupted from the house this morning to rush around the garden, reclaiming their favourite play places. Becky sympathised. She might not shout and run, but she found herself moving around the house, running her hand along the back of the chairs in the parlour, reordering the flowers in the bowl in the hall, straightening an ornament here and a cushion there.

The parlour needed no more attention than any other room, but she twitched a fringe on a tablecloth, shaped the carvings at the side of the mantelpiece with her finger, and tucked a rose more firmly into the bowl of flowers on the sideboard.

Becky was startled by an unexpected noise. Snuffling behind the curtain proved to be a miserable little girl, curled up on the cushioned seat in the deep window embrasure.

"Belle, baby, whatever is the matter?" She swept her daughter onto her lap. At three and a half, Lady Isabelle Overton normally strongly objected to being called 'baby,' and Becky measured the child's distress by her willingness to overlook her mother's slip of the tongue.

"The big girls told me not to bother them, Mama," Belle complained, "and I miss Mary."

"We shall invite her to visit, dearest. And when you learn your letters you will write to her."

"But that will be forever," wailed the child.

"I know! I shall find you some paper and you shall draw her a picture!"

When Hugh joined them they were at her desk in his study, Becky leafing through a pile of correspondence, Belle working intently on a drawing for her friend that looked like a collection of misshapen blotches, but was really, so Belle said, an image of the carriage that had brought them home.

"Becky, my love, I thought I'd ride out. Just for a look around." Becky smiled. Hugh, too, felt the need to circle his estate and reassure himself that home was still home.

"Take Belle?" she suggested. Lord Chirbury rode out most days with his son and heir. The Earl's tenants had known their future lord and master since he was old enough to perch on the saddle before his father, and at nearly seven, young Viscount Longford already expressed opinions about the wool clip and the wheat harvest.

"The Overton tenants should get to know their future lady, Hugh."

Hugh chuckled, and ran an affectionate hand over his daughter's head, who brushed it away, intent on her drawing. "She need not worry about the estate, Becky. We shall find her a good husband, when the time comes."

What a typically male thing to say. "Belle will be the baroness, Hugh. In her own right. She will be responsible for passing on the title and the estate, intact and improved, to her children. Belle. Not her husband."

Hugh looked wary, as well he might. "I only meant..."

"Do you think women are less competent than men?"

"No, but..."

"Or less intelligent?"

Hugh shook his head. "Definitely not."

"More fragile, perhaps?" she asked, sweetly. "Or do you believe your daughter less capable than Lord Chirbury's son?"

Hugh spread his hands in defeat.

"Very well. I surrender. You are right, heart of my heart. You are the least fragile person I know. And you and I working together run this estate and the mill better than ever I could on my own. We shall train our daughter. Though, what the tenants will make of it, I do not know." He turned to the little girl.

"Lady Isabelle Overton, is today a good day for your first lesson in how to be a baroness?"

Belle looked up at the use of her full name, eyes slowly refocusing. "Papa?" she asked, not sure what he was asking.

"Would you care to ride with your Papa, my sweet?" he asked.

With the little girl on one arm, Hugh stopped to give his wife a fierce hug. "We will not go far today, Becky."

He brought Belle home two hours later, tired but starry eyed, chattering so fast about what she and Papa had done and seen, and who they had met, Becky could only understand one word in three.

"Belle seemed to enjoy herself," she said to Hugh, as she finished dressing for dinner, and he lounged against the wall of her dressing room to watch.

"We visited the Turners and the Wilsons, and we met up with Mrs Dean and her son bringing in the cows. They love her already, Becky. They all knew about the Letters Patent, and they are as happy as we."

She smiled at his image in the mirror. "I am so glad, Hugh."

"Do you know why?" She turned to face him, and shook her head.

"Turner told me. He said she is the image of you, Becky, and if she grows up to be just like you, then Overton is safe for another generation."

Becky's smile widened into a grin, and she held her hands out to her husband, blinking away happy tears.

He bridged the gap for a kiss that lingered and deepened, leaving her breathless. The physical attraction between them was never far below the surface. The lightest touch, even a look, reminded them of the joys they found in one another. Another kiss and they would be late for dinner. And not for the first time. The cook would not be amused.

Hugh's next words sealed the cook's fate. "I agree with Turner. I hope Belle grows up to be just like you. I am so proud to be your husband, Becky."

Becky opened her arms to her baron. There would be other dinners.

THE END

Please consider taking a moment to write a review of *A Baron for Becky*—even a sentence or two. Honest reviews help other readers to choose books they will enjoy, and help writers to gain visibility in a very cluttered book market.

News and special offers

Subscribe to my newsletter for information about publication dates and more. As a subscriber, you will receive advance information about release dates and special price periods as well as exclusive, subscriber-only special offers. I send a newsletter no more than six times a year.

Subscribe to my newsletter

Acknowledgements

Thank you to my beta readers: Carol, Sue, Jocelyn, Tray-Ci, Sandy, Angie, Cathy, Jo, Jocelyn, Jan, and Doreen. Your comments and suggestions led to many changes that made the book stronger.

Thank you to Catherine Curzon, who played a story game with me and created the germ of the idea. My Becky is no Mrs A., but Catherine will recognise one or two of the events that prevented Aldridge from consummating his desires before he arrived in London with Becky, and the concept of a man brokering a marriage for his mistress also came out of our game.

Thank you to fellow Bluestocking Belles, especially Mari and Carol, who let me ramble on about plot ideas, talked me through holdups and hiccups, and encouraged me when I panicked.

Mari also worked with me through multiple rounds of editing, fitting this into a tight timeframe without a word of complaint.

As always, a special thank you to my husband, without whose support I would probably forget to eat when I get stuck in the early nineteenth century, and to my sister Sue, who is always my first reader.

Bluestocking Belles

If you love historical romance, then you'll love the Bluestocking Belles.

We're a group of Regency romance authors providing high-quality, entertaining novels of many different styles—and heat levels—for readers who love the Regency world as much as we do.

Our blog, *The Teatime Tattler*, publishes at least twice weekly, with exclusive news, interviews, and scandals set in and around the Regency. We host a monthly book club. The Bluestocking Bookshop is a Facebook Group where writers and readers create impromptu Regency storylines as you watch.

The Belles have committed to publishing at least one box set per year, the first in time for the 2015 holiday season. Proceeds from the Belles' joint projects go to the Malala Fund, to support education for young bluestockings around the world.

Find the Bluestocking Belles online:
www.BluestockingBelles.com/
Friend us on Facebook:
www.facebook.com/BellesinBlue
Follow us on Twitter:
@BellesInBlue

Malala Fund

The Bluestocking Belles have chosen the Malala Fund as the charity we support, and to which we donate communal royalties. Periodically, we take on projects intended to directly support this cause, which exemplifies our personal values and intentions: the right of girls and women to do whatever they choose with their lives.

For more information about the Malala Fund and the founder, Malala Yousafzai, winner of the 2014 Nobel Peace Prize, go to www.Malala.org

Published books

Candle's Christmas Chair

When Viscount Avery comes to see the best invalid chair maker in the southwest of England he does not expect to find Minerva Bradshaw, the woman who rejected him three years earlier. Or did she? Older and wiser, he wonders if there is more to the story.

For three years, Min Bradshaw has remembered the handsome guardsman who courted her for her fortune. She didn't expect to see him in her workshop, and she certainly doesn't intend to let him fool her again. Even if he is handsomer and more charming than ever.

Farewell to Kindness: Book 1 of *The Golden Redepennings*

Rede believes he has turned his back on compassion and mercy. But he is distracted from the hunt for those who killed his family by his growing attraction for Anne. His feelings for her are a weakness. Or could they instead be a source of strength?

Anne protected her family from scandal and worse by changing their identity. Can she keep Rede from discovering who they are? Can she give him her heart without trusting him? Can she trust him when he has closed himself off to love?

When their enemies link forces, Rede and Anne must face the past in order to claim the future.

(Excerpt below)

Coming in 2016

A Raging Madness: Book 2 of *The Golden Redepennings*

When Alex Redepenning comes to the funeral of Ella Melville's mother-in-law, he does not expect Ella to turn up in his bedroom, seeking help. They have met twice in the last ten years: once when she married one of Alex's fellow officers under dubious circumstances, and once when she arrived too late to attend her husband's deathbed. They parted rancorously each time.

After what he said at their last meeting Ella had hoped never to see Alex again, but an overheard clandestine conversation leaves her with nowhere else to turn.

Danger follows them; Ella's in-laws want her confined to Bedlam, and someone wants Alex dead. Joining forces is sensible. If they can survive their enemies, the only risk is to their hearts.

Encouraging Prudence: Book 1 of *The Virtue Sisters*

David and Prudence, operatives for one of England's shadowy spymasters, are sent to investigate a spying ring that blackmails aristocrats for access to secrets. Both find friends and family too close to the investigation for comfort, including David's brothers (the legitimate sons of the duke who sired him).

After what happened last time they worked together, both David and Prue are determined they won't surrender to the strong physical attraction between them. They're professionals. They'll find the blackmailer and the spy behind him, and part again.

It is not until the danger that lurks in Bristol takes Prue that David realises what she means to him. But finding her again may mean choosing between his country and his woman.

Lord Danwood's Dilemma: Book 1 of *Danwood's Daughters*

On inheriting from a distant cousin who had no sons, Anthony Simon Wentworth, the new Earl of Danwood, finds his predecessor had a unique way of stacking the odds so that a grandson of his would one day be Earl. Tony has inherited the title and the entailed land, but has no way to support it. To win the non-entailed wealth, he must marry and have a child with one of the former Lord Danwood's eight daughters.

The legitimate daughters live at Danwood Castle in the North York Moors, and in a nearby coastal village, the former Earl had a second family by his wife's sister. The eldest daughter, Sophia, keeps life on an even keel for her two sisters and two brothers, despite a lack of money and the general disapproval of the village.

Tony thinks he will settle the by-blows somewhere out of sight and marry one of the legitimate daughters. But he is distracted by the need to rescue his baseborn relatives from smugglers, the coastguard, an angry farmer or two, the machinations of their aunt—and his growing appreciation of the feisty Sophia.

Farewell to Kindness—excerpt

Prologue

London, 1801

George was drunk. But not nearly drunk enough. He still saw his young friend's dying eyes everywhere. In half-caught glimpses of strangers reflected in windows along Bond Street, under the hats of coachmen that passed him along the silent streets to Bedford Square, in the flickering lamps that shone pallidly against the cold London dawn as he stumbled up the steps to his front door.

They followed his every waking hour: hot, angry, hate-filled eyes that had once been warm with admiration.

He drank to forget, but all he could do was remember.

One more flight of stairs, then through the half-open door to his private sitting-room, already reaching for the waiting decanter of brandy as he crossed the floor.

He had a glass of oblivion halfway to his lips before he noticed the painting.

It stood on an easel, lit by a carefully arranged tree of candles. George's own face was illuminated—the golden shades of his hair, his intensely blue eyes. The artist had captured his high cheekbones and sculpted jaw. "One of London's most beautiful men," he'd been called.

He stalked to the easel, moving with great care to avoid spilling his drink.

Yes. The artist had talent. Who could have given him such a thing?

As he bent forward to look at it more closely, something whipped past his face. With a solid thunk, an arrow struck the painting, to stand quivering between the painted eyes.

George dropped his glass as he started backwards, flailing to keep his balance, and trying to turn at the same time to see behind him. There. In the shadows behind the door. A silent gowned figure with another arrow already nocked and ready to fly.

"Who are you? What do you want?" The drink thickened his voice. "If I shout, I'll wake the whole household."

"The household are all either below stairs or well above. And you will have, at most, one shout before I put this arrow between your eyes. I have demonstrated I can." It was a woman's voice, low and determined.

George glanced back at the arrow, and swallowed.

"You won't shoot me. You're a woman."

"I will shoot you with pleasure, if I must," the woman said. "But shooting you is not my first choice."

He pulled himself straight, glaring. "You won't get away with this. Don't you know who I am?"

"Do you not know who I am? I am the woman you owe a future to. And I mean to collect. You will give me either my future or my revenge."

He took a step towards her, leaning forward to peer into the shadows. She lifted the arrow point fractionally, saying, "No closer!"

He stopped. "I don't even know who you are. What crime have I supposedly committed? What do you want from me?"

She gestured to the chair by the fire with the point of her arrow. "Sit," she commanded, and once he'd complied, she moved out into the light. "Now do you know who I am?"

She looked familiar. But no, George couldn't place her. He shook his head.

She was silent for a moment. When she spoke, her voice was stiff with outrage. "Perhaps I can help your memory. You killed my brother. You sank my reputation into the gutter. You left me with sisters to care for and a baby to raise. Remember me now, guardian?" She sounded like a heroine from a Gothic novel. Come to think of it, it was a Gothic novel, and he was the villain.

"You're Stockie's sister." His voice was resigned. Really, he might have guessed that Stockie would find a corporeal way to haunt him. "But wait; you don't understand. I didn't mean to kill your brother. I was drunk. I misfired. You can't blame me for that."

She said nothing.

"He challenged me. I had to meet him. It was a matter of honour. I didn't mean to kill him."

She looked at him coldly. "I am not here to discuss the past. I want somewhere to live; somewhere in the country where you do not go. On the table at your elbow is a letter to your land steward in Gloucestershire. It tells him to give life tenancy of a suitable cottage to me and my sisters, with sufficient land to feed us. Read it. Sign it. Then toss it over here to me."

George frowned, drawing his brows together. "But Selby said he'd take care of everything."

"My cousin told you what he had planned?"

"That he would find you a place to live until the baby was born, and make sure there was no scandal."

"That he would lock us two older girls away, sell the baby, and marry our little sister to his loathsome son."

George had met the son. He wouldn't put a dog he didn't like in that boy's care. He had given her dying brother his promise that he'd leave the girls alone, but surely Stockie would expect him to come to their rescue?

"Then let me see to it. I am your guardian. And your trustee."

"We do not want you. And we do not want our cousin and his plans. Just leave us alone."

He examined his feet, ashamed to meet her scornful eyes. "I didn't mean to hurt anybody. I was drunk. I wasn't thinking."

"Sign the papers."

"I thought... I told the governess to meet me. In the dark, I just assumed... "

"Sign the papers," she repeated.

"I am sorry, you know."

"'Sorry' does nothing. If you are sorry, then sign the papers."

He reached for the papers; began to read.

"And do not think to renege on the bargain," she went on. "A cottage and some money for us to live on to make it possible for me to look after my family, and I will go away and be quiet about what you did. But if you try to take back the cottage, or to harm any one of us, I will make sure the whole of society knows.

"Do not think I am afraid to speak," she added, as he opened his mouth to tell her she had nothing to fear. "You have made certain our place in society is lost. Take away what little we have left, and I will take you down with me. I know society blames the innocent maid rather than the rake that ruins her, but they will care that she was your ward; they will care that you killed another ward, her own brother."

"Look, I've signed." George rolled the papers and tossed them at her feet. "You said you want money. I... I'll give you a letter for my bank. How much?"

She gestured with her head towards the purse he'd dropped as he came in the door. "What is in that?"

"My winnings from tonight."

"It looked heavy."

"I had a run of luck. Three thousand guineas, more or less."

"I will take it."

George frowned. "Three thousand? Will that be enough?"

"With the cottage, it will be enough. I don't want anything else from you except your absence from our lives."

"I'm still your guardian."

"For the sake of us all, I suggest you forget that. I will look after my sisters now."

He couldn't meet her eyes. He studied his hands, instead. What if he broke his promise to Stockie?

"I could marry you. That would fix things."

Stockie's sister—damn him if he could remember her name—shook her head, looking at him as if she found him loathsome, then said, "Take off all your clothes."

George gave a surprised laugh, one that turned automatically to a leer. "Sweetheart..."

She drew the bowstring that she'd allowed to relax, re-aiming the arrow at his heart. "All your clothes. Now. Take them off... Gather them together... Good. Now throw them out of the window."

Even through the drink, even at the point of an arrow, the thought of being naked in front of this woman caused a little stirring in the portion of his anatomy that had caused the problem. Her face was fiery red. Showing and then undoing his corset was embarrassing. More and more, in his casual liaisons, George was disrobing in the dark. His mistresses, of course, were paid to make no comment about his growing paunch.

He obeyed her instructions, opening the window and leaning out to drop his clothes. The bundle unfurled and spilled down the front steps into the street. Behind him, he heard the door shut, and the key turn in the lock.

Without much hope, George tried the door, and then the door to the bedroom. Both were locked. She hadn't missed a trick. He couldn't get out on his own. The servants were too far away to hear him. And, without his clothes, he could not try to attract attention from the street.

He wished her every success. Perhaps another letter to his land agent, instructing that she be given every care? No. That would only draw attention to her. Better let her handle it.

It was chilly in the room. It could be hours before the valet tried the door. But he had most of a decanter of brandy to keep the cold and the ghost at bay.

Perhaps, if he stayed away from Longford and kept the girls' secrets, his betrayed friend would stop haunting him?

Chapter one

London, 1807

Stephen Edward John Redepenning, 8th Earl of Chirbury, took up yet another paper from a stack that never seemed to get any smaller and brandished it at the portrait of his predecessor.

"You self-centred prick, George. Couldn't you have dealt with some of this before topping yourself?"

The portrait was an odd decorative choice.

It was fine enough, showing the golden hair and blue eyes all the Redepenning cousins had in common, and the elegant bones that helped George to cut a swathe in the bedrooms of the ton. But it was marred by a cut between the eyes, as if something sharp had been punched into the canvas with some force.

Mind you, George probably never saw it. The mess in which he left the estate suggested he'd not so much as entered the Earl's study in years.

Rede sighed at the brimming desk. In the four months since he'd stepped off the boat from Canada to find he'd inherited the earldom, one problem after another had surfaced. Some days, every waking moment was devoted to cleaning up the mess his cousin had left, coming to grips with his duties in the House of Lords, and making sure his own business interests and his all-important hunt were not neglected.

Despite his efforts, he'd barely made inroads into the papers his predecessor had left behind him. He'd stacked them in piles on a bookshelf, with the overflow on a sideboard. They must be all well out of date now, but they needed to be filed or thrown away, and someone needed to work out which was which while he focused on the current work.

He needed a secretary. Perhaps David or Alex might know of someone trustworthy and capable.

He began leafing through the report in his hands, skimming for the salient points. Something made him glance up. Nothing so definite as a sound, perhaps just a change in airflows. David Wakefield was standing across the room from him, leaning against the wall beside the door.

"David. Good to see you." He rounded the desk to shake his visitor's hand.

"My Lord," David responded, his quick grin mocking the formal salutation even as he gave it.

"Rede to you, always, as you well know," Rede protested. "Take a seat, David, and I'll ring for refreshments."

"This is a nice room," David commented. The furnishings were not new, but solid and well proportioned, the wallpaper between the ranks of shelves a green on green that complemented the darker green damask hangings pulled back from the window to let in the spring sunshine.

"George neglected it in his redecorating of the rest of the house. Thank God. From what I can gather, his man of business used it, but George never came in here."

The butler entered, and was sent away with an order for refreshments.

"Not much for business, your cousin."

"As you say. He had most of the house done in the Egyptian style. Both parlours are plagued with jackals and crocodiles, and even the hall bristles with sphinx heads and lions' feet. You take your life in your hands just walking to the bedchambers."

"I saw the front hall and the drawing room when I met you here in January. It's very fashionable in France, they say."

"It's gruesome—or at least his version of it is gruesome. Though the master bedchamber is worse: I think the style might be called French bordello. I had John set me up with one of the other rooms. I'd rather sleep with mummies than mirrors. The whole place needs to be redone when I can find the time."

The butler returned, leading a short procession of maids carrying trays. The two men were silent while he rearranged a group of small tables between them, and supervised the unloading of sliced bread, cold meats, cheese, slices of a meat pie, pickles, a bowl of fresh fruit. The maids came and went, one adding a large pot of coffee, with a sugar bowl and a jug of cream, and another bringing cups, plates and cutlery.

Their task completed, the maids dimpled at Rede's nod of thanks, and left the room. The butler took up a position beside the fireplace.

"Thank you, Parrish. We'll serve ourselves," Rede told him, firmly. "Please shut the door on your way out."

He poured David a cup of coffee. The two men had been friends for a long time—since the taller, older Rede had come to David's rescue at Eton when Rede was fifteen and David an undersized fourteen. David had learned a few tricks since then.

He was still slender, and of less than average height, but Rede had seen him in action during their days as youths on the town. He knew how to use his wiry strength to take down men with twice his body weight. Rede was no slouch in a fight, but he'd rather have David on his side than against him.

They hadn't kept in touch during the years Rede was in Canada. Rede was surprised to see David's name on the list of thief takers his solicitor had found him four months earlier. But he was not surprised to find that David had a reputation for both success and honesty—many thief takers were barely more trustworthy than the thieves they hunted.

David preferred the term 'enquiry agent', and described his job as 'finding things and people'. 'Finding' apparently required the ability to move at any level of society, and to come and go unobserved when he wished to.

Rede handed his friend the cup. As usual, David's face gave nothing away; his mobile mouth slightly quirked in amusement as he observed Rede watching him, his brown eyes steady under his heavy brows.

"I think," Rede said, "that you're going to tell me that you didn't find what you were looking for in Liverpool."

"Say, rather, that I found for sure that what I was looking for wasn't in Liverpool. I've written you a detailed report, but the summary is that I was able to clear all five of the men I went there to investigate." David took a bite of the bread he'd loaded with cold meat and pickle.

"So it's the three in Bristol, then."

"Probably. It seems likely."

Rede made what would have been a rude gesture if his hand had not been holding a large slice of pie. "Come on, man. You've already cleared seven names in London, and now the five in Liverpool. You've eliminated every other suspect. It has to be them."

"One or more of them. Or someone we haven't thought of. I'll find the evidence if it's there, Rede."

"I've waited so long, David. I suppose I can wait a bit longer."

"I've only been investigating for four months."

"I've been hunting for more than three years. I landed here in London three years to the day since I found them dead. Killed so that some English tradesman could turn an extra pound." And still, every night, he relived the moment he came home to the smoking ruin of his home, the broken bodies of his loved ones. Every morning, he woke to the raw need to find those responsible.

"Give me time to find some confirming evidence, Rede. You've waited for three years. Surely it's worth another month or two so that you're not revenging yourself on the wrong people?"

"Not revenge. Justice." He waved off the uncomfortable thought that he was lying to himself. "I can agree to a month or two. When will you go to Bristol?"

"In a couple of days. I have some people to see while I'm in London. But I already have people in Bristol doing the groundwork. There's not much I can do until they're ready."

Rede shook his head. "No, I'm not asking you to rush. I just thought I might head part of the way with you. The House has two more sittings, then I've nothing to keep me in London till after the election. I've two more estates to check in person—Longford Court and the one in Cheshire. George, as far as I can tell, hasn't been to either estate for years."

"I have fond memories of Longford Court," David mused.

"It's only a couple of hours from Bristol; I could be handy when you want to report on what you're finding."

"We spent some good holidays there with your other cousins."

"We did," Rede agreed. The two of them were quiet for a moment, thinking about long summer holidays with the large family of Rede's youngest uncle.

"I'm meant to attend my aunt's ball later this week," Rede said, shaking off the nostalgia. "I can head down to Longford after that. Why don't you come with us on Thursday? An extra man is always welcome; society is short of them, with the war."

David looked amused. "Yes. Even we bastards occasionally find ourselves in demand. And a good-looking, wealthy earl. You're a walking target, old friend."

Rede shook his head, an expression of wonder rather than rebuttal. "Have they always been this bad and I just didn't notice? And the marriage-minded are not as bad as the ones who desire… a less permanent liaison. What they do to get a man's attention would make your hair curl!"

David laughed. "Are you seeking envy or commiseration?"

"Not envy. I wouldn't touch that pack of harpies with a ten-foot pole. So will you come?"

"I already have an invitation from Her Grace, so I expect I'll see you there. I will take you up on the offer of company down as far as Longford, though. What day do you plan to leave?"

"Next Monday, I thought. I'll send a message today to tell the house to make ready. Heaven knows what state it's in."

"You've a steward to see to it?"

"A land steward, a distant connection of the family. He seems quite competent, but then so did the one in Kent who was fudging the accounts, and the one in Norfolk who spent most of his time chasing housemaids, and whose books and reports were a complete fiction. I've no idea what's going on at Longford—or in Cheshire for that matter. George didn't pay much attention."

"From what I gather, he was only interested in spending his income."

"Beyond his income, more like. None of the properties are returning what they could, but he still spent as if there was no tomorrow, most of it on credit. I've saved the earldom thousands a year just by paying off his mistresses." And dug into his own personal fortune to give them a competence so that they could retire from the sex trade, if they so wished, but no need to mention that.

"I remember hearing about his mistresses! He kept mistresses near all his major houses and several in London, and visited them all by turn. Rumour has it that he sometimes entertained several at once."

"Rumour exaggerates, as usual. From what I can gather, he ignored most of them most of the time. He'd call on the closest one when the mood took him. And when he didn't call, they occupied themselves shopping and sending him the bills.

"There were two in London and one in Kent, near his favourite house. I don't know of any near the other houses. If there's one near Longford, she's been buried down there on her own for years, though there is an anomaly in the records—a tenant who hasn't paid rent in years. It's one of the things I'll be checking with the steward—Baxter, his name is."

David nodded thoughtfully. "I remember Baxter. He'd be old now, surely?"

"This would be the son. You might remember him, too. He took us fishing a couple of times. Apparently he had an accident recently—hurt in a barn collapse, which sounds like Longford has at least a few maintenance problems. His own son is handling the work at the moment."

"Father to son again."

"As you say. But inheriting the position doesn't mean he's good at it, or that he's honest. Though, to be fair, I've a stack of reports from him reporting on maintenance needs and a host of other things. Most of them still sealed shut when I found them on George's desk."

"So you'll go down and take a look for yourself."

"And I'll be handy for anything that develops in Bristol. It's not more than two hours' ride."

"You'll be further away from the rest of your empire," David waved at the laden desk. "It looks like you're handling the whole thing yourself."

"I am, in essence. My agent here in London died while I was still in Canada, and I got rid of George's man of business as soon as I realised how incompetent he was—which took less than five minutes, I assure you. I'm looking for a couple of skilled and trustworthy people to replace them."

"One for the estate, one for your business?"

"Or one really good man for both, if I could find the right person. Any ideas?"

"Not off the top of my head. I'll think about it and ask around."

"Meanwhile, I'll set up a courier run. It's a day's hard ride each way, with post horses. I'll get the information I need soon enough."

"You could say the same about my investigation."

Rede shook his head. "Your investigation is my priority. I've been hunting a long time, David. I'm so close now I can taste it."

"Revenge." David said the word without inflection, his eyes revealing nothing of his thoughts. Nevertheless, Rede felt the need to defend his quest.

"Justice. They'll never pay in court for what they did. English justice doesn't care about some half-breeds on the frontier, whatever evidence we find. But they'll pay. I swore it on the graves of my wife and children."

"I may find evidence of a crime against English law. If they've cut corners on the frontier, they'll have cut corners elsewhere."

"And if you do, you can take it to the law. That'll be a nice seasoning to the retribution I have in mind."

"I've never asked what you did have in mind."

Rede smiled—a cold stretching of the lips that didn't reach his eyes. "I've no intention of killing them, if that's your concern. They took my family for the sake of their business interests. I'll take their business interests for the sake of my family, and of the other families we buried because of their greed."

He could still see them: one burnt-out cabin after another, the bodies left carelessly for the carrion eaters. At every stop they'd had to decide whether to stop and hastily bury the poor broken remnants, or continue on the trail of the human scum responsible, perhaps in time to save a family further on. The rage that had consumed him when he finally learned that the killers had been employed to destroy his trapping enterprise rose in him again. So many died, and for what? To add a few gold coins to the coffers of the men he hunted.

"I'll destroy them piece by piece: one ship, one warehouse, one deal, one pound at a time. I'll strip them of everything they have, and see them begging in the dirt. I'll take their families from them, if I can; convince their own wives and children to repudiate them. And I'll do it all within the law, so—when they reach the bottom of the deepest pit I can dig—I can tell them why."

Chapter two

Longford

At the mill school, the children had been impossible, chattering and poking each other. The Great House was being opened. For the first time in their lives, Longford Court would host its Earl. Anne Forsythe, who taught at the school three mornings a week, kept her private anxieties to herself. She bowed to necessity and set the children spelling and counting exercises that involved the Earl and Longford Court.

Some of the mothers came to pick up their children and stayed to help Anne tidy the room.

"Mrs Tyler, she do look for bodies to clean house," one of them said. "I be going this afternoon."

Mrs Tyler, the housekeeper, had closed most of the rooms thirteen years ago when the last of the Redepennings moved away.

Anne had spent the morning wondering what the Earl was planning, and how it would affect her and her sisters. "Will she be taking on a bigger staff permanently?" she asked.

Those who had been at the inn when the land steward's son had announced the call for servants knew how many were needed—more maids, a footman and two grooms—but not for how long.

"Will he stay, Mu'um, think you?" one of them asked Anne, who was locking the schoolroom behind them. " 'Twould be grand to have Court open."

"I have no idea what the Earl's plans are," she told them. "What does Mr Baxter say?"

This made them giggle.

"Eee, he doesna tell likes of us."

Another nodded. "Clamber-mouthed are t' Baxters. Our Beks— she cleans for Missus Baxter—she says they doesna tell no-one."

"Perhaps they do not know either?"

They set off along the river towards the bridge, the children running ahead.

Another comment on the benefits of having the Court open brought a warning from the prettiest of the young mothers. "Aye, if'n Earl will leave the maids be."

This led to a discussion of the new Earl as a youth. There were seven cousins, Anne learned, the previous Earl, the current Earl, and the five children of their youngest uncle, whose wife had been *châtelaine* at the Court for many years.

"He were a fine young man, were that Stephen Redepenning as is Earl now. Not like last Earl or his Pa."

"The old Earl and his Pa before him, they didn't come here much. But they was two of a kind."

"After anything in skirts."

"Yes, and the drinking, and the cards." Fanny added.

"Best to stay in a group, my Ma said. And so I did."

"Me, too."

As they crossed the bridge from the mill side of the river and turned towards the village, they went on to reminisce about those who hadn't stayed in a group, and what had become of them as a result.

The walk passed quickly, and they were soon at the row of cottages where they lived. One girl was telling the story of an angry father confronting Lord Chirbury with his daughter's baby. She finished with a flourish. "And he couldna deny the truth any longer, for the baby had the Redepenning eyes!"

"I have to go, Mu'um," one of the others said hastily, not meeting Anne's eyes. The storyteller flushed and put both hands over her mouth.

Anne smiled calmly. She knew what they thought, but no-one had ever said it out loud, and after she and her sisters had spent more than five years being the most respectable women in the village, they weren't going to. "Thank you for your help. I hope you enjoy the rest of your day."

They mumbled farewells and hurried away.

Anne continued to her own porch at the far end of the row of cottages. Did it matter that the new Earl, as a stripling, behaved far better than his dead cousin? Thirteen years on, he might have changed.

In any case, a rakehell in London might be less of a danger to her family than the most respectable of gentlemen right here on her doorstep. It all depended on how deeply he intended to enquire into estate business—and what he would do with any knowledge he gained.

If he suspected who they were... George had, to her surprise, kept their secret. Perhaps he really had been sorry. But a new Earl could decide it was his duty to let their cousin know where they were hiding. As long as her little sister was still underage, the danger continued.

She gave herself a small shake as she reached home. She had saved them before and, if she needed to, she would find a way to save them again. Time to be cheerful for Meg and Daisy.

She opened the door to the smell of warm bread, with undercurrents of stew and some other kind of baking.

"Mama!" Daisy shouted, dropping the cutlery she was putting on the table to run across the room and hug her mother. Meg was close behind, reaching out for her own hug and kiss. Anne handed Daisy her bonnet and Meg her cloak, and sat on the bench by the door to undo her boots, calling out a greeting to Hannah, who was stirring something at the fire.

Daisy was a delightful little elf of a child, thought her fond mama. Not yet six years of age, she was clever and charming. She reminded Anne of Meg at the same age some sixteen years ago, before a fever killed their mother and robbed Meg of her wits. Daisy had the same intense curiosity, the same eager approach to life. And—apart from her colouring—she looked the same, too, with Meg's slender body, oval face, arched brows, and sweet snub of a nose.

Daisy couldn't wait to tell Anne about her morning. "I made bread with Hannah, and I helped cut the apples for the pies, and Meg made the marks on the pie lids, didn't you Meg?"

"Meg made bread, too!" Meg added, dropping the cloak in her eagerness to have her say. Daisy, who had clambered onto the other end of the bench to reach the coat hooks, turned from hanging the bonnet. "Pick it up and pass it to me, Aunt Meg. I'll hang it for you."

"Meg hang it," Meg insisted.

Just then the door opened again, letting Kitty and Ruth into the warm.

"Water's warm," Hannah told them, "and t'meal be served as soon as may be. Miss Meg, Miss Daisy, up to table, my lovelies."

From the scullery as she washed her hands and face, Anne listened to her daughter reporting on her morning, with Meg chiming in to echo and agree. They had, it seemed, spent a morning in the kitchen, 'helping' Hannah prepare the dinner.

As always, the family said grace before they ate. Anne smiled around at her family. Growing up in luxury as she had, she couldn't have imagined eating such a simple meal in the kitchen—or eating with servant, children and adults all together. Even her nursery fare had been more elaborate than stew and bread, with apple pie to follow. When she left the schoolroom, dinners had been in the evening, not in the middle of the day, and had commonly boasted several removes with a dozen dishes at each.

She'd been lonely when she left her sisters on the nursery floor. She'd dined with her brother when he was home, but she and Sam had little to talk about. She didn't miss the solitary splendour of her girlhood. She preferred it here in this warm kitchen, surrounded by the women she loved.

"How was your lesson today?" she asked Kitty.

Kitty's smile lit the whole of her lovely face. "Rose and I practised our duet. Ruth said we are coming along very well, did you not, Ruth? She says we may sing it at the Redwoods' on Tuesday."

"If you are asked to sing," Ruth warned.

Kitty waved off this reminder with another smile. "Lady Redwood likes to hear us—she says we brighten her day."

"Pride goeth before a fall. Perhaps you should embroider that on a sampler?" Ruth raised one eyebrow, and tried to look stern, but her eyes betrayed a twinkle. Anne chuckled. Kitty could sing like an angel, especially with Rose Ashbrook, the Rector's daughter. But her fancy sewing was truly abysmal, and even in plain sewing her stitches often had to be unpicked and done again.

"I am not being proud, Ruth, truly I am not. But I like singing for Lady Redwood. Poor lady. Fancy never being able to walk, and never going anywhere unless someone carries you. And I would not be honest if I pretended that Rose and I did not make quite a pretty noise together, especially when Emma plays for us." Emma Redwood was the daughter of Sir Thomas Redwood, the squire, and his invalid wife.

Ruth relented. "Indeed you do, my dear. Even if it is unbecoming to say so.

At this point, Daisy—who had made great inroads into her stew—started into another story about her morning, again ably supported by Meg.

On Kitty, the same features that blessed Daisy had matured into true beauty, the nose straight and the large eyes fringed with the same absurdly long lashes as her small niece. The tiny mirror they all used told Anne that she was, if not a beauty, at least not an antidote. Meg still looked a child, though she was fully grown. She was three years Kitty's senior, but something in her expression spoke of her innocence and lack of understanding.

Kitty, Meg and Anne shared the same light brown hair and hazel eyes. Ruth and Daisy were complete contrasts to one another. Ruth was dark and light: hair almost black and eyes of a deep brown against a porcelain complexion. Her head was currently bent close to Daisy's golden curls while the child's intensely blue eyes watched the piece of apple pie Ruth was sliding onto Daisy's plate. The startling colour was set off with dark lashes, a surprising combination with the golden hair. Redepenning eyes, the Longford residents called them, though not to Anne's face.

Hannah rounded the table to clear the stew bowls, before taking her own place again on the other side of Daisy. Dear Hannah. She'd come to them as Daisy's wet nurse, and stayed these five and a half years as maid-of-all-work. She was as much part of the family as any of the sisters.

"Mmmm," Kitty said, having swallowed her first bite of pie. "This is good."

"Meg pricked the crust. Meg pricked the crust." Meg was jiggling in her seat with excitement.

"Eat your mouthful, Meg darling. Ladies do not speak when they have food in their mouths."

Meg gave another couple of chews and a mighty swallow. "Meg pricked the crust."

Anne leaned over to give her a kiss on the cheek. "Well done, Meg."

"Anne," Kitty asked, "Did you hear the new Earl is coming?"

"They did mention it at the school."

"The whole village is talking about it. The last Earl never visited, not since he was a boy. But the new Earl is going to be here this weekend, and Mr Will Baxter has told Mrs Tyler to prepare for him to stay until the end of June. Do you think we'll meet him?"

Anne exchanged glances with Ruth. "If he is a good landlord, he will want to meet all his tenants, darling." If their luck held, he would not be a good landlord.

If only he had waited another two years, until Kitty was of age. If only he planned to stay a few short days. If only he would leave without ever setting eyes on Daisy or questioning the rent rolls.

Meg, who had been listening with a frown on her usually happy face, suddenly scrambled up from the table and rounded it, heading for the door.

"Meg!" Anne shot out a hand to catch her pinafore. "Where do you think you are going?"

Meg tugged at her pinafore, trying to get free. Her face was distorted with fear. "Meg going to hide. Earl is coming."

In an instant, Anne was out of her seat and folding her sister in her arms. "Not the bad Earl, darling. This is a different Earl."

"The Earl is a bad man," Meg insisted.

"The bad Earl is dead," Anne soothed. "He will never come. The bad Earl is dead."

Ruth joined them, to run a soothing hand over Meg's hair. "The bad Earl will never come," she agreed.

"A good Earl comes?"

Anne met Ruth's eyes, and her own thoughts were reflected. In their experience, a good Earl was an unlikely beast indeed.

"A different Earl," Anne said.

"You'll have to watch your nephew with the maids," David observed to Rede, as they sat in the late afternoon sun on Monday, sampling a mug of the local brew.

They'd made an easy ride of it, leaving London at first light that Monday morning, and making their last post of the day from Newbury in the mid-afternoon.

John Price, Rede's man, had written ahead so horses had been waiting for them at each stop, and he'd booked rooms for them at the Red Lion in Hungerford.

It was a good choice. Newbury was crowded with families departing for Bristol, Bath, or points further west. The King's decision to call an election had chopped at least six weeks off the Season.

"So I've been told," Rede replied to David's warning. "Nasty Nat, my cousins call him. But my sister assures me that the girls at Oxford were quite willing, whatever the Chancellor says." He raised his mug in an ironic salute to the illusions of a doting mother.

"Sent down, was he?"

Rede took a contemplative sip of his beer. Not at all bad. "Yes. And his father won't take him to Brighton to stay with Prinny, and his mother is off to Bath and is reluctant to leave him without a keeper. He has fallen in with a bad crowd, apparently."

"So Uncle Rede to the rescue."

"How bad can a seventeen-year-old be, after all?"

"How bad was George at seventeen?" David asked, wryly. "You do know that young Bexley was George's acolyte?"

"Yes, my cousins made sure to acquaint me with that small fact."

"On the bright side, three of my cousins have invited themselves down to help me keep him out of trouble," he said.

They sat in silence for a while, sipping their beer and watching the sunset. "I see you were much in demand at the Haverford ball," David said after a while.

Rede gave a short bark of laughter with little amusement in it. "The mothers with daughters to market were bad enough. But the married women... Is no-one in London faithful? If I had one invitation to cuckold some poor unsuspecting husband, I had a dozen."

"Very likely neither poor nor unsuspecting. Just busy doing the same to some other woman's husband."

"Possibly. Likely, in fact. Bunch of rakes and harpies. They undoubtedly deserve one another."

He shuddered. He'd thought he would be safe enough dancing with Baroness Carrington, whose husband held a barony near Longford Court. He vaguely remembered her marriage while he was still at Eton, and figured she must be old enough to leave him be. But either the willowy blonde had worn exceptionally well, or she was a mere child when she married. Each time the figures of the dance brought her close, she whispered innuendos in his ear, her 'accidental' touches reinforcing the hidden meaning.

Even if he'd had time for dalliance, even if he didn't draw the line at adultery, he'd avoid a predator like the Baroness, with her hard-edged glitter.

She hadn't taken the hint from his non-committal answers, however.

"There's no need to be shy, my Lord Chirbury. We're both adults. If you take my meaning."

The situation had called for a blunt instrument. "I don't dally with married women, Lady Carrington. If you take my meaning."

He shook off the memory. It was too pleasant an evening to think about the Baroness and her ilk.

"Who was your lady friend?" he asked David.

"Just someone I know," David replied.

Not something David wanted to talk about, then. Interesting in itself. Rede changed the subject again.

"John should be here with the luggage soon."

David, though, was following his own train of thought. "You'll have to pick one of them, you know—one of the maidens with the marriage-minded mothers. The title must go on."

Rede shook his head. "I don't need to marry for that, David. I have two uncles to inherit, and after them four cousins, one of whom has already set up his nursery. The title is safe for another generation.

"And I'd rather be single. For one thing, marriage wouldn't be fair to the woman. My vengeance has to come first. Anything left of me goes to my business interests and the earldom.

"For another… I'm a trader, David. I invest where I can expect a good return at a reasonable risk. I've been married once, and had children. Hostages to fortune. The risk is too high. I'll not ever marry again."

Read the rest of Rede's and Anne's story in *Farewell to Kindness*, available now in print and for e-reader at all major online retailers.

Connect with Jude Knight

Jude Knight writes strong determined heroines, heroes who can appreciate a clever capable woman, villains you'll love to loathe, and all with a leavening of humour.

After a career in commercial writing, editing, and publishing, Jude Knight returned to her first love, fiction. Her novella, *Candle's Christmas Chair*, was released in December 2014, and is in the top ten on several Amazon bestseller lists in the US and UK. Her first novel *Farewell to Kindness*, was released on 1 April, and is first in a series: *The Golden Redepennings*.

Follow Jude on Twitter: @JudeKnightBooks
Friend Jude on Facebook: facebook.com/judeknightbooks
Subscribe to Jude's blog: judeknightauthor.com
Subscribe to Jude's newsletter:
judeknightauthor.com/newsletter/
Follow Jude on Goodreads: www.goodreads.com/judeknight